MEMORIES, MAGIC AND MAYHEM

K. STARLING

About this Book

Propriety insists ladies should never sprint, exchange gunfire, or perfect a right hook. How dull.Since Penelope Sedgewick felt such arbitrary societal expectations were rubbish, she became a sleuth. When not avoiding dances or calls by tiresome would-be suitors, she investigates delicate matters for ladies—love nests, stolen jewels, missing husbands who may or may not have been eaten by dragons—the usual.

When a lady from another time falls dead at her feet, she plunges headlong into the past (quite literally) to unravel a mystery thirty years in the making. Penelope's skills will be put to the test as she wrestles with ghosts from her future, tiresome rakes, and even Fate, all while concealing her magical abilities.

Will she be able to prevent the girl's death without altering history? Or will she inadvertently step on one too many butterflies, harming her family forever?

Memories, Magic, and Mayhem is the second novel in the Alderwood Regency Mysteries—a series of cozy fantasies set in a reimagined regency world filled with dragons, magic, and intrigue.

ISBN (paperback): 979-8-9906466-4-3
ISBN (hardcover): 979-8-9906466-5-0
ISBN (ebook): 979-8-9906466-3-6

www.authorkstarling.com

First Edition: February 2025

Dearest Reader,

Within the pages of this novel, you will enter
a world where dragons pull carriages, ladies
frequent healers to erase wrinkles, and Parliament
debates the legality of truth tinctures.

There will be romps, casual references to
weaponry (in fact, you should presume that
every character is armed), and an opinionated
narrator who offers her unsolicited thoughts.
Oh, and because temporal displacement
is more prevalent than previously known,
our timeline is a bit mucked up.

If this is not your proverbial cup of tea,
may I recommend you return this book
and select a less frivolous novel?

It has come to my attention that seers are scarce
in your world, so be forewarned. There will also
be references to forced labour and imprisonment,
actual murders (off-page), and a bit of on-page
violence (of the gunfire and fisty-cuff variety).

Enjoy!

Chapter Titles

1. The Chapter with Hair Tonic

2. The Chapter with the Knots

3. The Chapter with the Tumbling

4. The Chapter with the Fall

5. The Chapter with the Healer
Who Had Men for Tea (Literally?)

6. The Chapter with the Fallen Maiden

7. The Chapter with the Forgotten Boot

8. The Chapter with the Temporal Displacement

9. The Chapter with the Chance Meetings

10. The Chapter with the Tour

11. The Chapter with the Escape

12. The Chapter with the Déjà Vu

13. The Chapter in the Cure-all Shop

14. The Chapter with the Running

15. The Chapter in the Eye of the Storm

16. The Chapter with the Secret Society (Shhhh!)

17. The Chapter with the Murderer (Maybe)

18. The Chapter with the "Illegal" Midnight Tour

19. The Chapter with the Wagon

20. The Chapter with the First Dance

21.   The Chapter with that Busybody, Fate

22.   The Chapter with the Sleep Serum

23.   The Chapter with the Kiss

24.   The Chapter with the Aha

25.   The Chapter with the Goodbyes

26.   The Chapter with the Gravestone

27.   The Chapter with the Tea

The Epilogue

Characters of Note

(AND A FEW WHO CRASHED THE BALL)

PENELOPE SEDGEWICK – Our sleuth

VERITY WALTERS – Her assistant, still stealing spoons

AUNT JOSEPHINE – Penelope's aunt and a rebel

UNCLE ARCHIE – Penelope's incandescently happy uncle

MRS ABIGAIL STEVENSON – Uncle Archie's amour

MR CHARLES SEDGEWICK – Penelope's father

THE FUTURE MRS SEDGEWICK – Penelope's mother

TOAST – A forest dragon and master of impersonations

MRS AGNES DEWAR – Birch Hallow's housekeeper

MR HORACIO HEEP – A pedlar of cure-alls

SABLE – A curmudgeonly healer who eats men for tea

BONNIE – A shop girl

AMBROISE – A dragon and rascal

CERBRUS – Not a three-headed dog

MR SCOTT – A yeti

As well as sundry drakes, Folk, dead lovers, and constables.

Chapter One

THE CHAPTER WITH HAIR TONIC

Mʀs Cᴇᴄɪʟɪᴀ's Hᴀɪʀ Tᴏɴɪᴄ
Sᴛᴀᴠᴇs ᴏꜰꜰ Gʀᴇʏ
Rᴇᴠᴇʀsᴇs Bᴀʟᴅɴᴇss
Eɴʜᴀɴᴄᴇs Cᴜʀʟs

{Use as directed. Excessive application may cause headaches,
fits of laughter, and baldness.}

A Hair Tonic Label ca. 1808

When Penelope Sedgewick set out that morning, she did not expect to spend thirteen hours sharing an attic stairwell with half a dozen spiders. However, as she was determined to report on the furtive movements of her client's husband, she planted herself on the ninth stair (after dusting it, of course) to peep periodically through a hole in the adjoining wall.

Had she known that the middle-aged merchant would do nothing naughtier than add sugar to his cup before pouring the tea, she would have brought a book. Instead, she paused to observe the gentleman as he switched between reading, dining on the tavernkeeper's scrumptious pasties, and stoking the fire. How dull.

She had hoped to satisfy his wife's suspicions—that his weekly disappearances were spent with a steady mistress or caught up in a string of torrid affairs. Alas, no. It would appear that this gentleman spent every Thursday reading and nothing more. Her client would be disappointed. Ladies with ample time and a lack of affection for their husbands do wish to feel slighted from time to time. (Or wish to justify their own trysts with the footman. Mum's the word.)

Penelope would have been happy to oblige. She would have loved nothing more than to discover that he led a double life as a stage actor or that he spent his afternoons as an assassin; however, it was not to be. Her investigations rarely uncovered anything that could be labelled as indecent. Instead, they often culminated in the mundane— addictions to charms, the illicit trade of magical items, and gambling.

As the gentleman was evidently *not* meeting a mistress, Penelope wiggled her toes and stretched her legs with care, easing out the pinpricks and waiting until sensation returned to her left foot. What sort of sleuth would she be if she successfully snooped for half the day only to be discovered when she tumbled down a flight of stairs?

She rose, yet the tramping of feet in the hall brought her to a halt. Her heart did not resume a more sensible rhythm until the door to the room adjacent to her hiding place whined in protest as it swung open and collided with the wall. Penelope lowered herself back onto the stairs to wait, brushing the cotton breeches and linen shirt she had adorned to disguise herself as a boy of fifteen.

"I suppose you'll be wanting tea?" A gravelly voice roughened by decades of shouting down inebriated patrons slid through the paper-thin walls. The tavernkeeper's wife, she suspected. A cursory glance through a wide crack in the boards confirmed as much.

Two days prior, Penelope had selected her hiding spot. The narrow stairwell crammed between the inn's finest rooms had seemed ideal for spying on a disappointingly dull husband, and her hopes had been satisfied. However, the goings-on of the second room were none of her concern. She intended to turn away. And she would have, had not a familiar voice met her ears. "And two ports. None of that bathwater you serve the gents when they're foxed, mind you."

With care, Penelope slid closer to the crack in the wall. Through the slit, she spied her assistant, Walt, or as her mum had addressed her when she had stolen sweets as a child, Miss Verity Walters. In spite of her sensible ensemble—a pale blue cotton dress with a brown waist-length coat—Walt had the bearing of a Greek goddess who had hopped out of a painting to take an evening stroll: black coiled hair, a fine figure, and eyes that attempted, and often failed, to disguise a propensity for mischief that would impress a village-worth of wayward boys.

She plopped into the wingback chair near the fire, draping her legs over its arm. The scrunch of the hostess' nose, visible even in the dim light of a fire, informed Penelope that she preferred Walt not to treat her furniture with such incivility. "I'll have my daughter bring it up."

Walt nodded her approval. "And if a young man asks for me, send him my way." From her reticule, she withdrew a polished pipe, which she began to pack with tobacco. She lit it. Soon its sweet fragrance wove through the cracks in the board, replacing the odour of must.

For the benefit of her spider co-inhabitants, Penelope raised an eyebrow. Though it was none of her business, to say she was intrigued would have been putting it mildly. Who was her assistant meeting in a tavern miles from her rooms? But no, Walt was her friend (and perhaps her only true one at that). She would not violate her trust.

Hence she slid the attic stairwell's door ajar a smidge, preparing to leave, only to draw it closed again when a couple distracted in an amorous embrace stumbled into the hall. Her second escape attempt was thwarted by the delivery of a tray to Walt. The third was halted by a patron collapsing against the entrance to her hideout. His ear-splitting snores nearly drove her to withdraw her pistol. However, as she had not shot at anyone in nearly three months, her weapon remained in her pocket.

A half-hour later, after the man had moved on, she rose once more. She adjusted her cap, ensuring it still hid her raven bun. Then she rumpled her clothes a bit so she would not appear too tidy, and reached for the door. However, Fate, it would appear, had a wicked sense of humour. At that precise moment, two sets of footsteps echoed in the stairwell that led to the tap room below.

"You'll find her behind the third door on the left."

Two slightly inappropriate terms and one word that would scandalize even a rake were mumbled under our heroine's breath. She had been quite determined *not* to spy on her friend. Really, she had. Which is why she would only glance very, *very* briefly through the slit at the young man, not much older than a boy, entering the—

The door to the attic stairwell swung open. There, lit by the lamp she held, stood the tavernkeeper's wife. At the sight of Penelope disguised as a boy peering through a crack in the wall into a room inhabited by a lady, her expression passed from surprised to outraged. Rather than bellow, she spoke in the sort of whisper-shout usually reserved for mamas scolding their children during Sunday services. "What are you doin' here?!"

An amateur would have mumbled a pitiful reply; however, our heroine was no amateur. Instead, she padded noiselessly down the stairs, slid near to the woman, inhaling a mixture of smoke, yeast, and sweat, and whispered conspiratorially, "Who is that woman?"

Used to the antics of drunks and cheats, she levelled Penelope with a stare. "And what's that to you?"

Penelope leaned closer before answering in a clipped accent she had perfected after a fortnight inhabiting an impoverished rookery in South London. "That young man's the son of a peer of the realm." She winked and tapped the side of her nose before continuing, "Who I've been paid to keep an eye on."

Not quite convinced, the tavernkeeper's wife lifted the lamp to her face. Most sleuths would have been concerned about discovery given how the woman's sharp eyes surveyed every pore and stray hair. However, as Penelope resembled a pixie, with her heart-shaped face and petite stature, she was not concerned, not in the least. This was one disguise she had mastered without the aid of magic.

A spindly hand shot out from the woman's apron, seizing Penelope's arm like a vice and yanking her into the dimly lit hall. "You know what I think? I think you're one of those lads who look through keyholes and windows hoping to catch an eyeful of something they oughtn't've."

Droplets of spittle landed on Penelope's face. It took every ounce of her self-control not to wipe it away with the lace handkerchief stuffed in her pocket. "Honest, ma'am. I've been paid to keep an eye on him."

"'Course you have."

As subterfuge had failed her, Penelope resorted to a time-honoured tactic practised by sleuths and grandmothers: bribery.

"Of course, if you were to . . ." Her eyes shot left then right, feigning to search for eavesdroppers. As the hall was uncluttered, swept, and polished, without a place for a speck of dust let alone a person to hide, she inched closer still. ". . . look the other way . . ." Her free hand withdrew a two-bob bit from her pocket. ". . . I could be on my way."

Not one to turn down ready money, the tavernkeeper's wife snatched the coin from her hand. Her chin jutted towards the stairs that led to the tavern. "Mary Jones. That's her name."

It was not, of course. Interesting. So while the woman would look the other way, she would not betray a regular patron. At least not for a couple of bob.

Once Penelope was free of her talons, she did not bow. Instead, she scurried away as a proper wayward lad might. Halfway down the hall, her escape was interrupted by the creak of a door swinging open behind her.

Walt strolled into the hall, pipe bobbing on her lip. "See that he's fed a hearty breakfast. He'll be on his way tomorrow morning."

While the women exchanged a few words and coins, Penelope slid towards the stairs at the end of the hall, hoping to avoid discovery. Waves of boisterous laughter mixed with chatter rose to greet her as she stepped onto the first stair.

She passed the fifth step when a *PSST!* at her elbow nearly caused her to tumble downwards. How Walt had slid noiselessly down the hall and materialised at her side confounded her. Even in the amber haze of the enclosed passage, her assistant's eyes beamed with delight. Inwardly, Penelope groaned; she would not live this bungle down for quite some time—if ever.

As the women fell in step with one another, Walt nudged her. "Whatchoo doing here?"

"Investigating a scandalous affair."

The embrace of the tavern greeted them. Men huddled in groups about the fieldstone fireplace, or at worn but tidy tables, cradling their drinks. Their camaraderie, evident in their relaxed expressions, tempted Penelope to pull up a stool and spin a yarn or two. However, as she did not want her aunt to suspect she had not spent the evening tucked into her bed reading, she decided to hurry home.

A handful of patrons nodded a greeting to Walt, who nodded back. "So did you follow the couple here?" she asked.

"No. There is no couple." Penelope side-stepped a gentleman whose face glowed the shade of a tomato as he gestured wildly, sloshing his drink. "Just a gentleman who loves to read in silence, away from his wife's chatter, and harbours a taste for scrumptious pies."

"Well, they are delectable."

Just as the pair passed beneath a carved candelabrum suspended in the middle of the room, Walt spun around, narrowly dodging her employer, to cut a hasty path in the opposite direction.

As she was in disguise, Penelope thought it wise to continue towards the front door while surveying the room. A whistle danced on her lips. One face after another appeared either too drowsy or too content to pay her much mind, let alone elicit trepidation.

That was until her gaze landed on a knot of men near the door. At the centre sat a weedy man with hair sprouting every which way, his eyes trained in Walt's direction. A look of rage contorted his already displeasing features so much so that he resembled a rabid dog with mange.

"YOU!!!!" he bellowed. In unison, a dozen heads snapped in his direction.

Without turning round, Penelope heard Walt's boots thump across the wooden floor towards the rear exit. A knowing look was exchanged among the men. Four drinks thudded on the pine tabletop, their contents sloshing over the rim before the men toppled their chairs as they stood to give chase.

{Narrator's Note: A libellous rumour has spread that Walt fled because she was no match for four men. Such a falsehood cannot persist. She was more than equal to the task. In fact, she would have enjoyed a brawl; however, her personal code of honour prevented her from kicking arse when she had been in the wrong. Thank you very much.}

They might have caught up with her, had not Penelope's extended foot snagged an oak-sized man and sent him careening into his friends. Like tenpins, the pack toppled over one another. Wood splintered. Cups became airborne. Men shouted. And our sleuth? Well, dear reader, she slipped through the front door without a hair out of place.

Two turns and a shortcut through the stable yard put her on a collision course with her assistant. With more dexterity than one would expect from a lady sporting a high-waisted gown, Walt sprinted around the corner.

"Whatever was all of that about?" Penelope began to jog alongside her, away from the shouts ringing through the empty lanes. Brick homes dotted the path, their fruit trees casting shadows across the packed earth. The moon danced overhead as wispy clouds threatened to ruin the streak of fine weather they had been enjoying.

Making a sharp left, Walt steered them towards the heart of Alderwood. "I might've sold the skinny one a bottle of what I advertised as acne eraser."

They ducked beneath a low-hanging tree draped across a narrow passage between two gardens. Mint bordered the path, its sweet perfume tempting passersby to pluck a sprig or two.

Penelope strained her ears, willing them to perceive the footfall of their pursuers. Nothing, except the rustle of leaves. They paused in the shadow cast by a dilapidated barn. "And was it?"

"Nah." Walt's eye darted up and down the lane. Her employer noted the mischievous thrill in her voice. "It was a hair-growth tincture mixed with sugar water."

Penelope ought not to have grinned; to do so would encourage her friend's habit of sowing mayhem. However, a wry smile might have peeked out momentarily. "Send an errand boy to his house with a couple of shillings and an apology. Then, I shall disguise myself as a wanton flirt. When I appear at the tavern and compliment his facial hair—"

Walt chuckled. "It's not just on the face."

The grin they shared did not linger. A shift of the wind scattered a darkness across the lane; not the sort perceived by the eye, but a pall that gripped hearts. Instinctively, the pair drew their coats tight across their chests.

Bathed in pitch, a knowing swept over Penelope. It set her nerves ablaze, urging her to flee. She touched Walt's elbow, gently, so as not to startle her. Since her assistant had keen senses of her own, she understood.

Noiselessly, they slid around the side of the barn, still clothed in darkness. The lane was empty, yet they eased behind a handcart to observe.

It was not the clatter that rose over rooftops nor the stirring of a mare across the way that demanded her attention. No, as Penelope crouched, swathed in inky shadow void of starlight, it was a building that awoke her gift. Looming above a sea of overgrown grass stood a brick building, long and broad. A bird dived through the gaping hole in its sparse, blackened roof. Despite its age, not a vine or a shrub climbed its walls. Even the grass dared not approach it, and gave it a wide berth.

Penelope knew this building, of course. There was not a shack nor lane she had not explored, mapped, and catalogued in the whole of Alderwood, as well as the surrounding county. However, she knew *this* building instinctually. Her ability to sense magic told her that this place, this unremarkable derelict building, had known power. To her sniffer senses, it reeked of rancid oil and rotting vegetation.

In all of her nearly twenty-eight years, she had never encountered a place like it. The remnant of whatever tale it held within its brick walls fanned out like smoke, choking her senses.

Until that moment, she had avoided this byway at all costs, rushing past it when necessity demanded. Yet tonight, as Walt's eyes roved up and down the lane, a foreboding leeched into her bones.

They waited. Penelope's hands curled into fists as she fought the urge to flee. The reverberation of distant cries, separated from them by time, not space, vibrated in her chest. Had not Walt jerked her head in the direction of a field and darted into it, Penelope might have screamed. She had never, not once, felt such a heavy premonition.

As she followed Walt's lead, each step carried her away from that place, loosening its vicelike grip on her senses. At twenty yards, the fragrance of the wet earth greeted her. At thirty, the breeze whisked away the lingering tension. And at forty, she wondered at her weakness, that a place should stir such terror in a rational woman. Ridiculous. Best to shove such intrusive ponderings behind the lists of nautical terms she had memorised on a lark.

"All's clear, I'd wager." Walt stretched her arms skyward and yawned.

Penelope ran an outstretched hand over the waist-high grasses. "Indeed."

The pair meandered for some time. Conversation was scant; they were not the sort of ladies who needed to while the evening away with prattle. If either spoke, they spoke with intention (to inform or poke fun), not to fill the silence. When they arrived at a crossroads, where one lane led to town and the other towards Penelope's estate, they paused.

"I think I've made enough mischief for one evening." Walt lit her pipe. "Best be off."

"Truth be told, I think you have made enough mischief for ten lifetimes." The corner of Penelope's mouth lifted. "And I suspect you have not the least inclination to give up the practice."

Her assistant cocked an eyebrow. "Look who's talking, Miss I-dress-as-a-boy-to-spy-on-gentlemen-and-my-assistant. Hmmm!"

With that, she pivoted and strode towards town, carried onward by the sound of Penelope's laughter.

Chapter 2

THE CHAPTER WITH THE KNOTS

"After our research, my esteemed
colleague and I propose that
psychometrists ought to be known as
temporal travellers, or time travellers,
instead."

Psychometry or Temporal Displacement? The
Facts, by the Honourable Earl of Alderwood
and Mr Archibald Sedgewick

To be employed by the Sedgewicks was to be employed by
one of the wealthiest families in the county. Naturally, such
a lofty position came with certain benefits—stability, for one;
generous pay, for another; and prestige, of course. As the
mistresses were not tyrants and the master was not given to
fits of rage, the staff had little to complain of. That is, except
for the oddities Birch Hallow kept tucked behind its doors.

With the patience of saints, the staff dusted the bell jars
containing all manner of toads, they mopped up foam overflowing from beakers onto the floor, and they gathered the

remnants of flying machines strewn across the front lawn. They were English; their heredity demanded a stiff upper lip in the face of such curiosities.

Hence, the housekeeper, Mrs Dewar, a stalwart woman who had the bearing of an admiral, though not the facial hair, did not start upon entering the library the next morning. No, she gave her master, Mr Archibald Sedgewick, a wide berth as he lay bound hand and foot on the floor whilst his niece, Miss Penelope Sedgewick, nibbled on a cake, a watch in hand.

Mrs Dewar went about her business at the sideboard; tea was refilled, cakes rearranged, and the faedragon's head patted without a bat of the eye nor a tut. "Will there be anything else, miss?"

Penelope, distracted by her uncle's attempt to free himself from his restraints, paid no mind to the dark circles under her housekeeper's eyes. Perhaps she too had been out late. "Nothing more, thank you."

With that, Mrs Dewar bustled from the room, noiselessly sliding the door closed behind her.

"No more playing about," Penelope signed to her uncle, a gentleman with salt-and-pepper hair who looked as though he had only just tumbled out of bed. "She has gone."

Seconds later, having freed his hands, Uncle Archie popped up, shaking the ropes from his feet. "Good. I do hate an audience." His hands formed the words with a rapidity that reflected the pace of his thoughts. Since her uncle had never quit Birch Hallow, even when her late father, the eldest Sedgewick, had inherited it, Penelope had learnt sign language from her infancy; therefore, following his hurried signs was second nature. How else would she have been able to communicate with her uncle, who had been deaf since birth?

After kicking his restraints aside, he dusted the lint from his coat. "What was my time? Minus the interruption, of course."

Penelope replaced her teacup in her saucer in order to answer, "Two minutes and ten seconds. A personal best."

Hurriedly, her uncle scurried to his desk in the middle of the room, scribbled the time on a piece of parchment, applied wax, and sealed it. Before he joined his niece at the breakfast table, he paused at the floor-to-ceiling windows overlooking the grounds. A shy morning sun hid herself behind a blanket of grey clouds as though she were a wealthy lady still abed. The gardener trimmed the hedges. A mother hare shooed her younglings out of the path of a handcart containing mulch for the roses. Time ticked on as it always had at Birch Hallow, quietly.

The odour of burnt butter carried by a puff of smoke rising from beneath the table drew her uncle's attention. "Tell me you did not slip Cerberus cream again. You know how dairy wreaks havoc on her digestive system."

"Never, Uncle." Penelope stroked the miniature faedragon's head, eliciting a coo. When her uncle turned to the sideboard to drizzle honey in a criss-cross pattern over a second helping of cake, she placed her finger upon her lips and breathed a gentle *Shhh*. Cerberus winked before once again tucking her nose beneath her stained-glass-patterned wings.

Once her uncle had turned to face her again, she signed, "Given the nature of this latest experiment, is it safe to presume that you and Lord Alderwood are debating knots or tensile strength?"

Plate in hand, Uncle Archie slid into his seat. Before he dived into his cake and fruit, he topped up his tea. "No. My exercise in the art of escapology was to satisfy a wager."

"Did you win?"

"Of course."

The pair turned to their respective papers: she to her daily allotment of news from all manner of journals, the sensational included, and he to his academic papers. As hers provided scant information and even less actual news, she glanced at the headline of the latest edition of the *Journal of Speculative Sciences* tucked beneath her uncle's teacup. Emblazoned across the cover, a headline read, "Psychometry or Temporal Displacement? The Facts."

To say that our heroine's interest was piqued would be putting it mildly. It was a wonder she did not snatch the paper from beneath her uncle's elbow, toppling his tea in the process. However, as she was a gently bred heiress, she summoned the most disinterested air she could muster before tapping the table to get her uncle's attention. "Have you read the article on the first page of the *Journal*, Uncle? It looks quite interesting."

Always eager to converse on matters of physics, her uncle set aside his cup. "Did you happen to notice the authors?" He waggled his eyebrows.

She had not, and indicated as much with a shake of her head.

"The Earl and myself, of course."

"Since you appear before me with all your limbs, I presume that in the course of penning the paper, you were not forced to meet in person." Her nose scrunched in delight. Oh, how she did love to tease her uncle, as a proper niece ought.

"In fact, we did meet in person," her uncle signed proudly.

{Narrator's Note: The Earl in question is the honourable Earl of Alderwood, equestrian, renowned philosopher, and advisor to the Prince Regent. When not entertaining royalty, he corresponds with Uncle Archie. On paper, they are dear friends. In person, they are mortal enemies.}

"Perhaps the next month's edition of the *Journal of Speculative Sciences* should explore how the pair of you managed to endure a meeting unscathed."

"It is a marvel." Uncle Archie paused to bite into a slice of treacle tart, sending a cascade of crumbs tumbling down his shirt. Much to his personal butler's chagrin, the shirt, along with his waistcoat, had wrinkled of its own volition. "Though I never insinuated that *he* exited the fray without a scratch."

A shared chuckle roused Cerberus from her slumber. As penance, Uncle Archie welcomed her into his lap, lavishing her with kisses and berries dipped in honey.

Whilst her uncle was distracted by his scaly companion, Penelope took a steadying sip of tea. Its tangy liquid fanned across her tongue, shushing her nerves. Despite having made a vow (which she swore was a loose promise at best) to confess her magical abilities to her uncle and aunt, she still had not done so. No, a secret was a burden, especially a secret of such a nature. Their shoulders bore enough; she would not add to the weight they carried.

However, her curiosity would not pipe down. It insisted she return to the subject at hand. The bitter dregs of her tea cleared the small lump in her throat. "As for the article, do tell me more."

Cerberus hopped back to her chair, exhausted by the exertion of moving before noon. Giving the faedragon a final pat on the head, her uncle fixed his attention on his niece. "After combing through hundreds of accounts and interviewing dozens of listeners, we hypothesized that objects do not carry memories at all. Rather, they are bridges of a sort."

He snatched a letter from the pile of papers, and tore from it a strip no wider than his thumb. "This is an object's timeline. A string would make for a more fitting representation, yet this will do." With a sweeping motion, he sent half of the contents of the table cascading onto the rug to clear space for his demonstration. His eye flicked to his niece sheepishly as he recalled her distaste for rumpled paper. Together, they organised the fallen items into a pile.

His weathered hands spread the strip of paper flat. "If this . . ." A finger jabbed the topmost edge. ". . . is the moment the item came into being, and this . . ." He tapped the bottom edge. ". . . is the moment before its destruction, then this . . ." His finger slid along the length of the paper, connecting the two points. ". . . is its timeline."

Penelope nodded. Of course, she was familiar with and shared his theory of time. A three-dimensional web of strings would have been a more precise illustration; however, as they were discussing a singular object's history, paper would suffice.

He extended the paper to her across the table. One end fell limp in his hand while his thumb and pointer finger pinched the other. A nod sufficed to instruct her to take hold of the fallen end. She did.

With his free hand, he signed, "An object can connect two people like a bridge. It can create a pathway from your past to my present, or vice versa. And I suspect that a listener can navigate an object's history, permitting them to visit any time or place where the object was present."

Though Penelope had enjoyed her fill of honey cakes for one day, she rose to add another to her plate. She was intimately familiar with the gift of listening. It had been on her eleventh birthday that she had first discovered she could perceive an object's history. At first, the visions came merely as flashes, so fleeting she had been hardly aware of them. They had been like wisps of mist slipping through her fingers. Mastery of her gift came with age and practice, much like her ability to sense the presence of magic. Year by year, she honed the art of pressing into the whispers until they became vibrant visions. Only recently had she been able to catch scents and sounds as well.

With her feet planted near the sideboard, she stood. What kept her frozen in half a daze was the notion that her uncle could be correct. On a handful of occasions, she had pushed deep enough into a vision that she had disconnected from the present entirely.

On one occasion, she had emerged bearing the evidence of his theory. The collar of her dress had been peppered with rain droplets. Naturally, she had blamed their presence on perspiration. Even still, between blinks, she could smell the wet earth, ripe with the fragrance of—

KNOCK! KNOCK! KNOCK! The sound of her uncle rapping on the table snapped her back to the present. When she turned, a smile plastered on her face, she beheld her uncle's head crooked to one side.

"Are you unwell?" he asked in a concerned tone.

"Not at all." She slid into her seat, clutching a plate piled high with fruit and cakes. A blueberry tumbled onto the polished table and rolled across it. "Your theory fascinates me, and yet . . ."

Uncle Archie's eyes twinkled with delight. Ever since her earliest years, he had welcomed questions—he was a mad scientist through and through.

After transferring a generous helping of berries onto the plate set for Cerberus, she continued, "I spot a fault in it."

Her uncle's fingers fluttered with anticipation.

"From testimonies I have read . . ." *and my own experiences* ". . . the listener does not pass through every moment of an object's history. That could take years or centuries. Instead, they only catch glimpses until they arrive at a moment into which they wish to delve further."

"Precisely! The Earl and I have long wondered if the listener's gift extends beyond observing histories to navigating through time. Like a rock skimming across the surface of a lake, the listener hops across the object's timeline, touching moments anchored by strong emotion. They plunge headlong into the one of their choosing, stepping for an instant into the past only to return to the precise moment they had left. We have considered terming it time travel. It has a nice ring, do you not think?"

Naturally, Penelope's head felt as though it might explode. A cup of tea and several hours wandering the forest in solitude would prove restorative. It was a wonder she did not dash from the room, teapot and cup in tow. And yet she could not. One question lingered. "How could one test such a hypothesis? The listener alone experiences the vision."

"We witnessed it."

"But how?!"

"The Earl and I visited a pair of twin sisters, listeners. Upon our arrival, they handed each of us a folded scrap of paper and asked us to place them in our coat pockets. We did so. Our interview proceeded." His signing paused while his steady hand refilled his niece's cup, then his own. "At the end of the interview, they offered us a demonstration. They handed us scraps of blank paper and instructed us to write a message to ourselves, fold the papers, and then place them on a tray. We did so, eyeing them across the rug to ensure they remained firmly planted in their seats."

"Naturally, you were tempted to unfold the papers in your pocket."

"Of course. When we had finished, one sister laid the papers flat on her open palm. The second sister covered the papers with her hand. They closed their eyes. Later, the Earl and I observed that an unearthly stillness swept over them, robbing them of expression and even breath." By now, even Cerberus had raised her head, intrigued by the tale her companion told.

"An instant later, they became animated once more. When they unclasped their hands, the papers were gone. It was then that the Earl and I withdrew the scraps we had been given upon entering the parlour. On mine, written in my hand, were the words I had penned not minutes prior."

When one discovers that one may have the ability to move through space and time, it can be a shock. A terrible one, in fact. One that ought to have robbed her of her senses. However, as a sleuth with a web of informants spreading across four countries, Penelope had grown accustomed to surprising news—which was why a quick sip of tea was all that was necessary to restore her.

"Fascinating, Uncle." She patted his hand. "Please, leave the article on my desk to read later."

He nodded, then resumed his perusal of a letter.

After slipping the remainder of her plate's contents into Cerberus's dish near the fireplace, Penelope retrieved a journal from her desk. A walk, she decided, was in order.

A scratch under the chin sufficed as a farewell to her scaly breakfast companion. Her uncle received an embrace. His wavy hair, jutting every which way, smelt of cinnamon.

"Shall we be seeing you at dinner?" he signed.

"Yes." Tonight she had no intention of gallivanting through Alderwood dressed as a boy. She paused. "And, Uncle, what message did you write on your paper?"

A sheepish grin picked at the corners of his lips. His eyes danced. "The precise dates and times I have fallen in love."

She raised an eyebrow, encouraging him.

"The first was thirty years ago when I gave my heart to a dazzling young woman who, sadly, married another. And the second . . ." His eyes became glassy, brimming with emotion. ". . . was the 2nd of October, 1783, at 11:59 in the morning—the moment I first held you."

Overcome by a love she felt she scarcely deserved, Penelope embraced him once more, pressing a kiss to his temple. As she crossed towards the door, a tear did not trickle down her cheek. Well . . . maybe one did, but only one (or two).

Chapter 3

THE CHAPTER WITH THE TUMBLING

"Once, during the purge of 1779, I hid in
a burrow for two months without setting a
toe outside its walls. After the first week, I
became so downhearted that I rewrote the
final acts of six of Shakespeare's plays so
that they might have a happy ending."

A Quote from John Stuart, Seer

If a witch had been in the market for a house made of ginger-
bread into which she could entice young children so that she
might broil them for tea, the Forest of Dean in 1811 would
have been the ideal location. It had narrow rock crevices
perfect for tumbling into during a chase. Then there were
the knotted trees aplenty, whose roots conveniently broke
through the dark soil with the intent of twisting ankles. The
resident ghosts appreciated the mist that clung to the forest
floor, providing sufficient cover for spooking travellers. All in
all, it was an author's fantasy.

Since such horrors kept half the village at bay, Penelope collected her bonnet, gloves, and spencer and struck out for the wood. Her feet were no strangers to the paths traversed by tourists or the rougher byways reserved for locals. It was one of the latter she selected that morn. In their shadows, where lurked the creatures of legend, she found the silence necessary to reassemble her scattered nerves.

Her uncle's revelation was not especially shocking—she had heard such notions circulated before. Previously, she had not once given the ideas weight; however, she had never known her uncle to leap to conclusions. If he had gone so far as to put his thoughts to pen and paper, his hypothesis would, in all likelihood, one day be established as a fact.

What tore her conscience in two was a thought—could the past be altered? If her true gift as a listener lay in an ability to cross the timelines of objects like bridges, could she undo the decision that had led to her parents' deaths? If she . . .

A branch splintering underfoot to her right drew her attention. Voices whirled through the air. Oh, bother. People.

"The pup had the audacity to suggest I would be better pleased with, as he put it, 'a lovely book with loads of pictures' rather than the book I had requested."

The velvety voice piercing a thicket of tangled vines could only belong to one woman—Mrs Stevenson. Which meant her companion was—

"Please do tell me you bruised either his pride, by putting him in his place, or his head, by turning the 'lovely book with loads of pictures' against him."

Ah yes, her aunt, Josephine Sedgewick.

An obliging log provided a ready seat, onto which Penelope lowered herself. Doubtless, the pair were on a well-travelled lane that intersected with her own path just ahead. They would pass soon enough, leaving her to her thoughts.

Not that she minded a tête-à-tête with her aunt or Mrs Stevenson. She generally welcomed the opportunity to spar verbally with either. Today, though, she wished for no other company than her own.

They did not pass by as she had hoped. The crunch of gravel underfoot informed her that they too wished to wander the quieter paths. Blast. Within a matter of moments, they would be upon her. Penelope arranged her sage muslin gown, adjusted her posture, and fixed a wistful expression on her face as though she had been swept away by the raptures of nature on the cusp of autumn.

When the hem of her aunt's black skirt peeked around the brambles, Penelope spoke. Her bright "Good morning. What brings you to this corner of the wood?" caused both women to start.

Grins replaced confusion as the ladies welcomed her: Mrs Stevenson with a kiss on the cheek and her aunt with a look that would have caused lesser mortals to confess their darkest secrets.

She fell into step with them, retracing the paths she had already trodden.

"The weather," Mrs Stevenson began, "has taken a lovely turn, has it not, dear?"

Penelope, aware of her aunt's preference for the summer months, did not even bother to reply. As anticipated, her aunt piped in, "Not in the least."

Their friendship had long tickled Penelope. They were opposites, or so the town believed. While Mrs Stevenson was heat, her aunt was ice. To counter each of her aunt's edges, her friend had developed curves. One paraded about like a wildflower and the other cloaked herself in midnight. Day and night. Silk and iron.

Those who knew them well, though, recognised kindred spirits. Their appearances and tones were dissimilar, yet their souls were not. They were mirrors of one another in the essentials: their courage, their honour, and their wit.

Which is why Penelope was not offended when Mrs Stevenson asked, "Are you wandering the forest in hopes of being kidnapped by a pirate, or have you entrapped yourself in a torrid affair with a delicious farmer?" The expression on her face indicated that she sincerely hoped it was the latter.

Penelope did not grin. To grin would be to encourage such teasing. "Is there no other reason a young lady can wander the woods?"

Mrs Stevenson's eyes danced with mischief. "None that are any fun."

"Come, she may lead a secret life as the head of a ring of smugglers." Her aunt ducked underneath a fallen tree swathed in moss. Vines draped across it, tumbling to the forest floor to create an archway. "Trysts are not the only fun that can be had by intrepid young ladies."

Her aunt's friend shrugged. Clearly, traipsing about the wood as a smuggler could not compare to the delight of secret embraces. At least, not in her opinion.

"Alas, neither. I wander this way often

to study webs." Penelope leapt over a fallen branch cast across the path in the last storm. "I find orb-weaver webs especially fascinating."

The downturn of Mrs Stevenson's lip indicated her disappointment. Her aunt, on the other hand, lifted her eyebrows, clearly unconvinced.

To allay her aunt's suspicions (and bore the pair to tears, so they might wish to be rid of her), Penelope described the engineering wonder that was a spider's web. Soon her companions' eyes glazed over with abstraction.

As they approached a crossroads, Penelope made clear that she intended to head in the opposite direction of her aunt and friend. "When you arrive home, do check the library. Uncle Archie has been honing his escapism skills, and I am concerned he will get himself into a bind from which he cannot free himself."

An expression that made our heroine blush flashed across Mrs Stevenson's face. "All tied up, you say? Interesting."

To prevent herself from dwelling on *that* visual, Penelope recalled the first twenty digits of pi in reverse. She preferred not to consider the particulars of the budding romance between her uncle and the widowed Mrs Stevenson. No, thank you. Whatever nonsense they got themselves into was not her business.

Much to her surprise, her aunt did not wince or cringe. Mouth pursed, eyebrows pinched, jaw taut—Josephine Sedgewick, with more brains than half of the House of Lords combined, was perplexed. "Tied up in knots, did you say?"

"Yes." She considered her aunt out of the corner of her eye. "He and the Earl have made a wager."

"The Earl?" Aunt Josephine had stopped.

Mrs Stevenson, not yet noticing her friend's peculiar behaviour, wondered, "What are they bickering about this week?"

"Temporal displacement," Penelope promptly replied.

"Temporal displacement?" Her aunt's eyes roved Penelope's face as though she were meeting this sprite-like creature with curious hazel eyes for the first time. "And the Folk?"

"Yes. He hypothesises that listener's true gift lies in their ability—"

"To navigate through space and time." A second voice whispered in Penelope's ear—younger, yet matching her aunt's cadence note for note, her speech word for word.

Her aunt's face blurred as a second arose behind it. It was as though Penelope stared through a window, her eyes unable to hold the reflection in the glass while gazing on the world beyond. The forest blinked in and out of existence, supplanted by moonlight. Smoke stung her eyes.

"Are you two quite well?" asked Mrs Stevenson.

The moment snapped and vanished. Shaking away the wisps of a vision she could scarcely understand, Penelope grinned. "Of course, just tired."

Mrs Stevenson was no simpleton. It was evident in the flick of her gaze between Penelope and her friend that she was unconvinced; however, she was also not a busybody. Rather than press the matter, she adjusted her bonnet and bade our heroine farewell.

Penelope began to turn onto the path that would carry her deeper into the wood when her aunt caught her hand to enfold her in an embrace. There were no murmured words nor stifled tears. After all, they were Sedgewicks. And yet never in all her years, save the months after her parents' death when her aunt would cradle her in arms as she wept, had Aunt Josephine held her like that. Confused, Penelope returned the gesture stiffly.

When they stepped apart, they did not linger. Her aunt fell into step with her friend, commenting on a ladies' society she chaired. Penelope wandered into the forest once more.

She had tumbled into a vision; of that she was certain. Yet to do so accidentally, well . . . that had not occurred in a decade, if not longer. If her uncle was correct, she had not merely caught a glimpse of the past, but she had stepped into a moment from her aunt's history.

Her path led her into the ancient groves, where dwelt yews as wide as carriages are long. She ducked under one such matron of the wood, whose trunk was knotted and bent with age. Autumn had already claimed several of her leaves, turning them red to reflect the sunset of another year.

A knoll resembling a lady's profile provided a welcome spot to lean against and reflect. One by one her mind called forth the scenes she had seen in the vision—fire, ash, darkness. And when she shut out the world around her, there were shouts.

Had her eyes remained closed, the entire course of her day, if not her life, might have been altered. However, Fate is a meddler with a schedule to keep. When Penelope's lashes fluttered open, she caught sight of an Irish elk loping past her resting place.

Of course, she had seen an Irish elk before. In her childhood, a mother and her calf had spent half the year roaming the edges of their estate, popping in on Sundays to nip a dozen crab apples from the orchard before being chased off by the gardener and his broom. It was the males, however, with racks spanning the length of a church pew, that fascinated her.

The one before her, who nibbled on the final blades of summer grasses poking through the fallen leaves, hardly rustled the foliage as he passed. A wonder, she considered, given his size.

Unable to resist the temptation to observe such a creature, Penelope padded alongside him, careful to maintain a safe distance. Magnificent. A true . . .

Had not the ground creaked underfoot, our heroine might have tailed after the buck for half an hour. However, forest floors ought not to creak or shudder. Which is why her nervous system began to shout CRAP! CRAP! CRAP! when her left boot crunched through the earth. Before she could shout or grasp a root, the earth beneath her gave way.

The elk peaked up from his midmorning snack to discover that the overgrown pixie clad in a bonnet had disappeared. He shrugged before he meandered onward in search of apricots.

Chapter 4

THE CHAPTER WITH THE FALL

"Irish elk, a species of deer of the genus Megaloceros, have roamed Britain's Isles since before man first set foot on her shores. Unlike the woolly mammoth, their numbers have not dwindled. This is due in part to the presence of forest dragons, who have guarded against the encroachment of mankind."

Megafauna: A Study by Alexander Pence, 1801

Penelope was pleasantly surprised by her experience of being swallowed by the earth. Firstly, she had not tumbled into a wyrm den, nor, despite Mrs Stevenson's ardent wish, a pirate's lair. Secondly, she had slid. Had the ground to her right given way, she would have plummeted straight down onto packed earth. Instead, our heroine tumbled down a steep wall of earth before landing on her derriere. Though not a pleasant ride, it had prevented her from being concussed.

{Narrator's Note: While protagonists in *other* novels can recover from concussions within an hour or two, the rules of our universe do not permit such nonsense. Nor can protagonists be run through with a sword a dozen times only to best a hoard of ogres. Sorry to disappoint.}

Finally, she had not landed in standing water. She abhorred soggy stockings.

Once the world had righted itself, Penelope discovered that she lay sprawled across the floor of a room. Before exploring her surroundings, she took stock of herself. Head fine. Ribs bruised. Limbs intact, though bloodied. Hands . . . well, they appeared as though they had waged war with a cheese grater.

Though she was not squeamish, the state of them caused her stomach to temporarily relocate itself to her throat. Two handkerchiefs were gingerly tugged from her pocket, applied to her palms, and secured with minimal wincing.

Rather than stand, she perused her surroundings. A single shaft of light pierced the darkness. Before her spread a room whose ceiling was held aloft by rough-hewn beams. A scent reminiscent of a cave inundated her senses, as did another odour—wet iron. Her eyes roved the walls. There, perched on roots that served as shelves, sat geodes, intended to warn or ward off enemies. Though their power had faded, their presence still tickled her nose.

At the far end lay two beds, their straw mattresses long repurposed by a family of resident mice. Nearer her stood a table and four chairs. Cross-stitched florals and pastel sketches hung from the fieldstone walls, giving a homey feeling to the otherwise dank space.

Eager to explore before she plotted her escape, Penelope attempted to push herself upright. Unfortunately, her wrist would not cooperate. Given that half her body ached, she had not attended to the throb radiating up her right arm. However, when she shifted to draw her feet beneath her, her wrist protested. A gasp escaped her lips.

She froze with her heart thundering in her chest, waiting for the pain to subside. Blast! Scrambling a fifteen-foot embankment in a muslin dress would have been a feat with two hands, an impossibility with one.

Despite her strict policy against scooting, the situation necessitated it. One of the chairs provided the support necessary to stand. Gingerly, she tested both ankles. Sound.

End to end, the room was not seven paces across. She explored what few nooks and crannies it held, hoping to discover a door or a ladder. None. The gaping hole through which she had fallen was the sole entrance. No rope or ladder remained.

As she could not save herself, she had one choice—shouting.

"Excuse me! Squirrel?" She strained her ear, hoping to perceive the pitter-patter of paws or the flutter of wings. "Hare? Owl?" Nothing.

While most ladies would have hoped for a gentleman on a white steed to come to their rescue, Penelope had no time for such follies. Besides, why hope for a man to wander through the woods when it was brimming with a steady stream of furry messengers?

She tried again. "Hello! I mean you no harm. I only wish for you to carry a message."

Silence.

Just as she was about to call out again, the silhouette of a fox peeped out from the skylight's edge. He cocked his head to one side.

Penelope curtseyed. "Hello, Sir Fox. Thank you for answering my call."

Sensing that before him stood a lady, he bowed. Though she could not discern his thoughts, the primordial power inhabiting these woods gave its furry and feathered residents a sort of sentience. Whether it was lent to them by the magical creatures who dwelt there or given to them by Mother Nature herself, Penelope did not know. Today, though, she was thankful. It allowed him to understand her well enough to convey her message, or so she hoped.

"As you can see, I have fallen and am unable to rescue myself. Would you be so kind as to circulate my whereabouts among your acquaintances? The young forest dragon who inhabits the fledgling wood south of here is my dear friend, as is the yeti called Mr Scott. Could you alert them to my predicament?"

Although her vision was marred by the midday sun behind him, which set his copper fur ablaze, she noted that he squinted at her suspiciously.

Fair enough. Most ladies did not traipse about the forest keeping company with dragons and creatures of lore. Her four-legged rescuer had every reason to be sceptical.

Rather than attempt to convince him that she was harmless (which, even in her injured state, she was not), she elected to appeal to his compassion. Hands unclasped, she stretched her palms high, the light illuminating her blood-stained makeshift bandages.

A pout formed on his lips. Without so much as a farewell, he scampered off.

Uncertain when one of her rescuers would arrive, Penelope set about what came naturally—she tidied. She had learnt as a young girl that cleaning provided a ready opportunity to investigate under the guise of being helpful. Furthermore, she found that organisation settled her nerves.

Not that she had nerves; she was fine. Why would she not be? True, she could potentially prevent her parents' deaths, but that was not unsettling. Not in the least. Or so she convinced herself.

Determined not to give this notion another thought, Penelope turned her attention to the room. Clearly, the subterranean chamber had been built as a hideout. Shelves stocked with expired jars of fruits, empty sacks of grain, and half-finished bottles of port confirmed as much. The quarter-century-old halfpenny tucked beneath one of the cots supported her theory, as did one of the sketches.

A sketch of a young woman hung from one of the roots by a periwinkle ribbon. Faint gusts swept through the room, twirling it like a dancer on the stage. Though Penelope was no dowser (Folk whose gift permitted them to find objects or to detect items with particularly interesting histories), her fingers itched to pluck it from its ribbon and listen to whatever tale it held.

After several minutes of pacing, she relented. With care both for her wounded palms and the age of the paper, she undid the ribbon to examine it. Age had been unkind to the portrait, yellowing it, curling its edges. Tracks raced down the paper, from groundwater, perhaps.

An echo sounded in her mind as she considered the portrait's subject. The girl could not have been of age, nineteen or twenty at most. Her neatly drawn eyes brimmed with laughter. She felt familiar, as though she were an acquaintance; however, the style of her collar and hat was that of the decades before Penelope's birth.

A tingling sensation spread from Penelope's fingertips, swirling the length of her arms to her heart. The girl's laughter tripped across the decades.

A shadow passed across the hole above, winking out the sun. With care, Penelope slid the paper into her pocket. Tomorrow would provide ample opportunities to listen to its story or, if her uncle was correct, to travel to the past. Now, though, someone approached: either her rescuer or a drake seeking a midday snack.

Anticipation hummed in her veins as her eyes roved the leafy umbrella of treetops stretched above the opening. Her senses stretched outwards. Above her, padding noiselessly across the forest floor moved a being of power—not Mr Scott nor a drake. A glimpse of antlers trimmed with vines confirmed her hunch.

"Greetings, Sir Toast. Have you come to rescue me?"

Head cocked to one side, he gave her a mischievous smirk that communicated, *What have you got yourself into this time?*

"Oh, I *do* beg your pardon." Penelope placed a hand on her hip in protest. She would have stamped a foot, but her knee ached more than she preferred to admit. "Are you suggesting that I am a gadabout?"

Toast, or so his two-legged friends called him, shrugged. *Well, if the shoe fits . . .*

A chuckle escaped her lips. "As I have interrupted your midmorning nap, I shall let that affront to my character slide." Several injuries cried out in protest. She winced. "You did not happen to bring a rope, did you?"

The forest dragon shook his head. Sunlight danced across his scales, reflecting the autumnal hues of a world breathlessly awaiting the snow. Even his leafy mane, once flush with the verdant colours of the summer, had, of late, reminded her of a sunrise—burnt orange, coral, and gold.

With a jerk of the head towards the embankment, he suggested she could climb.

"Unfortunately . . ." She raised her left hand. Stark crimson stains had seeped through the linen handkerchief. Her injured wrist remained cradled against her body. "I am a tad worse for wear."

He frowned, revealing an especially endearing snaggly tooth that hung over his bottom lip. Like her, he had spotted an impasse. A forest dragon's tail is not especially long, twelve feet at most. As Penelope was petite, a hand-length shorter than most women, she doubted they ought to attempt a rescue by that means. Had she had two uninjured hands, then perhaps.

It was then that providence offered a solution. A rustling drew Toast's attention. He gazed westward. After a moment or two, he turned to her once more, relieved.

"Good afternoon." A bass voice rumbled in the distance.

Though Penelope harboured no tenderer feelings towards Mr Scott than those of friendship, she did take pains (literally, as you may recall, since half of her was bruised) to dust away what dirt remained from her dress, adjust her hat, and blot a smudge of mud from her nose. A tumble into a secret hide-away was not a sufficient excuse to appear rumpled.

A second silhouette joined Toast's. Even with the sun at his back, she could spot the collar of his waistcoat, as well as locks of auburn hair curling over the cuffs of his sleeves. The weather, though pleasant, had not cooled enough to entice him to wear a coat.

"Good afternoon, Miss Sedgewick. I hear that you have been injured."

"Yes, though nothing serious. A sprained wrist and sundry bumps and bruises."

When he turned to Toast to wordlessly plan her escape, Penelope may have stared. Despite the half a dozen times she had encountered Mr Scott, the sight of him still astounded her. It was not every day that a lady, even a lady who lived in Alderwood, encountered a yeti, especially one who sported a hat and boots.

> {Narrator's Note: As there is no law forbidding a reader from reading a series out of order (even though it is a highly unattractive habit), permit me to explain the first sentence of the last paragraph. Dear Mr Ben Scott is a yeti blessed with the gifts of whispering and foresight. Whisperers can commune with animals, including dragons. Carry on.}

"Miss Sedgewick," he called. "Would you permit me, if I descended, to lift you so that our dear friend could curl his tail under your . . ."

Though only the thinnest strip of skin was visible around his eyes and under his curled moustache, Penelope would have bet her estate that the gentleman blushed.

To spare him the mortification of speaking the word "bottom" aloud, she replied. "Yes, I think it a sound plan."

Soon a pair of sensible boots followed by linen breeches poked through the entrance. Each foothold was tested. Every movement was taken with care. Foot by foot, Mr Scott descended until he reached the room below.

"Good morning." He bowed. His eyes flitted from her bloodied hands to the scrape on her cheek. "Would you prefer I tend to your injuries here or above? That is, if you would permit me to do so."

She curtseyed. "Above, if you please."

Mr Scott acknowledged her decision before she had spoken it. Seers. Ugh! Feet in the present. Heads in next week. At least he did not make a show of it, unlike others who shared his gift.

Between the three of them, Penelope soon stood under the ancient yew once more. The wounds on her hands were tended with minimal discomfort and a splint was applied to her wrist.

"That wrist may be fractured." Mr Scott commented, the lilt of his Scottish roots edging the corners of his words. "Sable could tend to it. Her house is not a mile hence."

Penelope had too busy a schedule to bother with a fractured wrist. How would she practice fencing or perfect her archery skills one-handed? No, a visit to the surliest healer in all of Gloucestershire would be wise.

With that, the trio turned their feet towards the edge of the wood. As they departed, Penelope slipped her hand into her pocket and stroked the edge of the portrait.

Chapter 5

THE CHAPTER WITH THE HEALER WHO HAD MEN FOR TEA (LITERALLY?)

"During my time observing the practices of healers,
it came to my attention that their gifts, even among
the most experienced, had limits; however, when two
or three healers combined their gifts, their power
multiplied, permitting them to heal even fatal injuries."

Field Notes from My Year Among the Healers,
Abel Haversham, 1803

Had not Penelope spotted the crooked chimney of Sable's cottage through a break in the trees, she would have known they had arrived at their destination by the tsunami of honeysuckle that threatened to capsize the house. Like a fishing vessel in a gale, it was caught up in streams of herbs, ivy, and fern swirling at its foundation, reaching for the roof line, intent on dragging it under.

As Toast had fallen behind to visit a mother badger and her young, it was on Penelope that Sable's lightning eyes first fell. A scowl sank her brow low. It was not that she especially despised our heroine. In fact, if one were to slip a few drops of truth tincture to this healer with a waterfall of white hair, she would confess that she liked the heiress. However, she had a reputation to maintain. If she began to smile, how could she preserve her position in the community as a hag who ate naughty children for tea?

The walk, though not strenuous, had exacerbated the ache in Penelope's knee, causing her to limp. Though Mr Scott could have carried her with ease, she had been reticent to ask. His honour would have not permitted him to deny her, despite how ardently he might have blushed.

Sable's keen eyes dipped to her soiled dress and wrapped wrist. A flash of compassion might have wandered onto her face before she turned to a bushel of string beans grown to twice their natural size. "What're you doing here?" Then again, perhaps not.

Other ladies would have been offended. Penelope, though, was not other ladies. Contrariness was a quality she shared with those she held dear. However else would she survive the endless string of balls, card games, and afternoon calls if not for her friends' cutting remarks?

"Good afternoon, Sable. I trust you are well."

Without answering, the lady continued to harvest the beans. Her weathered hands, spotted from years tending to her garden, caressed the vines, breathing strength into them.

Toast hurried out of the forest, eager for a snack. When the woman's eye met his, genuine delight spread across it. Even the yeti was granted a nod.

"Sable, my dear, you look well today." Mr Scott wrestled a chair from the ivy. After he had dusted it and checked that it was sound, he motioned for Penelope to take a seat. "We have brought you a patient."

Thankful for his thoughtfulness, she lowered herself into the chair. Mr Scott and Sable wandered to the cottage in pursuit of tea and cake while Toast chased a butterfly.

Alone, she let her eyes slip shut. The melody of the garden—the buzz of beetles, the rustle of petals, the tinkling of a stream—hummed like a lullaby. It invited her to rest a while. A whisper of wind carried upon it the scents of Mother Nature. Thyme, honeysuckle, wild rose, and rosemary mingled to create an intoxicating perfume.

A quarter of an hour later, her hostess returned, bearing a tea tray. The party removed to a gazebo built not by hammer and nails but coaxed from the earth itself. Instead of cross-beams, the root from an obliging oak had stretched across the expanse. Wisteria, clothed in an indecent shade of violet, provided a roof. Tables and chairs had not been constructed; instead, such comforts had sprung from the earth.

A cup of tea with honey was presented to the injured. Penelope accepted it. Before Sable served herself, she knelt at her patient's side.

"What'd you do this time? Wrestle with a swan?" With care, Sable pressed her hands, callused and tanned, to Penelope's knee.

{Narrator's Note: For our friends inhabiting another universe, permit me to caution you should you ever encounter the beasts. These vicious feathered fiends are among our most fearsome predators. Besides stealing picnics and making a racket, they have been known to break the arms of maidens. Should you ever encounter one, run.}

"No. Swans I could have handled." She flinched as Sable's touch made her knee twinge. "Chambers hidden beneath the forest floor are trickier to contend with."

"So you happened upon a burrow." Her hands slid to Penelope's ribs.

Mr Scott fixated on the seed cake, doling out equal portions onto three plates. "No, ma'am, an actual subterranean chamber with chairs and a table."

"A burrow," she insisted, cradling her patient's bandaged hands in her own. Her lashes fluttered as a pained expression flashed across her face. Healers could sense the discomfort of others, or so Penelope had read. "That's what they were called in my youth."

It was no secret that a network of safehouses to smuggle Folk out of the country had existed during the purges of the last century. Birch Hallow had one such space tucked beneath a flight of stairs. As a young child, Penelope had happened upon it during a game of hide and seek. She had been drawn to the magic its wards radiated. A bed, washbasin, and table with chair had furnished the room. Though it had been vacant, a hint of rosewater had hung in the air, as though the occupant had only recently stepped out.

"I discovered one once in Scotland." The gentleman placed a plate stacked high with cold meats, cheeses, and seedcakes before Penelope. "It had caved in."

Sable rose and threw back an unsweetened cup of tea in one swig. "Hid in one or two myself in my middling years. Preferred the ones in houses, though. Less dank."

A jar of salve was withdrawn from her apron's pocket. When the lid was removed, the odour of comfrey, frank-

incense, and calendula filled the space, settling Penelope's frazzled nerves. It was applied with care to her minor scrapes and bruises.

"Sable, how were your gifts discovered?" Mr Scott broke off a corner of cake to share with a russet field mouse who boldly had climbed onto his knee. It scampered off, its spoils in tow. "My mother had to relocate us to my grandfather's hunting lodge when my gifts first manifested themselves. Every maid quit within a week due to the assortment of spiders and squirrels I kept in my breeches."

The vision of a young (and less hairy) Mr Scott driving governesses from the house with pockets full of toads tickled Penelope. Just yesterday, she had observed a young girl of four or five taking tea with a hare and a racoon. Whispering was the gift every child envied. What child would not wish to befriend a woodland creature?

Then again, as Mr Scott was past thirty, he, like Penelope, had been born into a world that had not yet accepted magic. And though the purges had ceased in her younger years, it had not been until after her fourteenth birthday that magic had been legalized. Even still, she had never confessed her gifts to anyone, besides Walt. Magic was fine for those who had to earn their bread, but society had not yet acknowledged its existence among the upper crust.

Having finished the application of a variety of sundry salves and creams to Penelope's less serious wounds, Sable plopped onto the stool across from her, eager to tend to her more substantial injuries. As she unwound the bandages, she replied, "Not so much discovered as revealed."

Both the yeti and the heiress raised their eyebrows.

"None of that." She wagged a finger at them. "There was a young lady . . ."

The clatter of a carriage drew the party's attention. As Society had classified the existence of a yeti in the Forest of Dean as fiction, Mr Scott stepped behind a column of lilac flowers. The ladies waved. Well, Penelope did. Her companion likely brandished a rude gesture as the carriage went on its way.

When she turned to her hostess once more, the woman's irises—the colour of blue lightning, vivid enough to illuminate a night's sky—possessed her. When the elder woman spoke, her West Country accent had vanished, replaced by one more refined. "Had not two other healers and I combined our gifts, she would have succumbed to her injuries."

Behind her, Penelope sensed a presence flutter. A desperate "Please" stirred the curl at the nape of her neck. She turned. The garden was empty save for Toast, who was napping in the shade of an oak.

By the time the gentleman had returned to his seat and had topped up the tea, the moment had passed, leaving Sable's characteristic glower in its wake.

"So," she began. "You'd like me to heal your wrist and hands, I understand?"

Instead of taking the woman by the shoulders and shouting, "What the blazes was that all about?", Penelope plastered on a ladylike grin. Four guineas were slid from her reticule. "Yes, and the knee as well, if you please."

"The wrist is fractured . . ."

A smirk plucked at the corner of Mr Scott's lips, revealing his satisfaction that his diagnosis had been correct.

"Without another healer to help, it'll still be tender. Treat it with care and keep it wrapped for a week. It'll be fine." With that, Sable's eyes slipped closed. Readers will be disappointed to learn that the wind did not stir, nor did her hands glow with an unearthly light. No: to the observer, nothing peculiar occurred.

Penelope, on the other hand, felt the pain wick from her palms and wrist. Raw wounds folded closed, leaving behind fresh, pink skin. The throb in her knee quieted. When Sable's eyes fluttered open, darkness whirled across their surface, then dissipated like smoke.

"You'll feel peaky for an hour." The healer downed her third cup of tea. "Best rest in the hammock until the queasiness passes."

"I feel f—" Penelope clapped her hand over her lips to suppress the rising tide of nausea, a common side effect of having one's bones mended.

With the aid of her companions, she navigated her way through the garden to the hammock, careful not to trip over any number of discarded gardening tools lurking beneath the tide of greenery. A pillow was provided, as was a thin quilt. Once she had thanked Sable and bidden Mr Scott a good day, she permitted her eyes to slip closed once more, winking out the noonday sun.

Safe under the watchful eye of Toast, she succumbed to her fatigue (and a couple of drops of sleep serum that had been added to her tea). Before she fell asleep, she thought she heard second whispered "Please." However, the wind snatched it away before she slipped under Morpheus' spell.

Chapter 6

THE CHAPTER WITH THE FALLEN MAIDEN

"They say the fire at the teahouse was an
accident. Accident, my aunt Fanny! I saw
a gentleman with a wide-brimmed hat run
from the building as though the devil was
after him."

Paul Smith, Farmer, 1796

Warm baths peppered with lavender oil and soap chips possess
a magical quality of their own. Or so Penelope believed after
she emerged from her carriage a few hours later bathed, fed,
and refreshed.

As she was wont to do on a fine afternoon not dampened
by rain, she directed her feet to the heart of Alderwood in
search of subtly acquired information (in other words, overheard gossip). She meandered through the quieter lanes to
the thoroughfare.

Carved wooden signs advertising all manner of wares
and services hung over the cobblestone byways and alleys.
Whether it was a weathered plaque promising quality crockery

or a varnished sign in the shape of a spool of thread, each beckoned the throng to step inside.

Beneath one such sign, she paused, feigning interest in a brooch on display. In all reality, she did not give two figs about jewellery; however, she *was* intrigued by the hurried exchange between the daughter of a parson and the son of an opera singer.

A knot of silly girls spilt out of a ribbon shop. Their laughter suggested that they shared a delicious secret. They did not. One of the girls had repeated a naughty joke. And not even a good one at that.

Penelope continued to stroll up and down the streets, admiring the tidiness of the town. Though whitewashed brick and limestone were the predominant building materials of the region, the occasional red-brick facade crept in to maintain a semblance of variety. Anything to attract the tourists. After all, a day traipsing the forest in search of a will-o'-the-wisp or the fae left many a pleasure seeker eager to lighten their purses in a quaint country town.

Her feet directed her to a carriageway the council had constructed a decade prior. Green spaces hemmed by curated rose hedges stretched from the forest on one end to a fountain on the other. Pedestrian pathways curved through shrubs trimmed into the shape of unicorns and mushrooms. Then, of course, there were trees to provide shade when the sun elected to be cheeky and make an appearance.

Like most days, couples stole longing glances as they strolled, governesses minded their charges, footmen chased their mistresses' lap dragons, and elderly pairs fed the resident birds seeds from paper bags purchased for a halfpenny. And though dragons were not permitted to fly within the town, they pranced up and down the streets bordering either side of the park, towing their carts behind them.

Penelope had donned a white muslin frock and russet poke bonnet embellished with wyvern feathers. Leather gloves hid the fabric she had wound around her wrist, which was still tender. She looked the part of an heiress. No one would ever have suspected that on her person she carried no fewer than three weapons and would have happily used any one of them if given the opportunity.

On and on she walked. Nods were acknowledged. Smiles exchanged. Manners observed. By the time she had reached the fountain, she wondered whether a lady could die of boredom. Certainly, death would be more diverting.

Her gaze roved the windows and porches lining the square, hoping to spy anything of interest. Nothing. Window after window reflected the afternoon sun. That was until a commotion on a balcony of Alderwood's principal teahouse drew her eye.

At a height of twenty feet above the square, a lady stumbled towards its bannister as though she had been shoved. Though Penelope was no seer, her senses urged her to sprint. Other onlookers gaped like frogs, their mouths hanging open, though none hurried to the woman's aid.

The woman collided with the railing. It shuddered under the force of her weight. For an instant, Penelope thought it might hold. Then a crack reverberated across the square. The railing gave way, and the woman fell. Her skirt whipped in the air as she tumbled noiselessly to the earth below.

A gig cutting across our heroine's path momentarily blocked her view. When a *thud* rang across the square, announcing the inevitable, Penelope tensed. The driver, oblivious to the victim's plight, drove on, revealing a crumpled body on the cobblestones.

Free of her impediment, Penelope crossed the space and fell to her knees near the woman's head. The lady, who was more a girl, stared blankly. Through curtains of golden hair her eyes shone—vacant seas of cornflower blue. Dead.

Shouts filled the street as men, women, and children swirled around them. Aware that she had only a few precious moments before an idiot parading as a knight in shining armour shooed her away, she catalogued every detail.

Wrists bound at her waist by a blue brocade sash. Odd. Wounds? Only those to her skull from the fall: her face, torso, and limbs appeared uninjured. Nails? Clean. Hands? Not especially rough. Dress? Peculiar. It was fine, fashionable even, or it would have been had the year been 1780. The cut and style reminded Penelope of a portrait displayed in the hall across from her bedroom door.

And then there was the necklace. Tied to a satin ribbon hung about the girl's neck was a silver pendant bearing an imprint—a three-pronged fork with circles at its base. This, though, was no ordinary trinket. Despite the overwhelming odour of a dozen charms present in the swelling crowd, Penelope sensed that it possessed a power she had not encountered before. Though the sensation was familiar, the scent was not. What magic it contained, she could not tell. Her fingers itched to take hold of it.

A gentleman placed a hand on her shoulder, urging her to step aside. With care, she brushed the girl's hair from her face. She froze. Had a herd of woolly rhinoceros ridden by a troupe of torch-bearing pixies stampeded through the square at the moment, she could not have moved. Her hand slid over her pocket, confirming the existence of the sketch she had discovered in the burrow that morning. Before her, bereft of laughter, lay its twin.

Unable to concoct an excuse to remain beside the girl a moment longer, Penelope rose and stepped away. As rapidly as she dared, she committed the likenesses of the onlookers to memory. A couple of dozen familiar faces were noted, as were a few unfamiliar ones. Joiners, coachmen, and gentry stood on tiptoes, already circulating rumours. Had not a voice in the back of Penelope's mind urged her to keep her mouth shut, she might have climbed the fountain, brandished a pistol, and reminded them that death was not a pageant.

Eager to escape, she pressed through the swelling horde. The odour of dozens of unwashed bodies hot with the musk of intrigue hastened her pace. She had nearly reached the tearoom's steps when she caught a flutter of black silk in her periphery. She pivoted.

Tan breeches, pale muslin, and hickory coats encircled the body. Aside from the odd stovepipe hat, not a thread of black was present.

Convinced the vision was yet another apparition, Penelope turned towards the steps once more. She would have proceeded inside to confirm a suspicion, had not she seen her. There, in the shadow of the balcony, stood her aunt.

They held one another's gaze, neither betraying their thoughts. When her aunt directed her steps towards the park, Penelope did as well. The pair weaved through the stream of horses, carts, and men, mirroring one another's movements.

Their paths intersected at the fountain. Without a word, they circled it. All manner of neighbours mounted its edge, eager to catch a peek of the goings-on at the base of balcony. Penelope may have bumped one (or three.) of the more artificially pious onlookers into the water.

Once clear of the crowd, the aunt and niece stopped. The balcony was still visible, with a section of railing dangling overhead, presiding over the spectacle.

"You have spotted the issue, obviously." Her aunt's eyes were trained on the scene.

"Several." When the wind picked at Penelope's skirt, she felt the sketch's edge through the thin muslin. The charm that concealed the pocket did not prevent her from feeling its contents. "Though I presume you are referring to the shutters."

Aunt Josephine dipped her pointed chin.

"How long has it been since the second floor was removed? Fourteen years?"

"Fifteen." She turned and strode further into the gardens. "A fire in '96 damaged the upper level. It sat vacant for four years." A bench free of droppings was selected. Aunt Josephine swept it with a whisk broom she kept in her reticule before she settled onto one end. "After the legalisation of magic, Alderwood became the unofficial capital of lore and magickind. An astute gentleman purchased the building to construct the tearoom, but never resurrected the terrace."

Penelope perched on the other end of the bench. "I doubt a young woman dressed in old-fashioned clothing could climb the tearoom's walls without a single patron taking note."

"Especially given that her hands were tied."

Had not she witnessed the fall herself, touched the girl's skin, observed the state of the windows, she would not have believed the tale. The question that formed in her mind was not whether it had happened, but how.

When she turned, a wooden box had been placed on the bench between them.

Certain Folk, those known as sniffers, of which Penelope was one, could sense the presence of magic. Charms perfumed the air with the scent of florals, whereas wards had a metallic quality. Magical creatures carried the odour of their natural environments. Toast, for instance, inundated her senses with the fragrance of the forest after the rain.

And then there were the *other* items—those that dampened magic. The box blackened by fire was one such item.

She could perceive it with her eyes, but to the piece of her that walked a world that brimmed with magic just beyond the senses, it felt hollow: a vacant entity that simultaneously drew her in and repelled her. Her fingers fluttered, eager to snatch it—either to understand it or to smash it on the ground; she could not tell which.

Her aunt extended her hand and slid the box, no larger than her palm, nearer to her niece. "Take this. Open it in a quiet place."

"What does it contain?" Penelope's hands remained folded in her lap.

Aunt Josephine's expression danced with mischief. "Answers."

A pair of pursed lips served as a reply.

"My dear." The elder woman shifted nearer the younger, scooping her niece's hand into her own. "Do you remember the first time you leapt from the dock into the pond?"

She did. Their property was home to a stream-fed pond. With glassy waters teeming with lily pads and reeds, it was the sort of place artists tramp through fields to paint. Aunt Josephine would take her to picnic on its shores. On sweltering days, her aunt would slip into a simple pair of breeches and a shirt to take a dip. Penelope waded. She swam. Yet never, not once, did she dare leap from the dock into its cobalt waters.

One day, her aunt offered to leap with her, despite the havoc it would wreak on her raven hair. Penelope had agreed. Hand in hand, they leapt, squealing with delight.

While they swam ashore, her younger self confessed that she had been silly not to attempt it on her own. Her aunt, arms slicing through the water, shook her head. "Nonsense, my dear. Today, I lent you an ounce of my courage until you could discover your own."

Back on the park bench, her aunt continued, "This is me offering you my hand." She slid the box onto her niece's palm. "Take it."

"Well . . ." Penelope curled her fingers around the burnished surface and tucked it into her reticule. "If you insist. This is all quite cryptic, though."

"Yes. Is it not such fun?" Her aunt's gaze flicked to her face. "Must be off. Much to do."

The ladies rose, and, for the second time that day, the women embraced.

"Remind me to hug them often," her aunt whispered into her ear. After a final squeeze, she released her and turned to walk away.

Chapter 7

THE CHAPTER WITH THE FORGOTTEN BOOT

"Gifts, like wine and cheese, improve
over time."

Josephus Perry, Sniffer

Our heroine did not race through the streets of Alderwood to her private offices. She was a lady of nearly twenty-eight, not a silly girl. With a degree of self-possession which most women could only aspire to, she criss-crossed through its narrow lanes.

Whether she elbowed a lady who blocked half of an alleyway is inconsequential. That she flashed a dagger at a gentleman who smiled at her is neither here nor there. Neither of these occurrences, if they even happened at all, indicated she was in a rush, thank you very much.

Rather than gain access to her office via the front entrance, a reputable herbal shop frequented by half the ladies in the town, she nipped in the back entrance. She navigated the spotless workroom, where hung trimmed herbs in tidy bunches.

The recently mopped hall lined with doors opening to consultation rooms was vacant. On the third door hung a placard that read, "Please do not disturb."

This particular door led to a stairwell—a pristine passageway free of muck, footprints, and scuffs. It was up these stairs she ascended. A polished oak door greeted her bearing a sign of its own. "Mrs Patience Jones. Please knock."

She did not knock. She never had. Since Miss Patience Jones was a moniker, a figment of her imagination, a front, she barged in as though she owned the place (which she did).

Before she had the opportunity to shed her bonnet, reticule, or spencer, a dagger sliced past her face, burying itself in the door with an unmomentous *twang*.

"Are you and the door quarrelling again?" Her bonnet and then gloves were removed and stowed in their proper places.

Adorned in a bottle-green, floor-length robe, Walt stood, pipe bobbing from her lip. "Who says I wasn't aiming for you?"

"Has your aim so devolved that you could not even clip me at, what, five yards?" Penelope turned to hang her bonnet from its hook, as well as gather her assistant's spencer from the floor. After they had been properly hung, she turned to discover Walt sticking her tongue out at her, which she ignored.

"And what mischief have you caused this morning?" Penelope observed the half-eaten bits of toast on the mantel, the cold meats on a plate perched on the bookcase, and the half a dozen daggers stuck fast into the wooden target that was usually kept hidden behind a tapestry. "Have you even left your rooms?"

"Nah. After last night's escapades, I thought I deserved to lie about." After refilling her teacup and draining its contents in one go, Walt flopped into her chair. Her coral lips puffed a stray curl out of her face. "And what have you been up to this morning? Fancy lady things, I presume."

Reticule still in hand, Penelope crossed to her desk. The letter opener lay parallel to her pen, just as she had left it. "Not unless you deem tumbling into a hole, which I later learned had been a hideout for the Folk during the purge, being rescued by a dragon and a yeti—"

"What's that ole furball up to?" Walt packed her pipe. She lit it, careful not to set her raven locks aflame when she flicked the match into the fireplace.

"Mr Scott is much the same. A solitary figure forced to wander the woods alone—an outcast, a legend, a cautionary tale."

"Lord, Miss. Why'd you have to go and get all morose? A 'fine' would have sufficed."

While her assistant poured a cup for each of them, Penelope thumbed through her correspondences. Besides a letter from a duchess who had misplaced her lover, the remainder of the pile could wait. It read:

Dear Miss Jones,

At your earliest convenience, please communicate a time and location to meet privately. Your reputation precedes you; therefore, I will lay bare the facts concerning a matter which requires the utmost delicacy.

My lover, Mr Montgomery Thomason, has not contacted me in several days. He has been faithful in his correspondence for

a decade at least. We have not had a row, nor is he abroad.
Most peculiar of all is the discovery of a gravestone at the site
of our first meeting, a tree in the forest. It bears his initials
and birth year, though the date of death reads 1781.

Please do not delay in responding. Money is of no object.

A Lady

Despite the intriguing details, she laid the letter aside. That the stone bore his initials and date of birth was curious; however, she would attend to the matter later.

After she had collected the tray of cheese, meat, and fruit from the bookshelf (and straightened a handful of volumes), she lowered herself into her chair. Careful not to slosh her tea over the rim of her cup, Penelope stirred in a spoonful of honey. Again and again, she spun the delicate silver spoon around the rim, creating a whirlpool. Dared she open the box here, with her friend beside her, or ought she to—

"Are you alright?"

Her hand jerked. Tea leapt from the cup onto her saucer. "Quite fine." As she had not returned her handkerchiefs to her pockets after her fall, her hand plunged into her reticule to fetch one. The box brushed against her knuckles.

Though she could not sense what magic lay tucked between the folds of fabric next to her, she could perceive a pair of eyes watching her. There, legs draped over the arm of her chair, sat her friend. Her caramel eyes held no judgment.

"Except . . ." She withdrew the box and placed it on the spindly table between them. ". . . my aunt gave this to me."

Walt puffed on her pipe and nodded. Though her reply consisted of one word—"Interesting"—her tone said, "Why are you all a-tither about a piece of kindling?"

Penelope chuckled. "Perhaps it is nothing of import. However, today has been . . ." Her voice faded. ". . . peculiar."

"More than usual?"

"Only if you consider hearing disembodied voices or catching glimpses of the past to be out of the ordinary." Her fingers stroked the lid. Flashes of the young woman careening towards the ground filled her vision. "And then there was the murder."

"Not another one of those." Walt's nose crinkled as though she had caught a whiff of dragon dung. "Can't we stick to love nests or bribery? Or even a nice coup? Perhaps one set in a scenic coastal village? That'd be lovely."

Penelope refilled their cups. "If only."

Whilst Walt built a tower of meat and cheese sandwiched between sliced pickles and topped with an olive, Penelope's gaze meandered to the bookshelf. The sight of book after book neatly arranged soothed her edges. If the box had to be opened, it would be best to do it with a friend.

As though she were reading her mind, Walt asked, "So, are we going to open it or would you prefer to wring your hands and fret about it for another half an hour?"

Penelope's lips pressed into a line. "I was not 'wringing my hands.'"

{Dear Reader, she was, in fact, wringing her hands.}

The echo of her companion's eye roll could be heard across the town.

Penelope's fingers fluttered as they reached for the box. She lifted it with her fingertips to settle it on her lap. With care, she opened the lid.

Despite her misgivings, moss-tinted smoke did not seep through the opening, nor did a bolt of lightning fall. Sadly, opening the blackened box did not summon a single harbinger of doom. Instead, a presumptuous slip of paper peeked through the crack.

"Well, that was anticlimactic." Walt thumbed through a Radcliffe novel, unimpressed.

After she'd elbowed aside the rising tide of silliness she felt, Penelope threw back the lid. Two halves of a broken locket and two accompanying chains lay nestled beneath a folded scrap of paper. Though she had yet to touch either of the golden ovals engraved with intricate roses, she felt it—magic. Its scent reminded her of lavender, a fragrance she had yet to encounter. Unlike vanity charms and thief thwarters, or any magical item for that matter, the locket did not tickle her nose. Instead, it soothed her, unruffling the misgivings that had plagued her.

Apprehensive about taking up an item whose power penetrated her skin, soaking into her being, she unfolded the paper instead.

"Read it aloud then." Walt continued to flip the novel's pages.

Long elegant strokes were crammed onto a quarter sheet of foolscap. It was her aunt's hand; of that she was certain. Penelope began, "*My Dear Penelope, When I was a young woman, I made an error in judgment. It haunts me to this day.*"

The novel was returned to the table as Walt leaned forward to snatch a biscuit tin she kept next to her chair. "Now . . ." She crammed a biscuit into her mouth. ". . . this makes waking up before four in the afternoon worth my while. Carry on."

"Over the years, I have wondered whether a fresh set of eyes could discern the patterns I missed, the mystery I failed to solve." A furrowed brow settled over Penelope's face. "A mystery? What sort of mystery?"

"We could speculate on the matter, foiling one another with witty repartee." She eyed the uneaten slice of Leicestershire cheese on her employer's plate. *"Or* you could read the rest of the letter."

Penelope nudged the plate towards her. The slice, as well as a wedge of Double Gloucester, vanished. She read on. *"This locket is the key. It is my hope that with it you will uncover the truth."*

A hand snatched one of the necklaces from the box. Half of the locket dangled from the golden chain wound through Walt's fingers. "Ooooh, fun! All very cloak and dagger."

Walt ambled across the rug to her bedchamber, slipping the necklace over her head. Clunks and clatters soon filled the air. Alone, Penelope read the letter a second then a third time. Beneath her aunt's signature lay a postscript.

P.S. Bring gold and weapons.

A web of facts and theories took shape in her mind. The murder, the visions, the voices, and this letter were related, or so she hoped. While Walt continued to riffle through her chest of drawers, Penelope filled her cup to the brim. Its warmth radiated through the porcelain.

Minutes later, her assistant emerged dressed in a soft pink gown with a black velvet ribbon at her waist. She hiked a foot onto the chair, revealing a dagger strapped to her thigh.

Penelope looked up from her cup. "And where are you going?"

"With you, of course." In the mirror by the door, Walt swept her hair into a loose bun before pinning it in place. "Who'll be there to save your neck if I don't tag along? Besides, it sounds delightful, what with all the gold and weaponry. Wouldn't miss it for the world."

"And don't forget the disembodied voices or visions of fire and smoke."

"Perhaps it would be best if I popped down to a tap room during those bits." From under the bed, Walt withdrew the leather bag Penelope had given her the previous April. Into it, she placed a novel, three apples, a tin of savoury biscuits, and a box of bullets.

Though she would never confess as much, Penelope felt relieved. Harrowing adventures are best when taken with a friend, especially one with a wicked right hook.

She crossed to the bookcase. Three volumes were removed to reveal a wooden box. From it, she withdrew a pair of pistols that had belonged to her father, and a pouch of gold. After tucking the palm-sized pouch in her coat pocket, she strapped one of the weapons to her thigh. She placed the other beside Walt, who stood trying to pour a cup of tea whilst yanking a stocking onto one foot.

A faint voice, not perceived by her ears yet heard all the same, drew her to the box once more. It lay open. Light streaming through the window caught the roses etched onto the second half of the locket.

Since a gaping chasm had not split the sitting room down the centre when her assistant had removed the first half of the necklace, Penelope edged closer. Like a siren's song, a chorus of unheard pleas drew her. Her hand reached out.

"Should I wear my sturdier boo——"

Candles were not lit as dusk turned to dark, nor was the fire set. A solitary boot rested on the rug, bereft of its mate. And two cups of tea grew cold.

Chapter 8

THE CHAPTER WITH THE TEMPORAL DISPLACEMENT

"—ts?"

Moonlight bathed the four walls of their rooms in a silvery hue. Without a word, each lady armed herself: Penelope with her pistol and Walt with a dagger (after she gingerly lowered the lone boot in her hand to the floor). They stepped together, back to back, their eyes roving the familiar yet foreign chamber.

While the mantel and window were unchanged, the desk had disappeared. In fact, all of the furniture had. Their pair of delicate wheat-coloured chairs had been replaced by a sturdy wingback chair. (And when I say sturdy, I mean clunky and dull.) A round table with two chairs had been placed near the window. And on the glass. . . droplets accompanied by the patter of rain on the roof.

With care, Penelope stepped in the direction of the bedroom, whose double doors were ajar. The yawning darkness beyond swallowed light, revealing little as to who or what lay within.

"Where are we?" muttered Walt under her breath.

"When."

A muffled snore reassured her that while they were not alone, the person buried under a quilt slept, or at least pretended to do so. The pair retraced their steps, easing towards the entry door that led to the stairs.

On their way, Walt nearly toppled a tailor's dummy. A fussy half-finished monstrosity swayed until her hand steadied it. "When?"

Penelope dipped her chin. "Yes. A better question would be 'When are we?'" To her, this much was obvious: one of the Folk had charmed the two halves of the necklace to create a bridge between 1811 and this moment. Though Penelope had never heard of such a charm, it was possible, she supposed.

They froze at the murmur of a man's voice muttering something about "ponies" and "next Sunday." The bed groaned. Not wishing to explain themselves to a drowsy gentleman of undetermined morals, the ladies slid the door open and padded down the stairs.

Had Penelope needed further evidence that they had travelled to another time, the missing door at the foot of the stairs would have sufficed. It had been added after she had purchased the building five years ago. (Or rather, five years ago for her.)

At the base of the stairs, Walt made to turn left towards the back kitchen. A gentle hand on her elbow brought her to a halt. Penelope shook her head. "If my memory serves me well, the back half of the building was a set of rooms occupied by the shopkeeper and his family."

They turned towards what in September of 1811 had been Cecilia's Cabinet, a reputable herbalist shop peddling tinctures and charms to wealthy ladies. Instead, the room that spread before them contained all manner of curiosities—a ship in a bottle, vases, lamps, and . . . Drat! Silverware.

Penelope spun on her heel, nose-to-nose (more like nose-to-chin) with her assistant. "It is imperative that you understand—"

Walt's brilliant caramel eyes caressed the locked case an arm's length away. They lingered on a serving spoon whose handle was adorned with a gryphon.

"Walt," her employer snapped in her face.

Usually, Penelope turned a blind eye to her assistant's thieving tendencies. Often she found it amusing, especially as she had been unable to discover the reason behind them. However, as they were marooned in a century that was not their own, without family, friends, or rescuer in sight, she felt it quite unwise to steal within the first fifteen minutes of their arrival.

In her stockinged feet, Walt slid closer to a case that contained several sets of fine silver spoons, her own particular Achilles's heel. She nearly salivated.

"Walt!" Penelope hissed.

The wail of a bowing floorboard overhead activated the ladies like a shot. They padded across the store until they reached the front door. Thankfully, the key had been left in the lock. Walt tore it open and barrelled into the night, straight into a puddle, in her stockinged feet, no less. While Penelope locked the door and slid the key beneath the gap, her friend offended several stray cats and a pair of birds sheltering under an awning with a string of expletives.

Thankfully, the rain had driven the merrymakers and thieves abed. The street lay vacant. Rather than the bustling lane lined with shops and inns, the thoroughfare resembled a quaint village.

Where in 1811 stood an inn, there sat a vacant plot ravaged by weeds. What would become fashionable boutiques were quaint cottages. Whenever it was that they stood, Alderwood had yet to become anything more than a country town.

The pair slid along the building to the corner, taking refuge in the shadow of an alley. Content that they would not be caught unawares, Penelope took stock. Though she had fared better than her partner, having not shed her spencer or boots, they were underdressed for the weather—and the period, she hazarded. The half-sewn dress they had seen in their rooms (or what would one day become their rooms) suggested that they had travelled to the latter 1770s or the early 1780s. A newspaper would confirm as much, could she lay her hands upon one.

She turned to Walt, who had begun to shiver. "Which shall we procure first, boots or dresses?"

"Is procure a gentlelady word for pinching?" Walt's breath hung in the air.

Over the thatched cottages and down cobblestone lanes, a bark echoed from another street. The ladies held their breath. Besides the flicker of a candle in a lone window down the lane, not a creature stirred in the darkness.

"No," she whispered, her eyes roving the street.

Walt apparently did not believe her. "Won't purloining goods from the past rip a chasm in—"

"If you prefer to die of pneumonia . . ."

"Procuring it is, then." Walt sheathed her dagger before stepping out from the alley.

It would appear the moon approved of their "procuring", for she dipped behind a cloud, providing a blanket of darkness under which they could prowl the streets.

"If I recall correctly, a handful of dress shops and seamstresses lay near the fountain." Penelope led the way. They slunk along the buildings to avoid the steady rain.

"As I am an unknown entity in this time, can't I parade about as your brother?"

"While one could trust a wig for an evening of espionage . . ." The pair turned left, passing a plot that would one day house a renowned healer, yet today was half built, its walls standing no higher than Penelope's shoulder. ". . . I would not expect it to stay put during a storm."

"Blast! I cut a fine figure as a gent." She eyed a silhouette that passed a window lit by a fire in the hearth. They slowed their pace.

"Indeed, and in addition, when dressed as a gentleman, you do not need to worry about modesty when kicking a foe in the face." Penelope minded her steps, careful not to splash in a puddle lest they draw unwanted attention.

Despite her efforts, a slice of amber burst through an opening in the drapes as they were drawn aside. Not wishing to tempt Fate, they dodged around a corner towards their destination.

Once they sprinted the length of several cottages, they took refuge under the arch of a recessed door. Well, Penelope sprinted; Walt impersonated a deer in ice skates as she slid across the muddy roadway wearing nothing but stockings.

The door advertised cure-alls of dubious origin. Remedies for all manner of ills, from rheumatism to baldness, were emblazoned in red lettering across the wide windows. A newspaper clipping posted near the door touted a remedy for arthritis as the discovery of the century. It was dated 1781.

Penelope summoned every crumb of historical happenings she had memorised from that particular year. The weather indicated that they had arrived in the autumn, as did the bare trees and wilted flowers in the window boxes that had dotted their path. No wonder her friend shook with cold.

Eager to continue their quest for warmer clothing, boots, and a hot bowl of stew, Walt peeked around the corner. "The fountain ought to be—" Her face fell.

Penelope stepped out from the threshold. In place of a stone fountain rose a wooden beam. The moon slipped from behind the clouds to reveal a circle of chains at its foot. Even in the dim light, she could discern scorch marks, evidence of flames.

Her friend moved nearer her protectively. "Well, sh—"

". . . it." Penelope finished. Despite the frigid temperatures and the fact that they had arrived during one of the purges, a grin slipped across our heroine's lips.

"Isn't it?" Her assistant chuckled.

The clouds, quite fatigued of the burden they carried, let loose. Not to be outdone, the wind whipped itself into a proper gale, carrying the scent of ash across the lane. The ladies stopped laughing.

"Come along." Penelope nodded at the storefront opposite them. Its window displayed a striped dress and wide-brimmed hat. "We had better get you indoors."

Walt only nodded.

Chapter 9

THE CHAPTER WITH THE CHANCE MEETINGS

"If I be waspish, best beware my sting."

The Taming of the Shrew, Shakespeare

Unsurprisingly, the rain did not flee like a thief in the night. Instead, it settled across the countryside, determined to overstay its welcome.

A cosy inn welcomed them the evening prior. Penelope had been impressed by Walt's impersonation of a distressed damsel. With a tale on her lips of highway robbery by muscled bandits, she won over the innkeeper, his wife, and no fewer than three inebriated patrons. Her story explained their lack of a chaperone (a cowardly cousin who had fled) and their arrival before dawn. A bowl of porridge and a cup of tea later, they were tucked into a fine room, sitting before a roaring fire.

Though Penelope was eager to begin, her internal clock chimed ten in the evening—not especially late, yet past the

-73-

hour she preferred to begin an investigation. Besides, travelling across thirty years had left her a tad fatigued.

Her robe, pointy-toed shoes, and pelisse were shed before she laid down on the bed. She yawned. "Wake me by eleven."

Walt nodded as she skewered a slice of bread and held it near the hearth. "Gladly."

The song of the rain tapping on the window soon lulled her to sleep, her hand clasping the locket fastened at her neck.

BAM! BAM! BAM! "Miss! Miss! Are you awake?"

Penelope sprang from the bed, pistol in hand. The room was vacant. Walt, her cloak, and her umbrella had disappeared, leaving only a plate of half-eaten toast and cold tea. Though the lilac drapes had been drawn closed, she could hear the steady drum of rain on the slate roof overhead.

BAM! BAM! BAM!

She started. Certain that she was in no imminent danger, she padded across the rug to the door. On the other side stood a lad not a day above eleven in a cap meant for a man twice his size. "Are you Miss Clearwater?"

"Yes." She slid her pistol, hidden behind the door, into her pocket.

"A Miss Jones said to deliver this." His grimy hands extended a letter. "And to keep knockin' till you answered."

After she accepted the letter, she wrapped two biscuits in a handkerchief in lieu of a tip, and sent the young man on his way.

The letter, written in a lackadaisical scrawl, was signed W.

Morning Dear,
Errands have driven me into the rain . . .

Which Penelope understood to mean, I was bored out of my knob.

I shall return after I have seen to the matter of the pocket watch and called on a few friends.

The "matter of the pocket watch" indicated that Walt would pay a visit to local shops to pawn the gold watch Penelope had carried for such purposes. The "friends" she referred to suggested that she intended to solicit the local taverns in hopes of collecting useful information and sampling the ale.

Have I time to spare, I may visit the local dressmaker or haberdasher. Regardless, let us dine together this evening. W.

So, she intended to purchase disguises—a logical course.

Not one to remain idle, Penelope ordered a pot of tea with honey and a newspaper. She then took stock of their provisions. Since she had been unaware that her touch would trigger the charm, they had left several items behind: a tin of biscuits (which Walt had bemoaned more than her lack of footwear), a second pistol, and ammunition. Thankfully, the weapon strapped to her thigh had been her father's and hailed from the decade prior to this one.

It had been fortuitous that they had arrived on a blustery night and been able to make the excuse of highway robbery. Had they popped into the room midday and attempted to purchase dresses while wearing what amounted to underclothes in 1781, an eyebrow or two would have been raised.

Fashionable ladies of 1811 wore airy fabric with minimal bows and ruffles. However, Penelope observed that the gentry of this era relished in lace, stripes, corsets, and satin. Careful padding added curves that could not otherwise exist in nature. And the petticoats . . . Well, two toddlers and their dollies could have taken refuge under one.

A piping-hot pot of tea arrived, accompanied by a paper reading October 4, 1781. While savouring the tea, she perused the headlines. What first struck her was how little newspapers had changed in thirty years. Like the ones she read daily, this edition of the Gloucester Journal contained gossip, advertisements, and opinion pieces, as well as, surprisingly, a few well-written articles.

As she suspected, they had arrived during the middle of one of the purges that had swept the latter half of the 1700s prior to the legalisation of magic in 1798. Like other purges of the era, this wave had been brutal, forcing the Folk with less subtle gifts to hide or flee. A cartoon on the front page portrayed a woman being led to a pyre whilst a crowd heckled her. Penelope crumpled the page and cast it into the hearth.

After dressing and styling her hair, Penelope bade her hostess farewell. Thankfully, the rain had nipped out for tea, permitting her to stroll the town unaccosted by the weather. Dressed in a quilted skirt with a floral bouquet print, accompanied by a plain silk robe, a peacock-blue cape, and a hood that rested on her shoulders, she weaved through the familiar streets, careful to dodge the puddles.

This was the Alderwood of her childhood, older even. On the corner stood the ribbon shop her mother had frequented. Its buttermilk shutters and window casings gleamed—freshly painted, she speculated. Never once had she left without a length of ribbon to tie on Cerberus's tail.

Across the way from the building that would house her offices stood the tailor's storefront. Within its red stone walls, generations of Sedgewick men had purchased coats for hunting, for riding, and for marrying. On one of their final walks, her father confided he had worn a blue-jay-coloured coat on his wedding day to please her mama. The same he had worn during their first dance.

Its door swung open. Penelope paused as her uncle stepped into the street. Though thirty years younger, he was as untidy as ever. From across the lane, she could discern wrinkles in his coat. He paid them no mind, though he did attempt, and fail, to smooth his hair.

From her periphery, she spotted a lady in pink, strolling up the lane. He bowed to her, unable to disguise his admiration. He signed, "Good afternoon."

As she approached, Penelope's suspicions were confirmed: the lady was Mrs Stevenson, though still a miss as she would not marry for another year at least. His greeting was met with a grin and a somewhat clumsily signed, "Good day! I trust your sister is well."

Like a candle at midnight, she drew the gaze of every passerby. Even in her youth, she was voluptuous in a way that felt almost indecent in the light of day. Though her dress fought valiantly to contain her curves, her uncle (unlike several men who passed by) paid them no mind. He was bewitched by her eyes.

"Yes." He beamed. "She is well. And what brings you to town this blustery day?"

In her expressions, Penelope noted hints of a first breath of infatuation—the flutter of her lashes, the way her lips could not contain her joy. And when she incorrectly signed the word "ribbon," a blush brightened her cheeks as Uncle Archie's fingers touched hers to help her form the word.

"Ribbon is a serious business, or so my mother told me; however, I never had much use for it beyond fashioning sling-shots and nets as a lad." At his words, they shared a smile.

"Abigail." A voice called from the next lane. "Abigail."

Mrs Stevenson stiffened. Down the muddied street hurried a second lady—her mother, or so Penelope suspected. She was equal to her daughter in beauty though inferior in manners. Her approach fell across their conversation like a shadow.

"Abigail, dear," she said when she stood beside her daughter at last. A curt nod was all the attention the "lady" paid Uncle Archie. Penelope envisioned how delightful it would be to lob a handful of mud at the twit. "Bid this . . ." She took no pains to disguise the curl of her lip. ". . . gentleman farewell. We must be on our way."

Though Penelope had known for months that this rabid shrew had prevented their courtship, it did not lessen the sting of witnessing her slight. Had this hag in taffeta seen past his deafness, past his position as a second son, they could have built a life together. Perhaps they could have even had children.

Mrs Stevenson curtseyed and hastily signed, "Good day." No sooner had her hands dropped to her side than her mama seized her by the elbow to lead her away. Uncle Archie, ever hopeful, watched them until they stepped into their carriage.

Aware of the rising knot in her throat, Penelope hurried into the curiosity shop. A quick "Good afternoon" satisfied the shopkeeper. Likely he thought she was a lovesick girl intent on spying on her beau. A tangle of pelisses, vases, and pots cluttered her view as she gazed through the window.

Wetness clung to her lashes. She blinked it back. This was no time for sentimental nonsense. There was an aunt to save and a timeline to not bungle.

After feigning interest in one or two items, she turned to exit, only to be greeted by yet another ghost from her future—her aunt. Blast! Was every member of her family wandering the streets this dreary afternoon?

"Must we, Josephine?" said a young woman with a round face. "We shall be late."

Penelope's eyes slid past her to the woman in cornflower blue, Miss Josephine Sedgewick—as out of place in a cluttered shop as the sun would be if it tried to contain itself to a lamp. At fifty-five, her aunt was commanding; however, at twenty-five, she was striking. Though not a beauty by traditional standards, her bold features and crystal eyes reminded Penelope of Shakespeare's Katherine come to life. (Well, during the first half of the play. Not the second. That bit is rubbish.)

Their gazes met. A flicker of surprise flashed across her aunt's features before she turned to the shopkeeper. "Good afternoon. Have you the item I requested?"

Had Penelope lingered, she would have drawn unwanted attention; therefore, she slid through the door into the street once more. Waves of dark clouds crashed overhead, threatening to unleash their waters on the sleepy town. Wherever her aunt was heading next, she hoped it was not far.

With as much speed as she could muster in a voluminous skirt, she dashed behind a dragon-drawn carriage on the corner to wait. Minutes later, her aunt emerged. Her sharp eyes swept the roadway before she turned northward.

A map of her childhood haunts formed in Penelope's mind. Given her aunt's trajectory, she could safely assume that she was not homeward bound. Dozens of other destinations were eliminated owing to improbability. Once her aunt crested the hill, Penelope struck towards a path that would permit her to observe her progress from afar.

Through a corner window, Penelope spotted her veer further into the country. They were not heading for the forest, then. From the graveyard, she observed her aunt and companion take a lane that bumped Mrs Stevenson's childhood home from the list. Confident of the pair's destination, Penelope nipped through two gardens and one kitchen to arrive at the lane she had visited the evening prior.

Beneath an iron sign held aloft by two brick columns stood a man, and not an ugly one at that. And behind him, dearest reader, stood the derelict brick building transformed into a tidy factory.

Chapter 10

THE CHAPTER WITH THE TOUR

"A reliable lady of standing informs me that the
better half of the Ton have been in possession of
wrinkle reducers, blemish blotters, and the like for a
decade at least. Perhaps money cannot buy love, but
it can buy beauty."

The Times, 1799

"Good afternoon. Have you come for the tour?" called a
gentleman to a mother and son arriving in their carriage.
"Best to hurry inside before the storm lets loose." Livid clouds
loomed, promising a deluge. The pair darted through the
doors.

Penelope hesitated at the corner. Her last encounter with
this particular building (albeit a future version thereof) included visions of smoke and ash. Furthermore, as she had landed
smack bang in the centre of a purge, it would be an inopportune time to sneeze from an abundance of latent magic.

Before presenting herself at the gate, she skirted the yard
of the imposing brick structure. Knotted weeds had been

replaced by neat hedges. Sparrows no longer dived through a rotted roof. The windows gleamed, nary a smudge in sight.

It was not until she stood opposite its gates that she felt safe. She could tell now that no magic lurked in this place, or at least not enough to trigger a sneezing fit. Her gloved hand slipped into her pocket. There, as always, was a bottle of mint oil, kept on hand to mask the fragrance carried by certain sorts of magic.

"Good afternoon. Have you come for the tour?" The gentleman welcomed her. His eyes lingered on her décolleté. To call him handsome would have been an insult. He was delicious in the sort of way that led even sensible women into hasty marriages followed by "premature" infants. Thankfully, Penelope was not *merely* sensible.

Penelope summoned a coy smile. "Yes, indeed. I am quite fascinated by . . ." Past her host's shoulder loomed a mural painted in the most offensive shade of red fathomable. The bottle read *Horacio Heep's Herbal Remedies, Cure-alls, and Salves.* Below it, in bold lettering, were the words *Manufactured, not Magicked.* ". . . the science of medicine."

The momentary dip of the gentleman's round lips reminded her that clever women were considered as suspicious as the Folk. A girlish giggle she found repulsive bubbled from her lips. "My papa has told me all about zoology."

Confusion clouded his infuriatingly divine face. Perfect.

"You know, the study of the human body," she explained.

Her host, a man of forty-odd years, gave her a look that communicated, *Bless her.*

"Yes, miss. We do love it when young ladies take an interest in our work." The scoundrel winked. "After all, when you

have a house and children of your own, our bruise creams
will come in quite handy for the scrapes and bumps they earn
while playing out of doors."

She stepped through the doorway. "You . . ." *may require a
bruise cream yourself if you do not stop patronising me* ". . . are quite
right."

> {Narrator's Notes: A scandalous rumour has
> spread that our dear heroine, and by extension, the
> author, hate mankind. This is simply preposterous.
> Our heroine adores her uncle and father, as well
> as Toast and Mr Scott. Men worthy of her praise
> have always and will always have it. As for the
> blackguards and simpletons, well . . . will anyone
> *really* care if one or two go missing or are eviscerated
> by our author's pen? I think not. Carry on.}

A curtsey later and she stepped inside, just as she caught
her aunt arriving at the gate. When one is tailing one's aunt
(or anyone else), it is wise to arrive first whenever possible.

Before her spread no dank factory riddled with disease.
Instead, properly organised shelves lined the walls. Down the
centre stretched a swept aisle flanked by rows of neat work-
stations. Black stoves were spaced at intervals throughout the
room. Men and women bustled about wearing crisp aprons.

"Ladies and gentlemen, welcome." Their host, adorned
in simple navy poplin breeches and tailcoat, bore himself like
a learned man. The coat emphasised his physique, lithe and
athletic. He was likely a horseman, or so Penelope wagered.
If she had not suspected him to be a blackguard, the sight of

such order coupled with the perfection of his jawline might have tempted her to propose on the spot. "My name is Horacio Heep, and it is my honour to share with you my little corner of the world."

Certain that her aunt had noticed her among the gathering of a dozen tour-takers, she pivoted to face Mr Heep. Her aunt stood at his elbow, staring at her. Though most cowered under that gaze, Penelope could not. A voice within her shouted, "Stand your ground, girl." She did, and soon, her aunt's icy eyes sought another target.

"Before you lies our workshop—where cures are manufactured, not magicked." He pressed his fingertips together, creating a steeple. An eagerness enlivened every line of his face.

The tour commenced. Their host extolled the revolutionary strides the factory had taken in the science of pharmacology. Workbenches filled with precise rows of jars the size of a palm, powders in wooden boxes, and liquids in amber containers were host to a flurry of activity as medicines were packaged, ready to be shipped across England, Wales, and Scotland.

Our sleuth fell into step behind her aunt. In all of her years, she had never seen Aunt Josephine venture out of doors in any colour besides black. Acquaintances presumed she donned the shades of mourning in honour of her eldest brother—Penelope's father, Charles Sedgewick. She did not. Though the true cause was shrouded in mystery, it had become her habit before his death.

Towards the south end sat vats of bubbling oils. Men stirred in powders with care. Camphor, peppermint, and frankincense mixed with a hint of alcohol tickled Penelope's nose. A wiggly sensation radiated from her chest. Even though the odours were of nature, not nurturers, a decade of self-imposed secrecy had predisposed her to avoid sneezing in public at all costs.

"If your noses are twitching, fear not; you are no sniffer," Mr Heep teased. He flashed a flirtatious grin at a woman half his age. She giggled, as did her mama. "Our physicians have travelled from the highlands of Scotland to the shores of the East Indies in search of ingredients."

One by one, he invited the guests to step nearer the vats or to wander among the tables, encouraging them to ask questions of the assistants. Penelope browsed the workbenches, eager to observe her aunt. Was this tour connected to her aunt's letter and her error in judgment, or was it an afternoon spent with a—?

It was then that her aunt's companion, a curvy woman with a pleasant figure, turned. Without the blast of her aunt's stare to distract her, Penelope was able to place her face. There, dressed in a stripes, was Mrs Dewar.

Rather than conduct themselves as mistress and housekeeper, though, they spoke as friends, exchanging meaningful glances over a drum of what Mr Heep had explained would become a treatment for freckles and acne. Curious.

When it was her turn to inspect the concoction in the brass drum, she did so admirably. For appearance's sake, she even threw in an "Ooooh," though she withheld an "Ahhh"—one wouldn't want to overdo it.

At one station, she spotted willow bark being cut into strips. It was then distilled into a tincture. Flue pipes carried the smoke from the burners and stove up and away through the roof, leaving the room free of soot. A thoroughly modern establishment indeed.

Penelope had been prepared to decree the excursion a failure. Although Mr Heep's establishment was a delight, she had not travelled thirty years to marvel at swept floors.

It was then that a fortuitous gust burst through the loading-bay doors, dispelling the scent of peppermint and lemongrass. She breathed in the aroma of rain, and with it, a hint of something she had not detected before. When a second blast drove the group away from the door and into the belly of the warehouse, Penelope lingered. Yes, hidden beneath the fragrance of herbs and chemicals was a scent that had not been manufactured nor grown, but magicked. One of the Folk had been at work in this place.

Since the heavens had yet to burst, the tour hastily made their goodbyes. Each received a sample of hand cream as a parting gift. Eager to beat the rain, Penelope hurried to the exit. After all, she could spy far more comfortably dressed as a lad, and the earlier she changed her outfit, the better.

Careful to maintain the facade of a lady of leisure, not a sleuth on a mission, she strolled down the road. Just as she had reached the lane that bent towards town, the heavens surrendered. A single *PLOP* of rain on her nose drove her to seek cover under the eaves of a house. Within seconds, a torrent of droplets the size of plums pummelled the countryside.

Chapter 11

THE CHAPTER WITH THE ESCAPE

"As the Folk are predominantly female,
they naturally came under suspicion.
After all, females are conniving
creatures, prone to deceit."

Anonymous Letter to the Editor, The Morning
Herald, *1799*

Downpours are all fine and well unless, of course, one is encumbered by twenty pounds of fabric and boning. Mud, Penelope had decided, would not soil her recently purloined skirt. She decided to wait until the storm ended, lifting her skirts past her ankles to avoid splatter whilst she perched on a board to prevent soggy shoes.

Or that was her plan. A plan which she forfeited when a carriage appeared. Its black horses sliced through the sheets of rain, fog swirling at their feet as though they were prancing through the clouds.

As she expected, the carriage slowed when it drew near her. Rather than the coachman alighting to lower the step and offer her a hand, the door swung open. Her aunt, with an amused expression on her face, sat within, beside Mrs Dewar. "May I offer you a seat in my carriage, or do you prefer to take your chances in the whirlwind?"

Penelope pursed her lips and glanced heavenward. "This has not yet whipped itself into a proper whirlwind."

"Shall I return a quarter of an hour hence?" Her aunt waved her inside. "Come along. I swear, I am no bandit."

The task of squeezing her skirt through the narrow door whilst not muddying her hem offered a few seconds to compose herself and thank the Goddess of Sleuths (if such a deity existed). Not only had a ride been provided, but also an opportunity to be properly introduced to her aunt.

"Thank you." Penelope settled onto the black leather bench opposite her aunt and Mrs Dewar. She adjusted her gloves to cover the bandage on her wrist. "Even had you been a bandit, I might still have accepted your offer. I do loathe the sniffles."

Delight brightened her aunt's eyes. Perfect. Penelope had banked upon her esteem of clever women to ingratiate herself. "Josephine Sedgewick. Not a bandit nor a smuggler, unfortunately." She extended her hand like a Quaker. "A pleasure."

"Prudence Clearwater." She accepted the proffered hand. Thankfully, a future Aunt Josephine had practised the art of the handshake with her niece.

"Firm, but not a stranglehold," she had instructed a miniature Penelope with bows in her hair. "And for goodness sake, you are not a delicate flower—no noodle hands." Penelope applied this advice now, and was satisfied to see that her attempt passed muster.

Aunt Josephine smoothed her dress. "Charmed. This is my friend Mrs Dewar."

"A pleasure to make your acquaintance," said Mrs Dewar. Contrary to her outward appearance—rosy cheeks, round eyes, and soft features—both her tone and personality lacked warmth. It was as though her outward person had conspired to defy her inward temperament. Not unsurprising. Penelope had never known her to be especially personable. In fact, if slipped a truth tincture, she would have described her as taciturn.

"And where can I instruct my coachman to convey you?" Aunt Josephine tapped on the roof to signal his attention.

"The Hedgerow Inn." Penelope grinned. "My cousin and I are on a tour of the region."

After instructions were given, the carriage started. A puff of smoke erupted from her aunt's woollen lap blanket. "I do apologise." She chuckled. "Do permit me to introduce you to my newest acquaintance, Ambrose."

A familiar snout emerged from the folds of the blanket. The petit zilant, roughly the length of a Jack Russell terrier, cocked his head to one side.

"A pleasure to make your acquaintance, sir." Penelope inclined her head.

Ambrose mirrored her and bowed his head. His eyes were obscured by his mane, which was the colour of the seashore: iridescent browns and pearls. The smirk on his face communicated, *Sir? She must have me confused with someone else.* Unlike her aunt, who embodied propriety, Ambrose was the definition of a rascal.

Introductions having been completed, he tucked his nose beneath the blanket and snuggled between the women once more. A dip in the road caused the woollen cover to slip from his shoulder. There, tightly binding his left wing to his chest, was a bandage. Though she had never known a time when Ambrose had two functioning wings, to behold the evidence of his suffering tempted Penelope to propose that they "deal" with the man responsible.

Her aunt's hand righted the blanket. When Penelope's eyes met hers once more, she saw reflected in them the fury she felt stirring within her own heart. Since murder was not on her schedule—well, probably not—she brushed aside such musings.

Several minutes were spent getting through the niceties polite society insisted upon. They discussed the weather (decidedly foul), the local shops (mediocre at best), and the Forest of Dean (a treat). While she felt that such topics were, in general, about as stimulating as trimming one's toenails, she relished the opportunity to become better acquainted with this version of her aunt and, by extension, her father. The ghost of his smile hung before her as her aunt extolled the virtues of hiring a proper guide to visit the forest.

When the carriage pulled hard to the right, Mrs Dewar rolled up the shade to peer outside. "It appears the storm has made the juncture impassable."

The slightest curve of her aunt's lips signalled that she was not put out by the detour. "We shall take the longer route through the wood."

A comfortable quiet settled between the ladies. Penelope's hand involuntarily went to the locket hidden beneath a thin kerchief.

The locket puzzled her. Though it was a charm, and a powerful one she wagered, it did not tickle her nose as others did. Curious. She had grown so accustomed to its lavender scent that she hardly noticed it anymore.

She adjusted the chain, ensuring it was secured about her neck, then tucked it beneath the cloth covering her décolleté once more. "I do hope the Hedgerow Inn is not out of your way." Of course, she knew it was not. Part of the reason she had selected it was because it was nearest her estate.

"No, not at all." Aunt Josephine's eye lingered on Penelope's face. The expression was not one of suspicion. Rather, if she had to give words to the thoughts displayed in her aunt's eye, they would have been, "Hmm . . . Curious."

Determined not to squander the opportunity that had been afforded to her, Penelope steered the conversation to topics that could benefit her investigation. "The tour was interesting, was it not? I must confess, I was impressed by the orderliness of the factory."

Mrs Dewar's eyebrows rose as she exchanged a knowing look with her friend.

"Yes." A grin indicated that her aunt shared her esteem of order, which, of course, she already knew. "Mr Heep's endeavours have done much good in Alderwood. The town has never been so prosperous."

"I have seen his products advertised in the papers, but have yet to purchase them for myself. Are they as miraculous as advertised?" Penelope poked, hoping their expressions would betray their suspicions.

Unfortunately, even at twenty-something, her aunt and housekeeper were cautious. Her aunt replied, "Interestingly, yes, they are." Penelope discerned a hint of wryness in her tone.

A darkening indicated that they had entered the forest. She raised the shade nearest her, feigning interest in the scenery she had known since her infancy. Autumn's glow had taken hold of the forest, bathing it in gold hues. Even in the dim light, bright corals contrasted against the blue of the evergreens—a palette that rivalled the sunset.

Our sleuth did not turn her head, yet she sensed that her aunt studied her. She had half a mind to confess the truth; however, a movement in the mist distracted her.

Though the rain had lessened, darkness still enshrouded the thickets and pathways stretching before her. She leaned nearer the window, fogging the glass with her breath. Her aunt mirrored her, resting a hand on the door. Even Mrs Dewar leaned nearer, her eyes roving the undergrowth. They sat motionless. There again, deep in the forest, a shadow darted between two trees.

"Have you drakes in this wood?" Penelope asked. They did; she knew as much.

"Too tall." Her aunt's hand slipped into her pocket beneath the woollen blanket, likely to withdraw a weapon.

Without the slightest tremble in her voice, Mrs Dewar added, "That is nearer the height of a man or an elk, perhaps."

Not a word passed between them. They stared into the darkness, waiting.

Several minutes slid past. Bit by bit, the tension unwound itself, permitting Penelope's heart to resume a more rational rhythm. Thankfully, whatever had sped through the forest had taken no interest in them.

Aunt Josephine chuckled. "It appears we permitted our fancies to . . ."

The horses slowed to a trot, then stopped.

Without a word, the three women simultaneously drew their pistols. They had no intention of falling prey to whatever lay in their path, be it a beast with two legs or four. Though Penelope knew her aunt and Mrs Dewar survived this day, fear drummed in her veins. Save for the rustle of leaves as the storm exhaled its final breath, the world had gone still. Not a creature stirred.

The coachman alighted, shaking the carriage. Through the window, Penelope caught the flutter of his cape. His measured tread faded down the lane.

"Pardon, miss," he called. "There's a woman on the road. I think she's hurt."

Without hesitating, Aunt Josephine unlatched the door and stepped onto the roadway. Ambrose trailed at her heel, sniffing the air as he slithered through the mud. Penelope followed.

With his rifle braced against his shoulder, the coachman stood over the crumpled mass at the edge of the road. Back and forth, the muzzle of the rifle swept the forest, awaiting whatever prowled beyond their sight. Aunt Josephine stood at his side, surveying their surroundings. Despite an injured wing, the zilant circled his human companion protectively. Penelope vowed to spoil him with sugared berries and kisses when she returned home. Further up the lane, Mrs Dewar kept watch.

As Penelope approached the unconscious woman, her shoes were the first thing she noticed. Rather than sturdy leather boots, the woman wore a pair of slippers, their details hardly discernible under the layers of mud. Penelope squatted beside her aunt, who was attending to the woman.

"Strange, is it not?" Her aunt's eyes darted towards the forest.

"Are you referring to the style of her dress, or that she ventured into a storm wearing house shoes?"

A pulse was sought and found. Though her breaths were shallow, her colouring was not worrisome, indicating that she had not been out of doors for long.

A grin picked at the corner of Aunt Josephine's mouth. "Both. And her hood . . ." She gestured to the black fabric knotted loosely around her neck. "It is impractical."

It was. When properly worn, the arch-shaped hood would have robbed the wearer of her peripheral vision. Her dress, made of a light cotton fabric dyed black, was simple, almost religious in nature.

Penelope checked her head for wounds. None. Her chestnut hair had been braided and wound into a tight knot at the nape of her neck. And though her ears were pierced, the holes were empty; she wore no jewellery.

"Her skin is cold. We ought to—" Penelope stopped as her fingers brushed a rough patch of skin at the nape of the woman's neck. She bent closer. A blanched scar marred the skin just behind her ear. A scar in a familiar shape.

Heat spilled across Penelope's body. She had seen this symbol on the pendant worn by the girl who had fallen from the balcony. "What is this?"

At the sight of the three-pronged fork with circles at its base burned into the woman's skin, all colour drained from her aunt's face. "Interesting."

"Have you seen it before?" Penelope rose to search the roadway for clues. In the distance, the howl of a hound sounded.

"We must get her into the carriage." Though Aunt Josephine's movements were natural, her voice cut through the mist like a blade.

Without further prompting, the coachman handed her aunt the rifle before kneeling in the mud to scoop the woman into his arms. He had not taken three steps before Penelope perceived a rustling sound in the forest.

"Hurry," whispered Josephine. The pair hastened, while Ambrose raced after them. Mrs Dewar flung the carriage door open.

A beating sound in the thicket drew Penelope's eye. Just beyond a rise blanketed in moss, the brim of a man's hat bobbed from side to side. Blast!

Unable to assist with lifting the still unconscious woman, she beat a path to the opposite side of the carriage. She wrenched the handle, throwing open the door before she climbed inside. Though her dress caught on the trim of the door, she ignored it. With a fistful of fabric in each hand, she yanked the woman into the carriage, nearly toppling out in the process.

Her wrist shouted several improper words in protest. Sable had admonished her to take care for a week, and yet not twenty-four hours later, she was wrestling with a woman twice her size. She cradled it against her body.

She had not yet regained her balance when Mrs Dewar and Aunt Josephine climbed into the carriage and closed the door behind them. The woman's eyes fluttered as they rolled her against the bench.

"Shh. You must be silent. You are among friends," her aunt breathed as she draped her skirt and blanket over the woman. The housekeeper followed suit, concern clouding her round face and fine, doe-like eyes.

Shouts outside drew their attention. "Get 'em off me! Get 'em off!"

While Penelope slid into the seat opposite her aunt, arranging her skirts over the woman curled in a ball at their feet, her eye caught Ambrose leaping as high as one wing could carry him. A stout man who resembled a dwarf with an unkempt beard swatted at him.

"Here, Ambrose," called her aunt in a voice dripping with sugar. "Here, my darling. Leave the gentleman alone."

Ever the faithful friend, Ambrose spun once then leapt into the coachman's arms. As he was handed to her aunt through the window, he winked at Penelope. (See, a rascal.)

"I do apologise for my friend. He has been pent up for weeks, recovering from an injury. Do tell me you have not been hurt." Though Penelope could only catch Aunt Josephine's face in profile, the man's smile assured her that her aunt had blasted him with a full dose of maidenly charm.

While her aunt bewitched the gentleman with stories of her childhood terrier (a figment of her imagination, as Penelope's father was allergic to dogs), Penelope had a moment to assess the situation.

At her feet, the woman trembled, either from the cold or fear; she could not tell. A woman branded with an unknown marking and dressed in black, no less. Put together, it was quite ominous.

Outside, being quelled by her aunt's long lashes, was a man who would not have drawn her attention, except that secured to his belt was a pair of iron shackles. About his chest, he had looped a rope like a sash. His leather holster held a pistol alongside a blade as long as her forearm.

"And you, miss." The blackguard addressed Penelope directly. He sauntered nearer them, mere feet from their stowaway's hiding place. "You haven't seen a young woman dressed in black, have you?"

Determined not to betray his prey, she opened her eyes wide and pursed her heart-shaped lips. "Why, no . . ." *you vile excuse for a man. You hideous ogre with less charm than a colony of syphilitic convicts.* ". . . sir, I have not. How terrifying!" Despite the chill, she fanned herself for dramatic effect.

He preened, stroking his ginger beard. Doubtless he thought himself irresistible with his shackles. "'Twould be, to a gentlewoman like yourself."

"Pray, do tell, what crime has she committed?" Mrs Dewar leaned across the carriage. "Is there a murderess on the loose?"

"Worse." He stepped alongside the carriage, practically leaning against its polished walls. A toothy grin revealed the remnants of a hardy breakfast wedged between his incisors. "She's a mistress of Satan himself—one of those Folk."

"Indeed." The knuckles of her aunt's hands blanched as she balled them into fists. "The whole lot of them ought to be drowned in the Thames."

Beneath the blanket, the girl recoiled, tucking herself into a tighter knot.

"If you would be so kind as to excuse us, we must be on our way before the weather takes another turn." Aunt Josephine's voice dripped with propriety. "Good day, sir, and best of luck." The ladies bowed, radiating false thanks rather than the contempt they felt. Even Ambrose bestowed a good-natured grin as the coachman shook the reins.

With smiles plastered on their faces, the aunt, her friend, and the niece chit-chatted about nothing in particular. Minutes passed before they lowered the window shades and, with them, their facades.

"Stay still until we arrive at my home." Aunt Josephine patted the still-trembling girl. "There are those who can help."

Her gaze latched on to Penelope's. A question lurked behind the windows of ice. And though Penelope did not turn her head, she could feel the intensity of Mrs Dewar's gaze scorching the side of her face.

Penelope met her aunt's eye. "I shall not tell."

"I know." Josephine gathered Ambrose into her lap and stroked his head. In a tone that ladies usually reserved for discussing lace, she added, "Had I suspected you would betray her, I would have shot you myself and left your body for the drakes. Even predators deserve a treat from time to time."

Unable to repress her delight, Penelope permitted a grin to sneak out. "Should we continue our acquaintance, remind me to tell you the tale of a gentleman who perturbed a herd of field dragons."

{Narrator's Note: No, our heroine did not feed a bothersome man to a she-dragon. Yes, the remains of a gentleman were discovered near their grazing grounds. And yes, said gentleman had insulted Uncle Archie earlier that week. But that is neither here nor there. Miss Sedgewick did not have a hand in the matter. . . Well. Probably not.}

Chapter 12

THE CHAPTER WITH THE DÉJÀ VU

"The time at length arrives, when grief is rather
an indulgence than a necessity; and the smile that
plays upon the lips, although it may be deemed a
sacrilege, is not banished."

Mary Shelley

Penelope adored her assistant—truly, she did. Or so she
reminded herself when she arrived at their rooms half an
hour later. Strewn across the bedchamber was all manner of
clothing—shoes, stockings, skirts, breeches, and petticoats. In
fact, had this novel been of another genre, she would have
blushed and retreated to the tavern below for half an hour.

Instead, she sighed the sigh known to mothers, maids,
and associates of Walt alike. Like any rational human being,
Penelope could not rest, let alone think, until the room had
been organised.

From the simple wooden frame on the wall, she collected a glove. Its mate, she discovered, had been tucked into

a vase on the oak mantel, alongside a set of stays. After clearing a pile of coats and cloaks from the chair, she used it as a stool to retrieve a cotton waistcoat from a hook just beyond her reach. Throughout, Walt slumbered on, unaware of the curses slipping from Penelope's lips. Not a quarter of an hour had passed before the room had been made orderly again.

After a pot of tea and a tray of cold meats with fruit had been delivered, Penelope removed her shoes and placed them by the fire to dry, then poured herself a much-needed cup of tea. The full-bodied umber liquid swirled across her tongue. Had she felt unsettled after seeing her uncle with Mrs Stevenson and spending an afternoon with her aunt, the peace provided by a warm fire and a properly brewed cup of tea would have set her aright.

In her absence, Walt had been busy. Among the articles of clothing were a humble dress appropriate for a servant, two outfits for a lad, and a second pistol. A receipt for the dresses they had "procured" the evening prior sat on the mantel. The tale her assistant had woven to entice the dressmaker to accept coin rather than contact the constabulary was one Penelope looked forward to hearing.

With nothing to distract her except Walt's occasional mumbles and the pattering of rain on the window, Penelope organised her afternoon's discoveries into tidy piles, connecting them to facts and theories she had collected before traipsing into the past. Visions of the falling girl, the burrow, and the Folk in the forest swirled through her mind's eye.

Interspersed were visions of Mrs Stevenson signing to her uncle. Whenever Penelope considered that her mother lived nearby, a quiet plea rose in her heart. Would it be so bad if she . . . It would. She could not dwell on such temptations.

"Wha're-you-doin'-'ere?" A half-conscious Walt raised her head and leaned on her elbows against the pillows. Her voice was raspy, thick with sleep and ale.

"I have not the faintest idea what you just said." Penelope poured a cup of tea for her friend and placed it on the round table between the two overstuffed chairs near the fire. "Come and drink a cup of tea. You are no help if you cannot even form a proper sentence."

Whether Walt stuck out her tongue at her employer is neither here nor there, nor is it our business if the other lady answered with a grin. Even though her employer was biting at the proverbial bit to spill the tea, she permitted a few minutes to pass before she updated her friend.

"I see that you have made good use of your time." Penelope refilled their cups: her third and Walt's second. "Have we any money left?"

Walt packed a pipe with tobacco. Not her usual pipe, of course. That one had been left on her chest of drawers. "Plenty. That watch you brought fetched a pretty penny. So long as we're able to return home within a fortnight, we can eat like queens."

That particular hurdle needled Penelope. Though she had begun to piece together the skeleton of a theory concerning the mysteries surrounding her, what eluded her still was how to wield the charmed locket. Its power was beyond anything she had known. With half of her network of Folk in nappies and the other half too terrified to admit their gifts, she was uncertain where to turn for guidance.

As usual, Walt possessed little regard for her inner dialogue. "You haven't a clue how it works, have you?"

"Not the foggiest." Her fingers brushed the locket that hung about her neck. She lifted it to her eyes to examine it properly. A golden circle of roses was etched into its face. Within lay a cameo carved of bone, likely dragon. The woman depicted in profile felt familiar; however, Penelope could not place her.

"Mine only has the initials M.P.S." Walt crossed to the mantel. She grabbed the vase and shook it. The rattle of something metallic clanked against the milky glass. "Didn't want to risk losing it."

"Or risk it transporting you to another time without me." Penelope rose and headed to the wardrobe in the corner, a dark cedar piece as wide as the bed. "My morning was spent trailing my aunt."

"Did she suspect you?" Her assistant joined her, appraising their options.

"Perhaps." A plain, pale blue dress was selected, as were sensible shoes and a cape. "My aunt is as intelligent as my uncle, though her talents lie more in understanding people and social systems."

"Then she suspected you." Walt, dressed in her shift, began to redress as a lady of means—choosing a gathered petticoat with peach stripes, buckled leather shoes, false rump, and matching dress.

"Regardless, I had the opportunity to tour the factory just east of town."

"The hollowed-out building?" She sat to buckle her shoes before climbing into her padding and bustled skirt.

Penelope nodded. After a morning traipsing through the woods, she relished the opportunity to dress in the less restrictive garb of a shop girl or maid. "The same. During this period, it manufactures cure-alls."

"Of the dubious sort, I suppose."

"Actually, my aunt claims that they are quite effective." With care, she pinned her dress in place. "I suspect Mr Heep is lacing the ingredients with magic before combining them with more mundane mixtures."

Dresses were tied. Pockets were secured. And weapons were stowed. Two more cups of tea were sipped (or downed) before the ladies were ready once more.

Penelope followed Walt into the hall. As she turned to lock the door, Walt pushed past her and back into the room. "One moment."

She reached for the vase on the mantel and turned it upside down. The locket rang against the glass as it fell into her hand. "Don't want to lea—"

They blinked rapidly as a breeze picked at their skirts. White walls had been replaced by a narrow passageway between two gardens. Gravel lay under their feet rather than wooden floorboards. Even the exposed beams holding the ceiling aloft had vanished in favour of a roiling sky intent on ruining picnics.

While our heroine muttered a single scandalous word, her companion swore like a sailor in a squall. The sight of two women, arm in arm, hurrying away from them to the adjoining lane brought all cursing to an end. Though Penelope did not catch their faces, their garb and frames matched those of Mrs Dewar and her aunt.

"Where are we?" At the sight of a farmer shoving a handcart through the muddied lane ahead, Walt corrected her posture. She slipped the locket about her neck before smoothing her skirt.

The cottages were not especially memorable and nor were the gardens. However, their proximity to the forest, as well as the direction of the church bell clanging to the north, aided Penelope in triangulating their approximate location. At least in space, that is. Time, she decided, was another matter. "'When are we?' would be a better question."

The force of Walt's exhale startled a hen in the neighbouring garden. "Not that again. Please don't tell me we've leapt to another decade."

A gaggle of children burst from the rear door of the cottage, their harried mama in tow. Her dress and petticoat were similar to Penelope's in both fabric and style. On her hip, she carried a basket of feed, which she parcelled out to the chickens, then the goat. The children splashed in puddles, eager to play before the storm let loose.

Not wishing to draw undue attention, the ladies strolled towards the main road. "No, not another decade. It appears we have travelled to the same day."

"How do you work that out?" Walt, aware that her friend relished in the opportunity to outline her powers of deduction, humoured her, as a proper partner in crime ought. "But constrain yourself to a list. I haven't the patience for your ramblings."

Penelope preened. "My aunt wore that precise dress earlier today, as did Mrs Dewar—"

Walt arched a brow.

"My future housekeeper. Furthermore—"

"There's more?"

Naturally, she ignored her friend's rude interruption. "My aunt has a plan. A plan, which I suspect, does not include us racing up and down the timeline willy-nilly."

As they approached a lane, they paused, unsure of which direction to turn.

Over the hedge, the heads of two gentlemen bobbed—one taller, with wavy dark hair, and another whose coif appeared as though it had been struck by an errant bolt of lightning. Penelope froze. At the corner, they turned—her uncle and her father, the prior in the blue coat he had worn earlier that day when speaking with Mrs Stevenson.

"Which way was it again?" signed her uncle. He nodded a greeting as he approached. Whether his clothing was rumpled, she could not tell, for her eyes were trained on the other man.

"Down the lane." Ever the gentleman, her father tipped his hat—his hazel eyes reflections of her own.

As he brushed by her, regret came to call. It reminded her of the mundane moments they had spent together, now lost to time. The forgettable days that poured into weeks then years, each precious in retrospect, yet unappreciated until they had passed. How many times had she chosen to bury her nose in a novel, denying his invitation to stroll through the garden? How many mornings had she dashed out the door, bonnet in hand, neglecting to kiss his stubbly cheek or turn to wave goodbye?

She longed to embrace him—to confess that she was his daughter, to hold him until her strength gave way. Yet she could not. So she stood there, burdened by the weight of a grief she thought she had outgrown.

Walt did not speak, nor did she attempt to lighten the mood with a quippy phrase. Instead, she took her friend's hand in hers and held it. Side by side, they turned to observe her father turn onto another lane and disappear behind a wall.

"It was my papa's voice I miss the most," Walt offered as she weaved her arm through the crook of her friend's elbow, steering them down the lane after the gentlemen. "Not his stage voice, mind you, but the one he'd use to wish me and my siblings goodnight."

They had not taken three steps when Penelope halted. "Where are you leading us?"

"After them, naturally." Walt tugged her along. "It's no accident that these blasted lockets placed us on this path minutes before your father and uncle turned onto it."

Unable to think, let alone object, Penelope permitted herself to be guided down the lane. The two men were visible in the distance, their path directing them towards the outskirts of town.

Indigo clouds rolled across the sky, threatening rain. A faint halo in the west led Penelope to guess they had travelled to an earlier time on the same day. Another version of herself was wandering the town as she meandered through country lanes.

Though she could not make out their conversation, her uncle and father continued to sign as they walked. Penelope felt as though she could have watched them do nothing more spectacular than talk for hours. A thousand memories flitted through her mind, each one no more distinct than the fog rising from the lane. When a tear threatened to cloud her vision, she sternly reminded her heart that she had not been displaced in time by three decades to wax sentimental. It groaned in protest.

At a corner where two lanes met, they paused. Her uncle leaned against a fieldstone wall. From his pocket, he withdrew a watch. She was now near enough to see him sign a question. "When ought we to expect her?"

"Any moment." Her father stood, facing the lane. Despite her aunt's regular reprimands, he slouched a tad. "As to the matter of the toenails . . ."

An obliging fallen log, a stone's throw from the gentlemen, provided the ladies with a ready opportunity to rest their feet while snooping.

Walt, ever the expert at appearing innocent whilst stirring mayhem, withdrew a pocket-sized novel and began to flip through its well-worn pages. Though a passerby would have presumed she was reading an excerpt aloud, in reality she asked, "What are they discussing?"

"Toenails." Penelope squinted her eyes, pretending to stare into the distance. "They are debating whether a corpse's toenails will continue to grow after death."

While her assistant's tone was incredulous, her expressions were not. Her face remained placid, even bored. "Are all of you like this?"

"Like what?"

"Mad, but brilliant."

"Of course." Her heart-shaped lips suppressed a grin. "A dash of madness makes life more interesting. Do you not agree?"

Though Walt had a ready retort, it was at that moment a woman in a hooded cape appeared down the lane. Penelope observed her dress (well-kept but not fine), her posture (unrefined but not slovenly), and her shoes (sturdy). The hood prevented her from examining the stranger's face.

Her uncle indicated the approach to her father, who turned to greet her. His knuckles ran up and down the length of his stubbled chin—a nervous habit he would continue until her childhood. "Good afternoon, miss. The weather is fine, is it not?"

She glanced over her shoulder. "It is, sir."

He extended to her a satchel. As she accepted it, she turned. Though Walt assumed a vacant ladylike expression, Penelope behaved quite unsleuthlike when she stared, mouth agape, at her father, her uncle, and the lady.

{Narrator's Note: Remember, dearest reader, this was an era when men were not even sure women could think, let alone whether they ought to; therefore, the safest option for women when attempting to go unnoticed was to assume a vacant expression and smile. Where were we? Oh, yes.}

Penelope's hand slid into her pocket. Folded tightly in an envelope was the sketch she had discovered in the burrow, the one which matched the dead woman in the square—and this lady, who hurried towards town, her head bent low against the wind.

So as not to draw attention, Penelope waited for her uncle and father to resume their stroll— towards home, she would hazard—before she leapt to her feet and trotted after the woman.

Walt hurried alongside her. "I thought we were following your father and uncle."

The hem of the woman's cloak whipped around a corner in the direction of the shops.

"We were, until I ran across that woman for the third time in roughly one day."

"She's not the corpse, is she?"

They paused at the corner, not wishing to draw their quarry's attention by proverbially nipping at her heels. "Yes. Well, not yet, obviously."

Through a copse of trees at the corner of a cottage, they spotted her cross towards the main square. Carriages, carts, and townsfolk criss-crossed their line of sight, eager to beat the oncoming deluge. The ladies scurried along like the rest of them, dodging dragon dung and side-stepping puddles.

One wrong turn and two near collisions later, they arrived at the corner opposite Mr Horatio Heep's store just in time to see the woman duck inside, but not before she held the door open and curtseyed to a well-dressed lady. Greetings were exchanged and would have been forgotten had not the wind snagged a letter the lady held in her hand. The gentlewoman gave chase. Thankfully, the paper caught on the carriage wheel, permitting its owner to retrieve it.

As she straightened up again, the sound of Penelope's and Walt's jaws clattering on the road echoed across the square. Though they had travelled across a few decades, encountered her father, uncle, and aunt, and met a woman Penelope would later witness fall to her death, nothing could have prepared them for the sight of Sable the healer smiling.

A curtain of rain fell on the street, driving Sable and the mystery woman into the shop. Our sleuth, with her intrepid assistant, headed into an inn that lay across the way. Several minutes would pass before Walt would regain the power of speech to comment, "Wonders never cease."

Chapter 13

THE CHAPTER IN THE CURE-ALL SHOP

"Earl Alwin rose, and proposed his bill to establish
a council to oversee the manufacturing of 'cure-
alls' and 'restoratives' to ensure they were not of
magical origin. After a few observations from the
noble lord, the measure was passed unanimously."

*Lords Chamber, Volume 15: debated on Tuesday 20
February, 1778*

It would be three-quarters of an hour before the storm would
pass, permitting Penelope and Walt ample time to satisfy their
hunger and their daily quotient of tea. Upon entering the
inn, they claimed the table nearest the window. Neither Sable
nor the young woman exited during their respite, though a
gentleman did arrive and hurry into the shop before Penelope
could identify him.

The driving rain battering the walls, as well as the hum
of a dozen voices exchanging local gossip or criticising the

weather, provided sufficient cover for two temporal adventuresses to discuss the situation at hand.

"Are we sure it was Sable and not just her less curmudgeonly twin?" Walt slathered butter on a roll. In her other hand, she held a green apple. "I'd always assumed her face was perpetually stuck in a frown."

"No, she reserves her more pleasant expressions for Toast and other woodland creatures." Penelope withdrew her handkerchief to sweep the crumbs from her half of the table. Her companion's half was left untouched, considered a lost cause.

While her assistant bit into her apple and then the golden roll, Penelope perused the newspaper she had borrowed from another patron—the same paper she had read in her room hours prior. Thankfully, the yet-to-be-understood charms that hung at their necks had not transported them to another year. At least, not yet.

Having read the articles already, she took pains to analyse the advertisements. In her opinion, they were vital to understanding public sentiment. Beside a single-column article calling for information regarding a missing mother of six children stood an ad promising to cure rheumatism.

Through a mouthful of yeasty bread and butter, Walt mumbled, "Have you figured it out yet?"

Penelope raised a brow. Of course, she suspected that her assistant was curious about the charm that insisted on snapping them back in time; however, considering the source of the question, the possibilities were endless.

Walt's finger (perhaps even the middle one) tapping the locket about her neck sufficed as a reply to her silence.

"Somewhat." After a painstakingly long sip of tea, Penelope continued, "A future version of my aunt likely colluded with one of the Folk to charm the necklace."

"Then a past version of the locket is nearby?" Crumbs clung to Walt's lips, tempting Penelope to scold her like a governess.

"Yes. The locket is the bridge. It existed at this time and place, which is why we can travel here. The charm placed on it is a map of sorts. Rather than letting us pop into any old day, it guides us to specific moments."

The factory, the visions, her aunt, the healer, and the murdered woman swirled in her mind. Each one was a string, and try as she might, she could not weave them into a sensible pattern.

Flummoxed and a tad over-stimulated by the tea, she found her body itching for activity. "Shall we visit the shop? My previous self is in the forest rescuing one of the Folk from the clutches of her captor as we speak."

"And mine is asleep and has been for an hour or two."

The ladies paid the innkeeper before stepping into the lane-turned-river. With care, they picked a path across the street to the eaves they had taken refuge under the evening before. They did not glance towards the pyre that stood a few buildings away. And Penelope's eye did not flick to the cobblestone street where the mystery woman would lie dead in thirty years' time.

"You pose as a wealthy lady with a minor ailment, and I shall be your maid," Penelope proposed.

"Excellent!" Walt stepped aside so Penelope could hold open the door for her. "I do enjoy giving airs."

As Penelope reached for the handle, what felt like a pair of hummingbirds fluttered in her chest. Not that she was unsettled. After all, she was a capable woman equal to the task of solving three mysteries at once while navigating a time wherein her gifts were illegal and could see her burnt at the stake. No. Whatever sensation needled her was not nerves, thank you very much.

Neither a chipper shopkeeper nor an attendant intent on raking in a sale were the first to greet them as they entered the shop. Instead, it was the fragrance of mint, camphor, and cinnamon that first assaulted their senses. A thousand odours mingled together, tickling the nose.

Like the factory, the shop was the picture of orderliness. Waxed tables with attractive displays filled the centre of the store. Their tiered stands displayed a rainbow of coloured glass bottles in every shape imaginable. At the far end, shelving stretched to the ceiling. The mirrored walls behind it reflected the bell jars containing ingredients ranging from fungi to imported vanilla beans.

Near the window, Penelope spotted Sable being entertained (or at least distracted) by none other than Mr Heep. So he was the mystery man who had dashed into the store during the deluge. His wet hair clung to his neck. Infuriating man. Even drenched, he was alluring.

Sable's attire was fine: a silk petticoat and matching lavender dress. Rather than tumbling like a waterfall to her waist, her hair was styled elegantly, with strands of silver weaving throughout her chestnut locks.

While unstoppering a hair tincture, Walt bent near to whisper, "Are we *sure* that is Sable?"

At last, Mr Heep noticed Walt. Her fine taffeta dress, her pearl earrings, and her posture commanded his attention. His eyes traced her every curve.

He bade Sable farewell. The moment he rose, Sable's lips dipped into a frown so deep that it sank through Earth's bedrock.

"Oh, that *is* her." Penelope dropped her eyes, as any proper servant ought, in expectation of the gentleman's onslaught.

"Good afternoon, miss." He bowed, holding Walt's eye in a manner that was tantamount to a marriage proposal (or a proposal of something else entirely). Quite against her will, Penelope's neck flushed with heat. Her assistant fluttered her eyelashes, entirely composed.

"What brings you to our humble store this afternoon?" Mr Heep leaned near.

Walt's mastery of the art of duplicity was half the reason Penelope had hired her. It tickled her to no end whenever her assistant posed as a gentlewoman, which is why her impish face shone with delight when her friend replied, "Curl tonic, my dear. I simply *must* have curl tonic."

Confident in Walt's capacity to provide a distraction, Penelope wandered towards the window. Like in the factory, the fragrance of herbs and oils overwhelmed her senses, crippling her ability to perceive charms and wards.

Though to the observer she appeared to busy herself deciphering the cramped writing on a paper box, in reality she was searching for hints of magic. One by one, she snuffed out her senses—sight, touch, smell—as she might a candle. Her consciousness reached outwards, groping for the presence of a healer's touch. Then she felt it: the faint hum of power.

Like pinpricks of light in the night, she sensed dozens upon dozens of charms. All about her, contained in hundreds of bottles, was magic.

When she reconnected with her surroundings and replaced the box on the shelf, the corner of her vision caught a pair of lightning eyes scrutinising her. Penelope, a force of nature in her own right, turned to face her observer . . . Sable. They shared a wry grin—the look of women with secrets they intended to keep.

"Excuse me, Mrs Heep." This was spoken by a voice so demure, Penelope thought a pixie must have fluttered in from the forest. She turned to discover it was the mystery woman. "A boy delivered a note."

This prompted a sigh from Sable. (Or, as we have just learned, Mrs Sable Heep, apparently the wife of Mr Heep, pedlar of questionable "cures" illegally doctored by magic.) "Thank you, Bonnie. Please order my carriage."

Walt, who had been sampling a throat tonic, sputtered, drawing the attention of Sable, Bonnie, Penelope, and Mr Heep, who was now bathed in a minty spray.

"Oh, sir." She whipped out a lacy handkerchief to pat his lapels dry. "I do apologise. The mint tickled my nose."

"Not to worry. Happens all the time." His tongue licked a droplet from his perfect lips. "Shall we try another blend instead?"

With Sable's watchful eye still trained on her, Penelope was unable to communicate with Walt through eyebrow raises or winks. Instead, she observed as Bonnie, the assistant, dusted jars, straightened boxes, and refilled Mrs Heep's pot of tea.

Like our heroine, the girl was, to borrow a colloquialism, a "wee lass." Rarely was Penelope able to stare down an opponent eye to eye. (Or smile at a friend. She does not glare at everyone—just most people.) However, the petite girl with an open face and golden hair stood shorter than even her.

What could Bonnie have done, or what would she later do, to draw sufficient ire to warrant murder? And would this transgression happen soon? Penelope guessed it would, given that the Bonnie who stood before her now, full of life, was near the age of the crumpled body she would examine in 1811. Was this the mystery she was to solve, or was there another? And how had this girl been transported to the balcony?

The clatter of wheels on the cobblestone outside announced the arrival of a navy carriage, drawn by a dragon the colour of rubies. Penelope turned to observe Sable rise. Her husband, Bonnie, and a young man who happened to enter the shop all bowed or curtseyed to her. It was strange to see her being fawned over, when she would later be avoided like the plague.

Snug inside her carriage, Sable cast a parting glance at the store. Her gaze raked the red lettering, lingering on the slogan "Manufactured, not Magicked" emblazoned across the bottom. Waves of malice rippled across her face.

With their purchases in tow, Walt and Penelope exited the store. A parting glance at the sign told Penelope that it closed in two hours. "That was informative."

"Nah," began Walt. "I always guessed that the old crone had been married. What else could explain her dour disposition?"

"Blighted love is not the lone cause of man-hating." Penelope paused to give way to a rambunctious faedragon eagerly chasing a squirrel. "Just the most common." The dragon's owner reprimanded him from a distance, not concerned enough to intervene. Tired of the chase, the grey squirrel turned and hissed at the dragon, sending the scaly tormentor whimpering back to his owner.

When they arrived at the inn, a letter awaited Penelope. It bore her aunt's initials.

It would be my honour if you would join me for a gathering of like-minded ladies this evening at ten. If you are so inclined, please meet me at the Whispering Willow, a tavern at the edge of the forest.

J.S.

"Curious." Or at least, that is what Walt may have mumbled through a mouth full of cake.

After tossing the letter into the fire laid out on the hearth, Penelope crossed to the wardrobe to withdraw a pair of breeches. "The letter, or the confidence my aunt bestows upon me?"

"Both. Clearly, she suspects you are more than you appear." Walt began to unpin her dress.

"Of course."

"And do you intend to join her?"

Penelope's eyes shone with mischief. "Of course."

"Then why are we disguising ourselves as boys?" She shrugged on a cotton shirt. "Not that I'm complaining."

"Because I intend to follow Bonnie after the shop closes." Penelope wound her hair into a tight bun. "And if I must tramp through alleyways or forest trails, I prefer to do so with pockets and sensible shoes."

Chapter 14

THE CHAPTER WITH THE RUNNING

"I lost my right hand to a drake, my left
foot to a wyrm, and my ear . . . well, I lost
that in a brawl with my wife. If I had to do
it over again, I'd take my chances with the
drake any day rather than face her again."

Steven Johnson (Byname Peg-Leg Steve),
Alderwood, 1801

Like a grand lady abed after a late night dancing, the sun
tumbled out from behind the clouds an hour before sunset
that day. Twilight bathed the forest in a coppery glow reflected by a million crystalline droplets hanging like chandeliers
from the trees. A chorus of songbirds harmonised with the
rustling leaves to create a melody more enchanting than one
could dream.

Bonnie had stolen through the town and into the forest.
Her path was a familiar one, at least to Penelope, who followed
close behind dressed as a boy. It was the same she had travelled

recently (well, recently to her) alongside her aunt and Mrs Stevenson. The deeper they delved into the wood, the more sure she became of young Bonnie's destination.

"How much longer must we tramp through the woods?" Just like a mischievous lad, Walt took up a stick to prod an animal burrow at the base of the log behind which the pair hid. "The innkeeper boasts a scrumptious pasty I am eager to taste."

As Penelope had predicted, Bonnie had wandered off the trail towards a grove of yew trees. "I would hazard we are near." A *WHOMP!* that ought to have alerted the girl to their presence, but luckily did not, distracted her.

She turned to discover Walt splayed on her bum, staring incredulously at a mound of moss. Scratch that; a living mound of moss that cursed like a rogue. Penelope leaned closer to discover a brownie with a pointy nose and braided beard, wearing a cloak woven from lichen, moss, and leaves. Had he not been chastising her friend for disturbing his tea, she would have asked about the construction of his hat, which appeared to be a spotted mushroom cap adorned with crystals.

After a rushed apology, the ladies zig-zagged through the trees, taking cover where they could, until they happened upon a blueberry bush. The pair squatted behind it, peering through a break in the branches.

The girl had arrived at the base of the yew where lay the burrow. She shuffled her feet as though she had forgotten the precise location of the door. The clomp of her shoes against boards indicated she had found it at last.

A bit of clattering later, the door creaked open. It revealed a mane of shaggy ginger hair belonging to a young man near the girl's age.

"Her brother?" From the bush, Walt plucked a berry which neither summer nor the birds had claimed. She popped it into her mouth. The puckering of her lips indicated that she ought to have left it alone.

Having emerged from the subterranean chamber, the young man beamed at the girl. His feet had scarcely cleared the ladder when he swept Bonnie into his arms and kissed her into the next week.

"Hopefully not," Penelope replied. A wriggling sensation travelled from the crown of her head to the tip of her

toes. Though our sleuth had posed as a maid in a bordello, investigated a dozen scandalous affairs, and practised kissing with a roguish footman (for scientific research, of course), her experience with romance had been theoretical at best, causing her to squirm like a twelve-year-old learning about . . . well, you know . . . for the first time.

"You're blushing, aren't you?" The smirk that shone on Walt's face could have lit a ballroom.

"No."

> {Narrator's Note: She was, indeed, blushing. And, though this is a secret we must guard, the kiss with the footman was *not* for scientific purposes. Rumour has it that on the eve of her twenty-fifth birthday, the combination of the footman's delicious lips and curiosity proved too great a temptation for even her. Do with that information what you will.}

Hand in hand, the young couple wandered together to the stump of a felled tree, whereupon they resumed kissing with renewed vigour.

From their vantage point, neither Walt nor Penelope could hear much of what passed, which was just as well. Whispered conversations between lovers were inconsequential to their investigation and, frankly, none of their business. Besides, these might be the pair's final moments together.

The investigative duo chose a flat boulder as a seat. They sat in silence, entranced by a glow equal to a million candles burning below the horizon. The waning sun's rays transfigured the clouds into hills of precious stones—golden opals, amber, and coral hyacinth. As a column of light bathed her face, Penelope felt that all the art created by man could not compare to the splendour of solitary sunset.

Regardless of the damp lichen that clung to their breeches and wetted their backsides, Walt reclined across the boulder and tucked her hands behind her head. "Pretty, isn't it?"

"Pretty is too cheap a word for such wonders."

"You don't say, Miss Fancypants." She nudged her friend good-naturedly. "And what costly words have you to spend on this sunset?"

Penelope grinned. "Glorious, for a start."

"Glorious?" The word rolled across Walt's tongue. "I'll save that one for when I dress as a viscountess." She yanked a blade of grass from beside her to hold between her teeth. "How is the happy couple?"

A perfunctory glance over her shoulder informed Penelope that they were fine. Quite fine, in fact. "As amorous as ever."

Walt nodded. Her eyes slid shut against a shaft of light that pierced the canopy of leaves. "Does knowing her death will happen soon not tempt you to try and circumvent it?"

"Circumvent?" Delight danced behind Penelope's eyes. "Look who has a fancy word or two to spend this fine evening."

A pine cone colliding with the side of her head was her companion's sole reply.

Penelope rubbed her temple. "No, I doubt I could circumvent it."

"Thought as much." Walt shrugged.

"Oh, did you?"

"Course I did."

Arms crossed, Penelope awaited an explanation.

"If her future is our past, then we can't alter it, can we? I imagine the universe would become quite cross if we started muddying our own histories." Walt explained.

"I think 'cross' is putting it mildly."

A few minutes later, the couple rose and moved back towards the burrow's entrance. Penelope tipped her head in their direction and then rocked onto the balls of her feet, ready to trail after the girl once more.

Bonnie slipped the pouch Penelope's father had given her into her lover's hand. With a final kiss, he descended to the underground chamber again, pulling the door shut. Leaves were placed with care to disguise its location from passersby. With a parting glance, Bonnie struck out towards town.

She had not walked a hundred paces when the tramping of hooves through the dried leaves brought her to a halt. Though the sun had set, it still illuminated the sky, permitting Penelope to discern the girl. Her shoulders relaxed as the rider approached, an indication that they were acquainted. From a narrow gully emerged a horse as dark as coal, bearing a woman rider dressed in slate grey. Its gait slowed as it approached.

Not a stray word met Penelope's ear—each was snatched by the rising wind. The lilt of their voices, as well as their body language, suggested theirs was a casual conversation. They strolled side by side, conversing. Though the woollen hood worn by the rider obstructed her face, there was something familiar about the rise and fall of her tone, the cadence, and the speech patterns.

They had nearly passed from view when the horse stirred anxiously. In Penelope's opinion, horses and most other animals were more perceptive than their two-legged counterparts.

Creatures as tame as pixies and as deadly as wyrms dwelt in the wood. Better safe than sorry. As she had in the shop earlier that day, Penelope silenced her senses and stretched herself outwards.

At first, nothing, not even a hum of magic. Unconvinced, she waited. Soon, a sickly sensation rooted in the pit of her stomach swelled within her. Rather than withdraw, she pressed herself further. There to her right, and also behind her, lurked chaos in the deepening shadows.

"Drakes!" she gasped as her consciousness returned to her body.

Terror flickered behind Walt's eyes before she shooed it away with a smirk. "Nothing like a pack of ravenous predators to liven up one's evening."

"Better drakes than a sewing circle, would you not agree?" Penelope rose. "How should we alert the ladies?"

"Let me handle this." Walt, still dressed as a man, stumbled out from their hiding place. In a baritone that could have fooled even the most seasoned stage actor, she jeered, "Oi, you, lovelies!"

Poor Bonnie froze. Thankfully, her companion had enough sense to seize her by the sleeve and yank her up to sit behind her on the saddle. She lashed the reigns violently, urging her steed onward. They ploughed through the darkness, the horse's sense of self-preservation directing them away from the drakes that lay in wait.

"Efficient." Penelope clapped her companion on the shoulder. "Now, which tree shall we climb?"

Though she could not yet see the drakes, a scent of sweat and musk pressed upon her, urging her to run. A lifetime of wandering these woods had taught her that to flee would bring death. Instead, she darted to an ancient oak, a sturdy sentry able to withstand a hunter's onslaught. Through the undergrowth, she spied a glimmer of movement to her right. The pack was closing in.

She was at the base of the tree when she spotted the second one. His scales shifted with the shadows as he sliced through the forest, his gaze never wavering, intent on capturing his prey: them. Though no larger than a hound, the wingless beast was lethal.

Neither woman hesitated, nor did they speak. They climbed, hand over hand, foot over foot, ascending into the canopy above. As our heroine was more petite than her companion and nursing a tender wrist, she trailed her. Years of practice prevented her from slipping, while dread urged her on.

The pounding of paws against the earth beneath alerted her to the first drake's arrival. Penelope's arms encircled a sturdy branch. "Hold on!"

The beast collided with the trunk, clawing at the bark as it snapped at her heels. Walt, wedged in a fork, turned to her and extended a hand. She grasped it.

As the second beast leapt, her friend yanked her higher. Hot breath curled up her ankle. Ever upward they climbed whilst the hunters circled beneath.

"Are all of your limbs still intact?" Walt selected a perch, a sturdy branch beyond the drakes' reach. Though there were branches left unclimbed, they appeared less trustworthy than the one she had chosen. She straddled it, her back leaning against the trunk.

"Barely." Penelope wiggled into a fork where the trunk split into two. With her legs hooked around a branch, she paced her breaths.

A primordial force slithered through her veins. Ice leeched into her chest. Though drakes had devolved into animals, remnants of ancient magic still clung to them.

To distract herself (and maintain her sanity), she began to recall the stories she had read about the creatures. "Did you know that drakes were once keepers of the frost, created to protect the world while it awaited the spring?"

Walt lifted an eyebrow. Even she felt their power, as evidenced by her clenched hands and taut jaw.

The creatures' eyes shone in the moonlight, orbs the colour of glaciers. With every passing moment, the weight of their corruption wriggled further onto Penelope's chest. She exhaled. "However, greed tempted them to consume rather than protect."

Rather than pace as they had done before, the trio gathered beneath her. Penelope caught her friend's eye. A look passed between them, communicating their predicament. As the branches above them were less robust, they were within the hunters' grasp should the drakes coordinate an attack.

What would have happened must be left to speculation and overactive imaginations, for at that moment, a howl rent the night in two. It was no common call of coyotes or even wolves. The cry that sent the drakes darting into the night with their tails between their legs was one straight from the pits of the underworld. It would have been enough to make even Cerberus cower. (The three-headed hellhound, that is. Not the faedragon.)

Though relieved by the drakes' retreat into the forest, Penelope did not relax—another magical entity had entered the fray.

"Please tell me that's not a wyrm." Walt shifted to a crouch. She squinted, straining her eyes. "I've had my fill of ravenous predators intent on having me for tea."

Not a creature stirred, not the bats overhead nor the owl perched in a neighbouring tree. All was still, which ought to have been comforting, except that forests, especially ancient ones, are never still. In the distance, the source of the howl moved.

Penelope rose to her feet, her eyes roving the shadows. As she refused to quit this mortal plane before solving the one mystery that kept her up at night, she asked, "Walt, I must know. Why the spoons?"

"Well, miss," Walt began, her voice a strained murmur, "I intend to gather a troupe of musical spoon performers who will travel the continent and entertain royalty."

Her employer would have rolled her eyes at her assistant's ridiculousness had not her nose caught a hint of a fragrance so pure it made her heady. A presence disturbed the sea of mist at the base of the tree, fanning outwards in waves. Rather than claw the bark in desperation to escape, Penelope grinned.

Chapter 15

THE CHAPTER IN THE EYE
OF THE STORM

"Forest Dragons are cousins to field, hill, mountain,
and lake dragons, with distant ties to the dragons
of the nautical world. Like their cousins, they are
protectors of their respective realms. Though they are
not physically imposing, their power is equal to that of
dragons quadruple their size."

A Dictionary of Dragonkind, S. Kephart

When a pair of antlers attached to a dragon rather than an elk appeared, Penelope burst into laughter. "What ho, friend. Have you come to rescue us?"

Through a gap in the foliage appeared a toothy grin belonging to a dashing forest dragon. He puffed out his chest and waggled his eyebrows. *At your service.*

"Flirt." Penelope began to descend, careful not to reinjure her wrist, which shouted in protest and declared that it intended to lodge a formal complaint for having been forced to scurry up a tree like a squirrel.

Walt shimmied down the length of the trunk, landing with a thud. With her thumbs stuck in her pockets, she loped over to Toast. "You're late."

It is a little-known fact that dragons can roll their eyes, which Toast demonstrated gloriously.

"He is not." Penelope stood on her tiptoes to scratch the peat that poked through the scales beneath his ears. He dipped his head and nuzzled her neck. "Besides, I suspect he crossed a great distance."

The bob of his head travelled to the tip of his tail.

While Penelope stroked his beard of moss, orange lichen, and vines, Toast may have stuck his tongue out at her assistant, eliciting a full-bellied laugh.

"Her aunt didn't slip you a charm to transport you through time as well, did she?" From her pocket, Walt pulled out a fob watch. A jut of her chin indicated they ought to return to the inn. After all, Penelope had a clandestine rendezvous to attend.

Toast's eyes dipped to a fang fastened about his neck by a woven cord.

"I prefer yours to the dainty lockets she gave us." Walt sauntered by his side to inspect the tooth. "Is that one of your own?"

He flashed her devilish grin without gaps or holes. Penelope smiled. Though Toast winked and preened in the presence of humans, she had it on good authority that he became reserved and a bit clumsy in the company of she-dragons.

Despite the faint light of the waning gibbous moon, they discovered a path leading to the village. Never again would she take for granted the limestone-marked trails, the alarm wards, and the refuge towers that existed in her own time. Without them, she had nearly lost a foot.

The trio meandered along. Walt puffed on her pipe, whereas Toast nodded a greeting to various woodland friends—hares, foxes, wrens. One such friend, a milk-coloured moth, fluttered about his snout, likely communicating gossip. It danced excitedly, demanding the dragon's attention. Moths, according to Mr Scott, were tattlers, even worse than butterflies.

Since her scaly companion was engrossed in the conversation at hand and she was not one to interrupt, Penelope permitted her gaze to wander. Her hazel eyes adjusted to the golden cast of the moon draped across the grove. Mirrors of water puddled at roots, reflecting her amber light. A faint breath of air plucked a handful of leaves from their branches. They whirled to the ground, spinning like ballet dancers before they landed on a man's crumpled form.

Penelope halted.

"Drat!" Walt rolled her eyes.

As our sleuth darted to the body, Toast dropped into a crouch, his keen eyes searching for danger. Not to be outdone by a dragon, Walt drew her pistol. They were alone, or so Penelope surmised from the lack of gunfire or other such nonsense.

Though she did not revel in death, she did delight in puzzles, and suspicious deaths had inadvertently become a speciality of hers. The first thing she noticed was not the man's age (thirties) or the wound (a gunshot to the chest). Those were all fine and well. What fascinated her was his clothing.

For the second time in roughly eighteen hours, she had discovered a victim whose dress was mismatched to the era. In her time, Bonnie had fallen, her arms pinned with a sash, from a balcony while dressed in a gown from this decade. And today, a gentleman lay dead in a coat, hat, and boots common among the gentry of 1811.

His boots had no buckles; they were black and plain, though polished. His hat, which lay near his head, had a narrow brim and, unlike the fashions of this day, was free of adornment. This gentleman, whoever he was, was not from this time. Penelope, had she not been staunchly against frivolity, could have skipped with delight. Not at the poor man's demise, of course.

The elegant strokes of the letter she had received from a duchess seeking her lover floated before her. 1781—that was the year chiselled onto the gravestone.

To confirm her suspicions, she patted his pockets. As she'd predicted, his coat contained a watch. Etched inside its cover were the initials M.T.: for Montgomery Thomason, she supposed. Her fingers fluttered in anticipation.

Once her eyes slipped shut, visions of a smelter flitted past her. Another, of a jeweller, was paid no mind. It was not until a hint of rose water tickled her nose that she pressed the vision further. A ballroom shimmered before her, one she had visited in the next town over. The forest around her was driven away by candlelight.

She relinquished her hold on her present, immersing herself in the object's past. As she suspected, petticoats with ruffles were replaced by the styles of Grecian sculptors. A lady approached, dressed in the column-like silhouette popular in her time—the duchess. Her eyes were trained on the gentleman, a look of longing framed by black lashes.

Upon surfacing from the past, Penelope continued to inspect the corpse. Her breath hung in the air as she checked his hands for defensive wounds—none. She leant nearer the dead man; the scent of pipe tobacco clung to his clothing. Cold pricked at her skin. The threat of ice hung in the air—uncommon for October.

Finished with her inspection of the body, she called out, "As I suspected, he is not from this time. Perhaps I shall try to see the actual murder next."

When Walt did not reply with a snappy retort, Penelope turned. A sort of vignette unfolded before her. Her assistant, still disguised as a man in a brown coat and breeches, stood near, pistol held at her shoulder, her eyes unblinking, staring into the darkness. At the sight of her, a prickling sensation crawled up Penelope's spine. Her gaze shifted to Toast, who stood sentry. The moon's light cast his scales in an emerald glow. Even in him, an unnatural stillness prevailed.

It was then that she noticed that the melody of the forest, a choir of crickets, toads, and beetles, had fallen silent. The world, or at least the corner inhabited by Alderwood, had stopped spinning.

Her fingers trailed to her collar, seeking the locket hidden by her shirt. Even through the cotton, it felt warm to the touch. Though she ought to have been afraid, terrified perhaps, the knowledge-seeker within her could not shush her curiosity. What wonder had she inadvertently stumbled upon?

Penelope turned her gaze skyward. A clearing overhead provided a window to the sky. Rather than the pinpricks of stars dotting the heavens, streaks of light blazed across the aether. It was as though the Earth's axis had shifted, placing her at its centre—the eye of the storm.

Above her, a leaf hovered, unmoving. She plucked it from space. When she released it, it did not float to the ground below but hung suspended in the air.

Perplexed, even outright confounded, Penelope paced. Whether minutes or even millennia passed, she could not tell. However, by the time she had sorted out the most logical course of action, her feet ached.

Uncertain whether her plan would work or potentially spin the universe into chaos, she fished the locket from her shirt and held it at her eye level. Like a kettle left on a stove, it burned her fingers. She drew a shaky breath before tumbling into its abyss.

At first, a million moments blinked past. They slipped through her fingers like flour through a sieve. She struggled to discern the faces as they whizzed past, flickering for an instant before being replaced by another. Drawing on the strength of the earth beneath her feet, she willed them to pass at a more reasonable pace.

When a flash of Walt from earlier that day presented itself, she once again willed time to move more slowly. The evening crawled by—first the shop, then the drakes. At last, the moment before she had touched the pocket watch hovered before her. She drew a steadying breath before diving headlong into it.

She fell forward, somersaulting through the air. Several bones and essential bits of cartilage crunched when she collided with the ground. Unsure whether she ought to move, she remained still. It was not until she heard the thump of feet drawing near that she gasped for air.

Walt's face popped into her view. "Whatcha doin' down there?" While her words were snappy, concern lurked behind her eyes.

Paws shook the ground beneath her. Toast's snout nudged her, driving away the lingering cold.

"Apologies." She accepted her friend's hand and hopped to her feet. "It would appear that delving through time while wearing a charm permitting you to travel through time may not be the best idea."

Her friend brushed leaves and dirt from Penelope's waistcoat. "Obviously."

Not eager to be discovered at the scene of a murder, they turned towards the inn once more.

"Did anything exciting happen?" Walt asked.

"Unless you find time coming to a halt exciting, not especially."

The raised brow of the forest dragon paired with eyes the size of saucers, communicated, *Unless you mean that metaphorically, I find that horrifying.*

"What he said," added her two-legged companion, who holstered her weapon before removing a biscuit wrapped in a handkerchief from her pocket.

"It was not *that* bad."

Apparently, dragons can also scoff, or at least Toast could. He demonstrated as much when a puff of smoke erupted from his lips. In recompense, Penelope scratched his chin. Within seconds, she could have proposed challenging a troupe of unicorns to a brawl, and he would not have cared. Like a kitten, he purred as they walked along, barely sensible of his surroundings.

"Traitor." Walt winked.

{Narrator's Note: It may surprise the reader to learn that unicorns are not to be trifled with. While, yes, they may be lovely to behold prancing through a field, the reader would do well to remember that they have a horn attached to their heads—and a very pointy one at that. To date, no fewer than thirty-two people have been impaled by unicorns for no other offence than being annoying. So should the reader happen to come across a perturbed unicorn, my advice is to run.}

The glow of dozens of windows welcomed them as they emerged from the forest. With two hours to spare before she intended to meet her aunt, Penelope was eager to sit before a fire and wash the dirt from her hands. For though she would never have admitted as much, the past few hours had unsettled her.

Though she was troubled by the time murders (or so she had termed them), as they bade Toast farewell and promised to meet the following day, what nettled her most was her wrist.

During her time in the void, it had mended. Sable had told her it would take a week to fully heal, and yet, only twenty-four hours had passed. How long, then, had she paced when time had ceased? To her, it had felt like minutes; however, when she considered that her wrist had mended and even that her nails had grown, she wondered.

Chapter 16

THE CHAPTER WITH THE SECRET SOCIETY (SHHHH!)

"On the 24th of April, 1798, the House of Lords passed the Magic Act, permitting the practice of magic across the empire. As anticipated, the announcement was met with dissension. In several counties, judges were forced to sign stays of execution to prevent zealots from burning the Folk already imprisoned."

Gloucester Journal, 25 of April, 1798

When Penelope arrived at the Whispering Willow two hours later dressed as herself, Josephine Sedgewick awaited her, accompanied by Mrs Dewar and a footman who could have auditioned for the role of a barn.

Eyes ablaze with curiosity, Josephine curtseyed. "You have come armed, I presume."

"Naturally." Penelope patted her pocket. While she did not feel it necessary to itemise the weapons or investigative tools hidden on her person, two daggers and a kit for picking locks would have been on the list if she had.

"Good." Her aunt, dressed in a dark wool cape, struck a path leading north of the town. "If there is a gunfight, shoot any men and slack-jawed women first—except my footman, of course."

"Because they are the most likely to be foes?" Penelope skirted a puddle left from the storm. Criss-crossed by wheel ruts, it stretched across half the lane. "Or so that the real fun can begin?"

The echo of Josephine's boisterous "Ha!" woke a tabby slumbering in a window box. Its jade eyes scowled at her. A wicked grin animated her aunt's face. "Both." Her feet directed them towards the rolling hills of patchwork farms and orchards.

Mrs Dewar, with her round face and pleasant features, merely grinned. The years, Penelope noted, would not be kind to her future housekeeper. Her dress and manners indicated she led a life of leisure, perhaps as the daughter of an untitled gentleman or as the wife of a successful professional. The affluence she enjoyed in this decade would pass. By Penelope's eleventh birthday (her earliest memory of the housekeeper), an unknown circumstance would force her to work for her bread. And though housekeepers were upstairs staff with easier terms of service and better pay, it was nonetheless several rungs beneath her current position.

At a fieldstone wall, her aunt turned. The path led to a cottage silhouetted by a sea of stars—a million fireflies suspended in an inky expanse. The clouds had fled, ashamed by their overexuberant precipitation earlier that day.

At a kissing gate, Josephine whispered instructions to her man before leading the ladies to the front door. He dissolved into the shadows: a feat, given his size. When they stepped into the yard, the odour of metal tickled Penelope's nose, declaring the presence of wards.

The rhythm of conversation snaked through the window. From the predominance of female voices, one might have thought they were to attend a knitting circle or sip tea with friends. However, the late hour, the watchman at the door, the wards, and the woman with a rifle at the upper-floor window indicated otherwise. A nod to the stalky farmer and a whispered password delivered the ladies to the home's interior.

Josephine led the troop through the foyer to a sparse sitting room. Sundry candles perched on tables half a century old lit the space, as did a blazing fire. A mustiness suggested the house was not dwelt in by a regular inhabitant. In Penelope's day, the cottage would be let to various younger sons and widowed women.

A dozen ladies of all stations, from maids to the baronesses, chatted quietly. Mrs Stevenson whispered to a woman who was quite the siren. (A metaphorical one, not an actual siren. Those rarely stray far from the coast.) The woman's dragon-scale necklace indicated that she was a member of the upper crust. That and the way she stared in disdain at half the room.

Another woman, a nursemaid perhaps, dressed simply in tans and faded blues, spoke in hushed tones to a lady Penelope recognised as the wife of a knight. By her age and the frequent use of the words "wedding" and "bridesmaids," it appeared as though she was still a Miss, though she would become a Mrs shortly.

One lady after another was analysed and catalogued. In their features, Penelope spied either the profiles of women with whom she would take tea one day, or features they would share with their future daughters and sons.

Above the din rose a clap like a judge's gavel. A hush fell over the room.

Seated in a wide wingback chair facing the fire sat her aunt, presiding. In her hand, she held a metal bookend shaped like a lake dragon. "Ladies, welcome. Shall we begin?"

Had her aunt been born in a more progressive age, she would have marshalled legions. Instead, she held the reins of several renowned leagues (and a few discreet ones) whose associates held the ears (and the hearts) of half the House of Lords. Today, Penelope suspected, was the genesis of her endeavours to reform the nation through policies discussed over pillows and ideals preached in the nurseries of the future aristocracy.

With the poise of the Queen, her aunt turned to Mrs Dewar. "Agnes, would you be so kind as to update us?"

Across the room, the ladies shifted forward in their seats, eager for the first report. Despite the disparity in social standing, each lady shared a common feature—a pair of sharp eyes and, or so Penelope suspected, a fine mind to match.

"Thank you, Miss Sedgewick." She fiddled with the lace at her cuffs. "There are reports of further arrests to be made in the coming week."

Stifled gasps erupted around the room, as well as a few tuts.

"We would do well to offer shelter to those who are rumoured to possess gifts, particularly healers, seers, and dowsers."

"Do we know names?" piped up the nursemaid. She sat at the edge of the circle. The flickering glow of the fire changed the worried lines on her forehead into canyons.

Ms Dewar shook her head. "But my information indicates that another purge will begin shortly."

"Thank you. At the close of this meeting . . ." Josephine's gaze shifted from one lady to another, impressing the gravitas of her words upon them. ". . . it will be our duty to alert those we can and redouble our efforts to establish additional burrows. How many have we at present?"

The bride of a knight spoke. "Twenty-three that could withstand an inspection and could house a person for a week or longer. There are an additional eleven that could hide a person for a day or two. Not to mention those outside our county."

"See that their hostesses and hosts are prepared to receive additional guests," ordered Josephine.

Penelope had to will herself not to smile. Uncle Archie's brilliance was obvious to anyone whose intellect surpassed that of a doorknob. Her aunt, though, was often underestimated. Whether it was the fact that she wore skirts instead of breeches . . . Fine, it was emphatically due to the apparel she wore on the lower half of her body. And yet here she sat ascendant. At just twenty-five, she had accomplished more good than Penelope had at nearly twenty-eight.

Fate, it would appear, concurred. It dangled before her an opportunity in the form of her aunt's next report. "As to the Heeps, our tour of the factory yielded scant information. Furthermore, our associate installed within the shop has little to report."

A silhouette stepped from the shadows into the circle of light radiating from the fireplace—Bonnie, the shop girl. Yet here was no silly doll but a shrewd, capable woman. In the presence of equals, she had put aside her mask. "While we are confident that his products are in fact magicked and not manufactured . . ." She paused. Half the room exchanged smirks. ". . . we can't prove as much, nor can we be certain that his business is connected to the missing Folk."

"Have we no experienced sniffer to assist us?" asked another lady.

"None."

Contrary to popular opinion, crossroads do not create time anomalies: the stream of history continues to flow uninterrupted, regardless of whatever existential crisis a heroine faces. Or so it did for Miss Penelope Sedgewick. For years, Destiny had been shoving her closer to a tipping point, a moment when she would disclose her gifts. It was as though she had been running down a hill, the momentum of gravity drawing her onward at an ever-increasing pace.

Unable to resist its pull, she blurted out (quite rudely), "They are lacing the ingredients. Before they arrive at the factory, I suspect."

Though the snapping of heads does not make an audible sound, if it did, a *WHISH!* would have echoed off the striped papered walls as every lady turned in her direction.

Penelope folded her hands in her lap. Not because they trembled. No, the battalion of hummingbirds let loose in her body had nothing to do with her hands shaking. It was the chill of the night air and nothing more.

She turned to her aunt, trusting her to shield her, as she always had, if it came to that. Their eyes met, and in them she discovered interest, not surprise. Taking a deep breath, she continued, "Neither location has a concentration of magic significant enough to insinuate that healers are present."

In all likelihood, Miss Josephine Sedgewick wished to climb on her chair and dance. Unfortunately, she did not. Instead, with her lips curled at the corners, she turned to the room. "Ladies, may I present Miss Clearwater, a recent acquaintance and, apparently, a skilled sniffer." With a wave of her hand, she yielded her the floor.

"At the factory, I could not sense it at first. The scent of the herbs and chemicals was overwhelming."

"Our other sniffers have reported as much," interjected Bonnie, a spark of recognition reflected in her expression. "They've shared that it's impossible to detect charms fixed to perishable substances. Also, the odours of the factory make it difficult to catch their fragrance."

"While that is generally true . . ." Penelope began, ". . . with practice, sniffers can detect the presence of even the weakest magic, such as that present in salves and creams." Thrill had banished the butterflies. It infused her blood and marrow. "When an obliging breeze cleared the air at the factory, I caught a hint of it. This afternoon, I visited Mr Heep's shop. Magic radiated from the bottles themselves, yet not all."

"It makes a certain amount of sense." Bonnie withdrew two amber jars. Neither was labelled, but they were the sort Penelope had handled in the shop. Bonnie stepped forward, hand extended. "And these?"

Whether it was experience or luck, it was evident which bottle had been tampered with. Even with the lids sealed tight, she caught the fragrance of sandalwood. "The one on the right. I would hazard it treats aches well."

"It does. One of our best-sellers." The girl's doll-like features were enlivened with amusement. "The other's a base oil."

"Thank you, Miss . . ." Her aunt paused, signalling to Penelope that she had guessed her name was an alias. ". . . Clearwater. Every woman in this room appreciates the risk you take. Know that each of us has a stake in this war."

With her elbows resting on the arms of her chair and her hands folded, Josephine leaned forward. Her voice hovered at a whisper. "We must discover the source of the ingredients and whether, as we suspect, the Folk are being kept against their will."

Curious. Her aunt had neglected to mention the woman they had discovered fleeing in the forest. While a report was given concerning the forthcoming union between one of the members and a gentleman who would (from Penelope's recollection) go on to champion the legalisation of magic, her mind wove the information she had learnt into her web of theories. Though a pattern was emerging, several questions remained unanswered.

Half an hour later, the meeting drew to a close. One by one, the ladies disappeared into the night, some into carriages and others on foot.

Mrs Dewar departed for home with the nursemaid at her side, discussing how best to nurture compassion for the Folk in her young charge. Alone with her aunt, Penelope inspected a book of sonnets. "Why did you not mention the woman we discovered in the forest?"

"Timing." Her aunt extinguished a candle on the mantle. "Once we arrived at my house, the woman slipped into a sleep from which I preferred not to rouse her; therefore, I had little information to share."

"Do you suspect she has been held against her will?"

"Yes. And dozens of others, perhaps." Taking a candle in hand, Josephine led them to the door.

"And is Mr Heep the mastermind or merely a cog in the machine?"

They had reached the threshold. From her pocket, Josephine withdrew a key. "I cannot tell at present; however, I suspect whoever is at the helm has aspirations that extend far beyond profits."

With a puff of air, she blew out the candle.

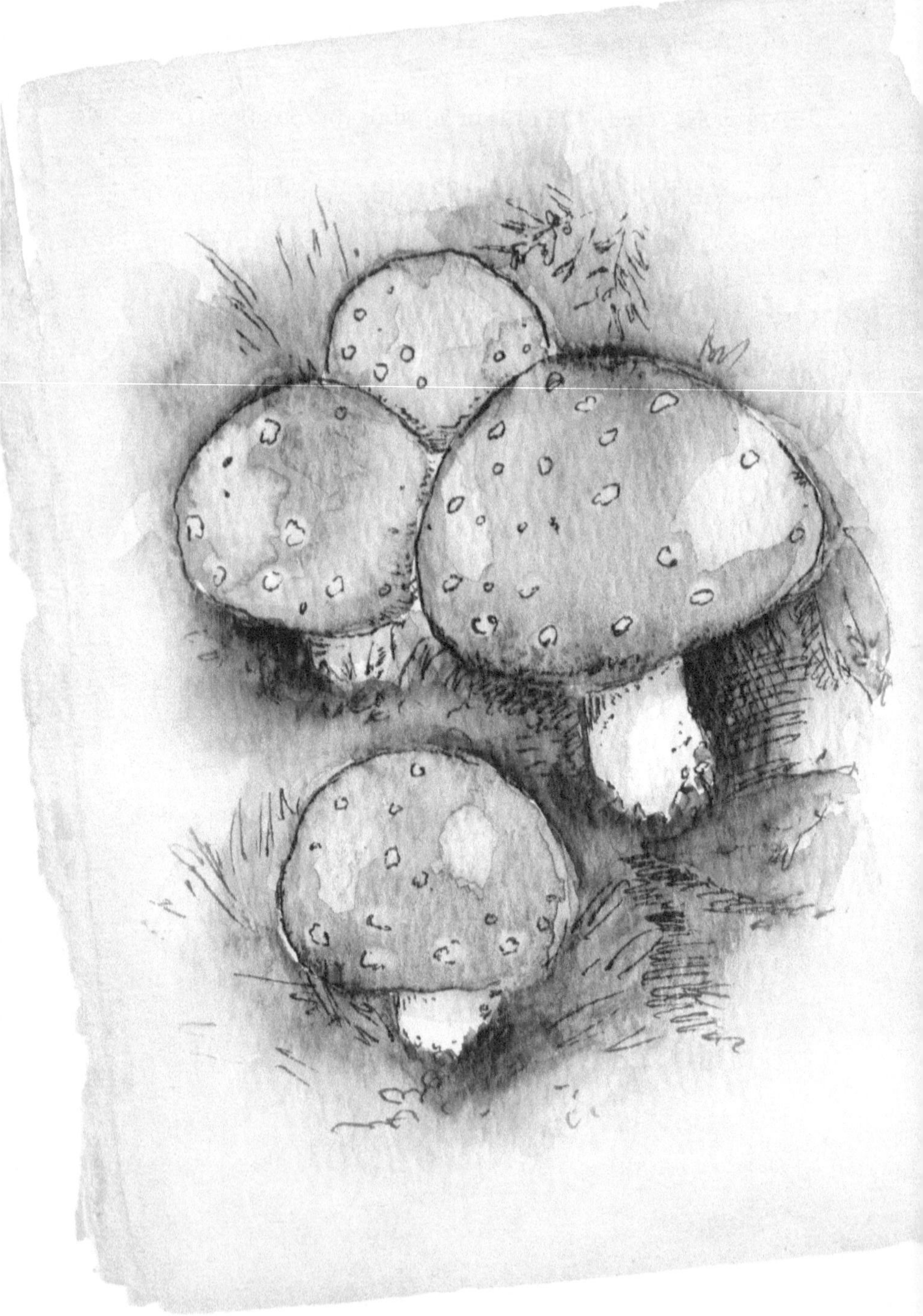

Chapter 17

THE CHAPTER WITH THE MURDERER (MAYBE)

"As decreed by the laws of this land, I
hereby condemn you to death for the
practice of magic. May God have mercy on
your soul."

*Justice William Pence at the Execution of
John the Cobbler, 1785*

As scheduled, the time-travelling trio (Oooh, that was a satisfying phrase) convened at nine in the morning at the edge of the wood. The human members dined on a picnic of honey cakes and berries. Though Toast had eaten his fill of leaves and grasses, he eagerly accepted a jar of preserved peaches.

"So you're telling me that the fate of the nation is steered by a society of women, not by all those crusty men in London?" Walt pitched a pine cone at Toast, who batted it through a window in the canopy above. The dragon wiggled his haunches while swishing his tail. Like the forest, his colour had shifted from greens to brilliant oranges, corals, and reds.

"Obviously." It was Penelope's turn to pitch, and she selected a pine cone that felt natural in her hand. "I suspect that the future passage of the Magic Act is due to strategic marriages and carefully placed governesses."

With the skill of a woman who had spent a decade honing her aim, she released the cone at a dizzying speed. It sailed narrowly past the tip of Toast's tail. Rather than stomp or grumble or set a tree ablaze, he pranced over to her and patted her head with his tail to communicate a hearty *Well done!*

A fork in a tree welcomed Walt, providing an ideal throne. Had a poet wandered past at that moment, he would doubtless have been inspired to compose a sonnet about a raven-haired maiden with chestnut eyes. Whether he would have finished it is a matter of speculation, as men who fawned over Walt had a habit of incurring black eyes or bruised . . . well, quills.

"Why haven't we the vote then?" she wondered. Her pipe was withdrawn from her pocket and packed. "Or the right to enlist, for that matter?"

"I suspect it is a work in progress." Penelope wandered to the edge of the clearing, where she reached out for a falling leaf the colour of a sunflower on a summer day. When she released it, a gust caught it like a lady's hand at a ball. It spun and twirled until it joined its sisters and brothers to carpet the forest floor.

She turned to discover Toast sweeping leaves into a pile. Though his tail was as effective as three garden rakes, she gathered armfuls to add to the mound.

A blast from his lips, which were set in a pitiful pout, drove Walt to her feet. She loped, pipe bobbing on her lip, to an untouched pile of leaves. "Until this little misadventure into the past, I had underestimated your aunt."

"Even I do, sometimes." Guilt poked her in the ribs like a smelly ogre. Until yesterday, she had not known the breadth of her aunt's work. It had been hinted at yet never laid bare. Like the masses she often railed against, Penelope too had discounted her. Worse yet, she wondered, had she allowed those same voices to justify her lack of initiative?

The vision of Toast bounding across the clearing into the mound distracted her. With a great splash, he dived into the pile. Leaves flew into the air. He rolled on his back, batting a leaf with his paw to keep it aloft.

Over the rustle, a noise in the distance tickled Penelope's ear. At first, she thought she had imagined it. After all, she had recently encountered several spectral visions from the beyond. However, Toast's stillness confirmed her suspicion. He, too, tilted his head, listening. Their eyes met. *Men.*

Walt hastily shook the contents of her pipe into the dirt, stomping on it with her foot. Another cry, one of pain, echoed through the trees. The tramping of horse hooves joined the voices of at least two men.

Without a word, the dragon and his two friends darted behind a rise topped with brambles. Despite his size, he vanished before their eyes, his colouring shifting to match his surroundings. His scales even mimicked the shadows cast by the trees overhead.

As the ladies were dressed in stripes and blues, they tried to hide themselves by curling into tight balls. They needn't have, though, for as soon as Toast had settled onto his haunches, he swept his leafy wing over them, leaving a slit through which they could view the men passing by.

Walt scratched him behind his ear as thanks.

"If you try and run again, I'll shoot you on the spot," spoke a man just beyond their view.

A second man, whose voice felt familiar to Penelope, added, "'Twould be more fun that way, and save us all the hassle of a hearing."

The rogues laughed. At the edge of the clearing, she spotted them. While she did recognise one of their party, the greasy fellow who had pursued the woman the day prior, her eye was drawn to the redheaded young man bound with ropes—Bonnie's love. Blast!

"Nah. It's more fun to watch them burn," added the fourth man. He rode a knackered pony with one foot in the grave. Its ribs and hip bones protruded through its skin. At the sight of it, a low growl rumbled in Toast's throat.

Though the humans could not detect the warning, the pony could. It jerked at the reins, eager to flee.

"What the—" cried its rider as the pony reared its front feet.

Distracted, his companions did not perceive their captive break into a run. At least, they did not until he had nearly crossed the clearing.

While the rider struggled to regain control of the mare, the others began to sprint . . . Perhaps sprint is too generous a word. The bungling pair of greaseballs ploughed across the forest floor with as much grace as trolls in a hooped panniers.

Walt drew her weapon and rose to a crouch, prepared to pounce. Before Penelope could join her, Walt's skirt snagged on a branch, yanking her onto her derriere with a thud. Peculiar, or so thought her friend.

When the . . . (This word has been redacted so as not to offend stodgy assemblies of meddlers who cannot abide ladies reading scandalous material. Suffice to say, the word penned by the author began with the first three letters of "bass" and the last four letters of "custard." Let us continue.)

When the cretin struck the pony, Toast bore his fangs. Though forest dragons were not violent by nature, they had been known to literally eviscerate those who harmed the creatures under their care.

A tad nervous for his safety, Penelope placed a hand on his shoulder. A quick shake of her head warned him to remain still. He settled into the dirt once more.

Her two-legged friend, though, who was less easily tamed, stood. Murder seeped through every pore of her skin. When she stepped from beneath the shelter of the dragon's wing, her shoe caught on a root. Though it did little to delay her, it sparked a wave of heat to burst across Penelope's skin.

Whether it was her connection to time that warned her or her instinct, she could not tell; however, her gut demanded they not interfere. Her hand shot out, catching Walt's elbow and yanking her to the ground.

Enraged, Walt muttered, "Let me—"

The crack of wood splintering drew every eye upwards. From the tree under which they crouched, a massive branch fell. It landed with an ominous thud not an arm's length away, crushing the brambles behind which they had hidden.

Toast hooked Walt with his tail to draw her beneath his wing, which he swept over them once more. Through a gap,

Penelope spotted his lip curl into a menacing snarl. The pounding of boots and hooves was all she heard above the parade of her own heartbeat.

Neither woman spoke. A half smile demonstrated one lady's thanks, while a shrug sufficed as a "My pleasure."

When Toast lifted his wing, indicating that the men had moved on, the ladies stood, dusted their dresses, and stared. Had Walt not been pulled back, she might have been killed, or at least seriously injured. They circled the branch. It was as round as a child's waist.

"Fate, it appears, would prefer we not meddle." Penelope's gaze met her friend's. "We would do well to be cautious."

Walt nodded.

The roar of a mob rang in the distance, and the trio exchanged a look. The ladies sprinted in its direction—the heart of Alderwood.

After having bidden Toast farewell at the forest's edge, the pair were drawn onwards to the main square. A lad brushed past them to join the crowd ahead. As they turned into the thoroughfare from a narrow alley, they paced themselves. Ladies, after all, did not dash down streets.

Carriages and carts blocked the lane, abandoned by their drivers. Men and women, straining to catch a glimpse of the commotion, formed a wall of heads and hats. The second-floor windows were jammed with mamas dangling their babes on their hips as they stared towards the square.

With a few well-placed elbows and the careful application of a stare, Penelope and Walt soon gained a position at the front of the line. Beside the pyre stood the greasy urchin from the forest. His hand held a fistful of the young man's ginger hair. All his flight had earned him, it appeared, was a fresh bruise on his cheek and a bloodied lip.

Hundreds of faces reflected the enslaver's hatred. Men of all classes shouted their support. Loathful women jeered. Even the children mimicked their malice. Humanity at its worst, or so Penelope felt. Walt apparently shared her opinion, as evidenced by her fists balled at her sides.

Though the overall sentiment was one of support, here and there Penelope spotted a downturned countenance, a glassy stare, or, among the brave, a frown. Such expressions were noted on a cluster of faces she knew well—those of her aunt, her uncle, and her father.

They stood opposite her, arms crossed, exuding disgust. Her father, perhaps, could have stepped forward: she half expected it of him. Instead, he smoothed the stubble on his chin and signed, "This is cruel."

"*This* is the state of our justice system," Josephine replied. If looks could kill, hers would have ignited half the town where they stood. "*This* is why you must seek a position in Parliament. We need good men to lead, not reprobates who crave power."

Startled cries mixed with jeers drew Penelope's attention to the poor lad. The ogre-like fiend stood over him, sneering. Spit dripped down the boy's cheek. As his hands were bound behind his back, he could not wipe it away.

A small figure broke from the crowd—Bonnie. Rather than wrap him in her arms and weep, the woman, withdrew her handkerchief to press it to his cheek. For a fleeting moment, they held one another's gaze, communicating their devotion. Without so much as a sigh, she turned, crossed the square, and pushed through the crowd.

When Penelope sought her aunt once more, she had vanished.

The white-washed storefronts reverberated with the clopping of hooves on cobblestone. From a side street, a man on horseback appeared. Rich and poor stepped aside, creating a path. When he reached the crowd's edge, he dismounted.

He was wealthy; everything from the mare he rode to his saddle and clothing made that much clear. The magistrate, she supposed. With a disinterested gait, he approached the accused. Under his arm was tucked a riding crop.

"What have we here?" He spoke louder than needed—for show, Penelope supposed. A quiet scoff near her shoulder indicated that Walt agreed.

"One of those deceitful seers, sir." The constable shoved the young man to the ground. His body slammed against the cobblestone. "And a murderer."

A groan escaped the young man's lips as he rolled onto his side. Blood bloomed across his cheek. Before the gentleman's crop fell across his shoulders, Penelope winced in anticipation.

"Be quiet, you servant of the Dark One." The magistrate's face transformed into a grotesque mask. Hatred rippled outward, animating the crowd.

Penelope started at the sound of her aunt's hushed voice at her elbow. "The only servant of Satan I see here today is the man beating a defenceless boy."

A dip of her chin was Penelope's sole reply.

Under the pretence of taking her arm, her aunt bent near. "We have observed an increase in arrests since Mr Heep's enterprises have prospered."

Though the boy had scarcely moved, let alone spoken, the magistrate raised his riding crop above his head whilst his associate laughed.

"Enough!" A familiar voice rang across the square, silencing the crowds. At the sight of her father—her gentle father—stepping from the line of onlookers, Penelope's throat grew tight.

"Since when have we p . . ." He stuttered. Ps had always given him trouble. His throat bobbed as he steeled himself. ". . . permitted ourselves to devolve into a mob rather than a nation governed by law?"

Though the magistrate in his black garb was twice his age, her father was the owner of one of the most prosperous estates in the county, and to cross him would have been unwise. Rage broiled under the gentleman's thin veneer of civility. Had her father been a less influential man, Penelope felt certain the man would have turned his riding crop against him.

Instead, the diseased slug stuffed in a waistcoat bowed. "Wise words, Mr Sedgewick."

A collective exhale passed from one onlooker to the next. For all their shouts and threats, mobs are nothing more than the weak armed with force of numbers. Any remaining resistance vanished as her father crossed to the captive to press his own handkerchief to the lad's cheek. By the time he had hooked a hand under his arm to help him to his feet, half of the crowd had melted into their shops and rooms.

The boy's captor, sensing that the tide of public sentiment had changed, shooed the remaining crowd homeward. "Off with ya!"

Aunt Josephine tugged on Penelope's arm, drawing her away from prying ears. Penelope's assistant, ever the professional, had distanced herself upon her aunt's approach. They had agreed previously to meet at the inn should they be separated.

Once clear of the dispersing crowd, her aunt spoke with such brightness that passersby would have assumed they were discussing the weather. "I must go. There is much to do."

Penelope tittered like a schoolgirl for the benefit of an austere couple walking their twin miniature sapphires. "Will they harm him?"

"Unlikely." Her aunt nodded at a passing acquaintance, the future parson. "Seers tend to disappear before they are burned. To where, we have not discovered."

"Healers, too."

"Yes, which implicates Mr Heep."

"Though the disappearance of listeners does not," Penelope added.

"Correct."

They paused at a window to permit a gentleman to pass them; one who followed them a tad too closely. To put on a convincing front, they marvelled at the craftsmanship of a schooner in a bottle displayed in the window. Their shadow stepped into the shop.

Satisfied that the gentleman had genuine business, they struck a path towards the inn. In the warmth of the sun, most of the puddles had disappeared, though the mud remained, caking itself onto wheels and hooves.

In the shade of a tree arching across the roadway, her aunt released her arm. The two women faced one another—one appraising, the other attempting to appear innocent and failing miserably. Seconds ticked past. Penelope nearly spilt the proverbial tea, feeling an almighty urge to confess not only her second gift and that she was, in fact, Josephine's niece, but that she had stolen brandy as a young woman and had bet on horses at least once.

Thankfully, her aunt's eye flicked over Penelope's shoulder. Her gaze lingered for a moment before returning to her niece's eyes. "Have you plans for tomorrow evening?"

"No. I have no engagements at present."

"Good." Her aunt curtseyed. "I shall have an invitation to my ball delivered to the inn. I do hope you will be able to attend."

With that, she darted past her niece. On the corner of the country lane opposite stood Penelope's uncle and father. Her aunt did not look back. Instead, she accepted her eldest brother's arm whilst Uncle Archie railed against the magistrate, and they departed for home.

Chapter 18

THE CHAPTER WITH THE "ILLEGAL" MIDNIGHT TOUR

"Faerie torches, by this humble Folklorist's observation,
are dear not because the fair folk are unwilling to part
with them, but because few humans possess the necessary
currency (namely, leases on ancient trees, secrets, and
unicorn hair) with which they may be purchased."

On Fae, Fair Folk, and Fairies, Sir Richard Canty

At nine o'clock in the evening, in defiance of the earlier hours
when the sun had reigned triumphant, a torrential downpour
descended on Alderwood. Though the townsfolk railed against
the heavens, shouting curses and grumbling under their breath,
the clouds continued to let loose their floodgates. Hope for dry
laundry was universally abandoned. Many planned midnight
trysts were rescheduled.

One trio, though, was undeterred. When the clock on
the mantel in the inn struck ten, none of the rain-bedraggled
customers noticed two skinny boys nip out the back. Nor did

a single town-dweller notice a dragon trailing alongside them as they cut across fields and lanes.

"Am I understanding you correctly?" Walt, dressed as a young man with her hair tucked into a cap and her chest bound, hopped over a puddle. "You believe that the purge is, at least in this region, a cover for illicit activities?"

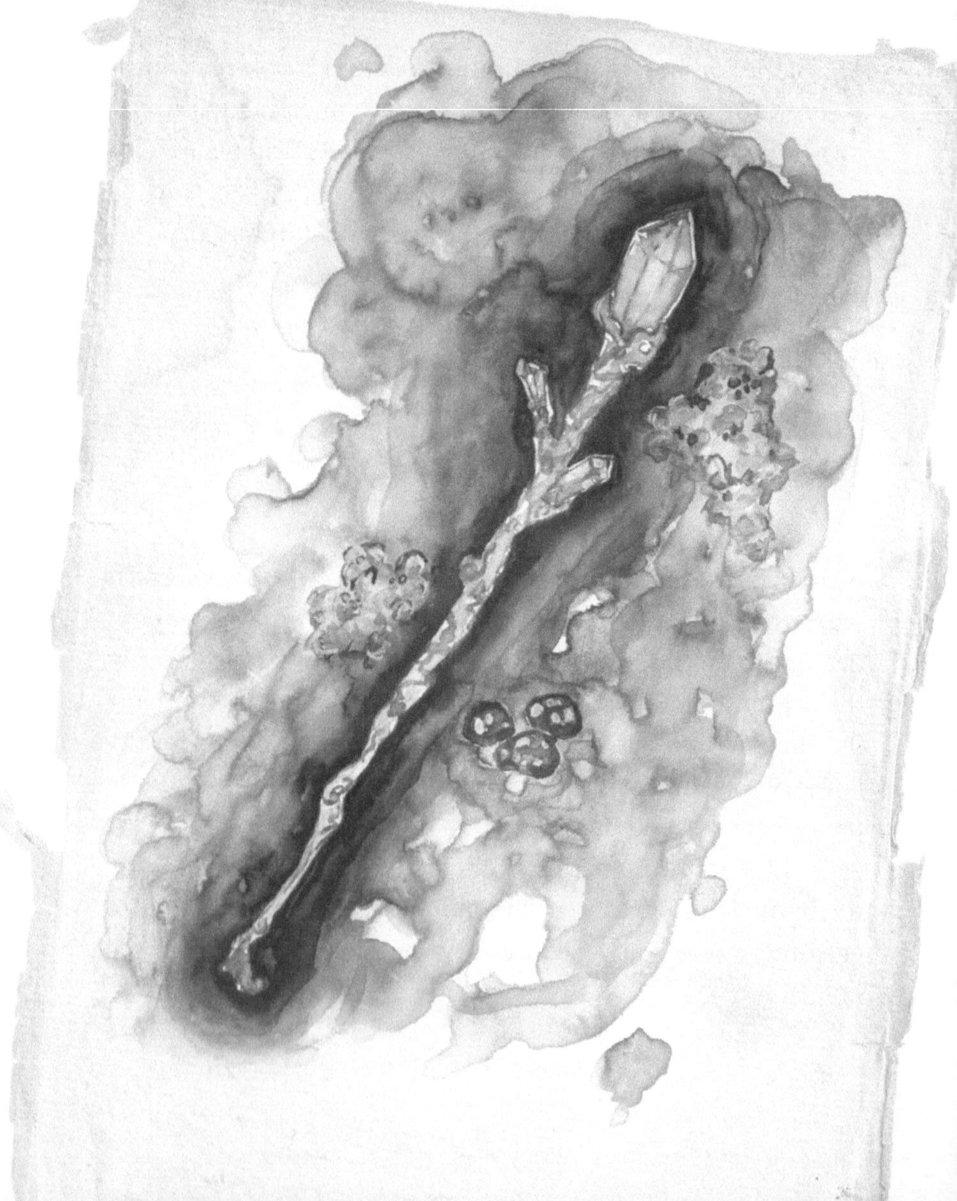

"Yes." When Penelope was dressed as a boy, her sprite-like features were especially obvious: her pointed chin stuck out and her mischievous eyes gleamed. "How better to build a criminal enterprise?" Her eyes roved the horizon, discerning little besides a few lit windows in the distance. "When a man or woman is forced to either work or face the pyre, hope spurs them towards captivity rather than certain death."

Toast huffed a hearty *Obviously* with a puff of smoke bursting from his nostrils. Ever the gentleman, he had extended his wing over the ladies' heads.

"And why only the healers, the seers, and the listeners?"

With a roll of the eye, their scaly co-conspirator insinuated, *The healers—isn't that one obvious?*

"None of your sass." Walt wagged a finger at him. "It's bad enough that I have to take it from her."

A sort of apology was offered when he nudged her shoulder with his nose. It was reciprocated by a pat on the neck, signalling that all was forgiven.

Penelope held up a fist, bringing the party to a halt. Near a barn tucked at the edge of the wood, there was movement. Without a moon, the building shrank into the blackness of the forest. Had it not been for a lamp hung from a hook near the door, she would not have seen it.

A circle of orange light cast long shadows as men moved in the darkness. They carried crates from the barn to a covered wagon. What appeared to be ears of corn peeked out of the slats.

As they were not far off and accompanied by a dragon, they crouched low in the furrowed field and waited. After a final crate was added, the barn doors were shut tight against the rain.

Our sleuth observed the wagon in silence, curious as to its destination. When it turned northward towards the countryside, she directed her steps in the opposite direction, towards the factory. "It is my hypothesis that someone has discovered the true nature of listeners' and seers' gifts."

The assistant dressed as a young man and the forest dragon posing as an umbrella sported a pair of raised eyebrows.

Penelope obliged. "If listeners can hear an object's history, thereby travelling into the past, logic would guide us to suppose that seers can—"

"Travel forward in time." Walt interrupted. "Makes sense." She held her arms stretched outwards at her sides to balance on the ridges of soil. Rivers of muck and debris had transformed the furrows into streams.

Toast bobbed his head in agreement.

"What if these gifts were used to create charms?" Penelope's hand trailed to the locket tucked beneath her shirt. "They could permit one to travel forwards or backwards through time. Think of the power one could attain, knowing the outcome of wars or the past misdeeds of a business associate."

They walked in silence, considering. Lives could be shattered or empires built with the correct information wielded masterfully by a diabolical hand.

Toast broke their reflections by tapping Penelope's shoulder with his tail. They paused under the eaves of an outbuilding that bordered the road. With a stick, he hastily scribbled a drawing of a man with Xs for eyes and his hat cast aside. For a sketch in the mud, it was quite well done.

"Are you wondering whether the murdered gentleman could be the victim of a scheme?" Penelope asked.

He nodded his head so enthusiastically that he accidentally sprinkled his friends with a shower of rainwater that had collected on his scales and wings. A sheepish smile served as an apology.

"Yes, as well as Bonnie's and others, I suspect. In the paper, there was an advertisement offering a reward for the discovery of a missing woman. And at the meeting, my aunt spoke of others who had disappeared."

The sight of the factory, dimly lit by the windows of the neighbouring homes, hushed their conversation. Rather than approach from the road, they cut through another furrowed field.

Breaking the silence, Walt spoke in low tones. "Remind me of the plan again." She stretched her hand out from under Toast's wing. The rain had slowed to a drizzle.

Penelope rolled her eyes. One would have thought that they had not meticulously discussed the plan. There had even been a sketch of the factory's floor plan, for goodness' sake. Toast turned his head skyward to disguise an amused grin. Traitor.

"Our guard dragon will remain outside the factory to serve as a sentry," she began. "You and I shall peruse the office and factory floor for clues as to the whereabouts of the healers."

"And what're we searching for?" Walt drew out a handful of nuts she had wrapped in a kerchief, and popped them into her mouth.

"Labels, shipping invoices, ledgers, trap doors, and the like." The trio had arrived at the stone wall that surrounded the property. They hunkered behind it, peeking their heads over to survey the yard and building for a guard. None. That the building was left unattended suggested that either nothing nefarious happened within its four walls or that Mr

Heep was a greater simpleton than Penelope had thought. "Are we ready?"

After a brief scratch under the chin, the ladies bade their friend farewell. They made easy work of vaulting over the low wall. Crouching, they darted across the yard until they reached the back door. Locked, as anticipated.

Penelope extracted a set of metal rods she had stowed on her person and handed them to her associate. Though she was excellent at picking locks, Walt was better.

Not two minutes later, the lock slipped open. It would appear that like the factory floor, Mr Heep kept even his hinges in good repair. When the door slid ajar, there was no creak or whine to sound an alarm. A tad disappointing, really.

A jerk of the head indicated that Penelope would enter first, with Walt on her heels. After a glance over her shoulder to check on her watch dragon (whose head bobbed just above the overgrown grasses), she disappeared into the belly of the factory.

They plunged headlong into darkness. Without a moon or candle, the factory was as black as a cavern buried deep within the earth. Penelope, of course, had anticipated as much. From her pocket, she withdrew a crystal bound by dried vines to a claw-shaped branch. When she whispered a word taught to her by the fair one who had sold it to her for a secret and a millennia-long lease on a fine oak located on her property, starlight burst from its core.

Walt blinked rapidly to clear the spots from their vision. "Do you always have one of those?"

A shake of Penelope's head was countered by a mumbled "all along" and a "muck about in the darkness."

Once their eyes had adjusted, they surveyed the space that spread before them. The rafters and support beams arching overhead reminded Penelope of the ribs of a sea dragon in a tale she had heard as a child. In the tale, the young adventuress was swallowed, boat and all, by the monster.

Like the day before, the aroma of herbs and chemicals filled the air. Rows and rows of work tables and shelves, neat and ordered, stretched before them. The glow of the light cast sharp shadows on the walls. They stretched like fingers, reaching for the rafters.

The ladies padded on tiptoes across the length of the room to the corner, where a raised platform overlooked the factory floor. Though embers still glowed in the cast-iron bellies of the stoves, a chill nipped at Penelope's fingers and nose. Before ascending the stairs to the platform, they paused. Not a creak nor a whisper—above was empty, or so they hoped.

With an unmistakable hint of disdain in her voice, Walt said, "Orderly, isn't it?"

"Yes. It is divine." Penelope's voice hummed with delight. She padded up the stairs, ignoring the scoff from behind her.

At the fourth step from the top, her gaze swept the space above. Tables, chairs, and crates were lined in rows, and not a scrap of paper lay on the floor. Though Penelope understood that Mr Heep was likely a nefarious scoundrel who imprisoned Folk for profit, she could not disparage the management of his business.

Once they had arrived on the platform and triple-checked the nooks and crannies, they split apart—Walt to a locked cabinet and Penelope to the ledgers.

Walt plopped on the floor in front of the sturdy wooden cabinet banded with iron. Leaf carvings adorned its door and frame. Withdrawing her tools once more, she set to picking its bronze lock. "Have you checked for wards?"

Of course our sleuth had checked for wards; she was no amateur. A pair of pursed lips were answer enough.

For a quarter of an hour, Penelope sorted through the papers on the desk. Most contained correspondence from tradesmen and merchants. Bound ledgers were laid open and scrutinised. Even a perusal of the contents of the cabinet—mostly deeds and contracts—proved fruitless. Careful not to leave a trace, the women returned each paper to its rightful place.

"Nothing." Walt slid the cabinet shut, locking it once more. "Not a trace of anything untoward."

"Surprisingly, no. The worst offence I discovered was a half-drunk cup of tea with a—"

On the corner of the desk nearest the safe, where once had sat a plain cup with a silver spoon balanced on the saucer, now sat the untouched cup and the saucer minus the spoon.

Walt stared at the rafters, her hands shoved in her pockets. As Fate had not cast any of the wooden beams down upon her head, it would appear petty larceny was beneath her notice. Penelope's conscience shrugged.

They advanced to the stairs, intent on searching the factory floor for trap doors, when the faint call of a field dragon floated across the yard, through the brick walls, and to their ears. Without a word, Penelope grabbed her assistant's coat sleeve and dragged her towards a stack of wooden boxes marked "fragile".

"Whatcha doin' that for?" She shrugged her arm free.

In a shout impersonating a whisper, Penelope explained, "The-warning-signal-is-a-field-dragon-cry. Which-you-would-have-known-had-you-paid-attention."

{Narrator's Note: Yes, the ladies did hear a field dragon call, NOT a forest dragon. Toast is a skilled impersonator of several species of dragons and other large animals. And his impression of a troll . . . magnifique.}

A sliver of light streamed through a side door. As though Medusa's eyes had turned them into stone, the ladies froze mid-step. When a lantern held aloft poked its way through, they dived behind the boxes. Rather than jam her fairy torch into her pocket, Penelope shook it to snuff it out, pitching them into utter darkness.

Afraid to speak, they strained their ears to discover the intruder's whereabouts. Penelope measured her breaths, willing her heart to stop panicking. True, they were trapped in a factory that likely enslaved Folk, and during a time that was not their own, but still, that was no reason for a tizzy.

It was not until the first step on the stairs creaked in protest that the whereabouts of the other person were made known. Thankfully, a gap between the boxes permitted her a view of the stairs. From a second gap, nearer Walt, they had a clear view of the desk.

Like the rising sun, the lamp's glow rose over the floor of the loft. It revealed not a thief nor a ruffian, but a familiar face. Sable, cloaked in a navy-coloured hood and dress, strode up the stairs as if she owned them (which she did). Gone were the pleasant smiles and polite words. The woman who swept past the boxes towards the locked cabinet had a look of intent.

With little to do except watch, the pair waited. A key was withdrawn from her pocket and inserted into the lock. From the corner of her eye, Penelope swore she spied her assistant mouth the word "cheat."

Sable did not leaf through page after page of receipts and deeds. With the speed of a woman who knew precisely what she sought, she located and reviewed two documents before stuffing them down her stays.

While she replaced the papers she had disrupted, a second cry echoed across the field outside. The ladies exchanged a glance. It would appear they must endure a second interruption. Drat!

Sable replaced the lock and paused at a table to review what appeared to be a deed. She studied them until the sound of hooves clomping on the cobblestone could be heard. Fear flashed across Sable's lightning-blue eyes. So Mr Heep was not aware of his wife's midnight wanderings, Penelope surmised.

At the sound of men's voices piercing the loading bay's doors, the healer hastily folded the document. Not far away, rough wood scraped across brick. Sable rolled her eyes and blew out the light.

Thankfully, she elected to nip behind a second pile of boxes at the opposite end of the loft. It would have been quite awkward had she chosen to share their hideout.

A blast of night air whipped through the factory, causing Penelope to draw her coat tight across her chest. In the silver cast of the moon, who had decided to wander out from behind the wispy clouds, she spied Walt silently chewing. The evidence of her inopportune snacking lay sprinkled across her lapels—scones, or so Penelope wagered.

When Walt caught her employer's eye, she signed, "What?! I was hungry and had nothing better to do."

Half of Penelope bristled with frustration while the other half—the half that had been too excited to take tea—considered snatching the second currant scone from her assistant's hand.

"Where do we put 'em?" one man called to another in a raspy voice.

"Stack 'em neatly by the shelves. Just there."

Grunts and the scrape of wood filled the air. With little to see and even less to do, the ladies listened. Since neither of the men was of a loquacious temperament, the minutes ticked by at a snail's pace.

A second protest from the massive wooden doors signalled the men's departure. Penelope sighed when the sturdy doors cut off the icy gusts of wind. No sooner had the bolts and locks been secured than Sable darted from her hiding place and vanished down the stairs.

Soon enough, the door through which she had entered was opened, then shut.

The ladies rose and stretched their arms overhead. Pinpricks danced across Penelope's feet and up her knees. Before they left, she swept the platform to ensure they had returned every item to its proper place. "Well, shall we search for trap doors?"

Rather than help (or return the spoon she had nabbed), Walt juggled four wads of paper she had pinched from the bin. For the benefit of her audience of one, she added an expertly executed spin to her routine. "Nah. I dou—"

Three crumpled papers fell to the floor.

Chapter 19

THE CHAPTER WITH THE WAGON

"—bt there are any."

As our reader may have guessed, the locket once again saw fit to waylay the pair's plans in favour of its own agenda.

Rather than deliver them to a cosy inn where they might order a bowl of stew, it relocated them to the middle of a puddle. Fortunately, they had donned sturdy shoes meant to withstand the elements. Unfortunately, they had not the opportunity to rail and shout, nor even mutter a curse, for within an instant of realising they had been transported once more, they noticed a cornflower-blue skirt disappear around the corner of a brick building.

Though the wearer had disappeared before she spotted them (hopefully), the ladies still leapt behind a grouping of barrels tucked beneath a building's eaves. They crouched low, listening. A chill radiated through Penelope's shirt as she pressed her back to the red-brick wall. Walt tucked her hands into her coat, her breath hanging in the air.

They had nipped backwards *again*, or so Penelope suspected. The weather and the phase of the moon, which peeked from behind a cloud, suggested they had been transported to the same evening. And they had not travelled far. Penelope supposed they were just outside the factory.

As the mystery woman had not returned, guns blazing or otherwise, both women exhaled. Penelope was the first to rise, her eyes locked on the corner. "It appears we have moved to earlier the same evening."

"Whenever I meet whoever charmed this locket, I intend to give her a piece of my mind." Her assistant's gaze swept the yard.

In the distance, Penelope perceived Toast, her faithful watch dragon, pacing the field. "You presume it is a she who is behind this scheme."

"Naturally. Only a woman could be so diabolical."

Noiselessly, Penelope withdrew her pistol, holding it low, her finger on the trigger. She tiptoed to the edge of the building to peer around its corner. A shake of the head indicated the coast was clear. The mystery woman dressed in blue had disappeared.

"Who was she? Too tall to be Bonnie." Walt wondered.

"Not Sable; she was dressed in navy and entered through the opposite door." At those words, a thought occurred to Penelope. The cry of a field dragon confirmed it. Without slipping or sliding across the rain-drenched yard, she sprinted to the opposite corner. She arrived just in time to spot Sable, hood raised against the drizzle, unlock the factory's front door.

They had indeed moved backwards in time, yet only by a matter of a quarter-hour, a half at most. Once Sable had darted inside, she turned to call Walt.

An expert in mayhem, Walt had noiselessly apparated at her side. A cry of shock burst from Penelope's lips when she turned to discover her at her elbow.

Tickled, her assistant doubled over, clutching her side in laughter.

"Do not do that again." She bumped her elbow good-naturedly. "I would hate to shoot you, especially accidentally."

"Have you considered shooting me intentionally?" Walt wiped a tear from her cheek with the back of her hand.

The expression of a chaotic sprite slid over her face. "Often."

It occurred to Penelope that each time the locket had moved them through time, they had arrived at the perfect moment—in the alley and now at the factory. Had they arrived seconds earlier, they would have been caught. Even the first day they had arrived had been opportune, placing them in a familiar location the day before significant events swung into motion. This moment, then, had been selected. Had they missed . . .

Before her mind could form a plan, she began to sprint around the back of the building to the opposite end.

"What?!" Walt's feet slapped against the wet gravel that bordered the building. "Are we being chased or is this for exercise? Because if it's the latter, I think I'd prefer a nap instead."

"Neither." As she suspected, the clopping of hooves rang in the distance. "I think it essential we watch the men unload the crates."

They reached the corner of the building nearest the loading-bay door. On a hill not a quarter of a mile away, a pair of horses' ears peeked over the rise. Penelope sank into the shadows cast by the building, dissolving into the darkness.

"D'you think they'll lead us to wherever they're keeping the Folk?" Walt asked between pants.

"Likely."

With each passing moment, the cart drew nearer. The women steadied their breath. Since the prior version of themselves had experienced this moment and had heard the cart depart, Penelope knew they would not be caught. However, she did not wish to push her luck.

After what felt like an eternity, a familiar covered wagon and its driver turned into the yard. Nothing was especially uncommon about the wagon. Like a thousand others in the county, it sported a larger pair of wheels at the rear. Planks served as side walls, preventing the boxes from spilling out. All in all, it was nothing spectacular. Which is why Walt stared, dumbstruck by the triumphant grin her employer took no pains to disguise.

As before, the bay doors were opened. And on cue, the man with a raspy voice asked, "Where do we put 'em?"

To which the driver replied, "Stack 'em neatly by the shelves. Just there."

Penelope was a patient woman. She had to be. In 1811, nothing happened quickly. That evening, though, she cast patience to the wind. When the men disappeared into the belly of the factory, she darted towards the low-lying stone wall and leapt over it with ease. Soon enough, Walt landed with a thud beside her.

A stray curl staged a revolution and escaped from her associate's cap. Walt tucked it away again. "Rather than make me guess what your brilliant intellect has deduced, can you give me the abridged version without all the exposition?"

With her hands cupped over her mouth, Penelope imitated the call of a barn owl—a signal she and Toast had agreed on earlier that evening.

While they waited for the men to finish their work and for the muscle of the operation to discover them, Penelope obliged her friend. "The wagon loaded at the barn earlier this evening when we cut through the field and this wagon are one and the same."

"Could be a coincidence." The expression on her assistant's face declared, *I know this is not; however, as it needles you, I prefer to be contrary.*

"It could be. However . . ."

Even before Penelope heard the rustle of damp grass to their left, she caught a hint of power in the mist that clung to the ground. The fragrance of a forest dragon was that of wet earth, fern leaves, field daisies abloom, and warm sap on a summer's day. It was the perfume of the Sedgewicks' forest: now his forest as well, as she had entrusted it to him.

He waited several yards away, likely unwilling to spook the pony towing the cart.

"As I was saying," she continued, "why would a farmer deliver crates of corn to a factory at night? It is not as though they had come from afar and were delayed by the storm."

Nearby, the wooden doors swung shut as before, raking across the ground at the threshold.

"The hour is intentional. Besides, why would a tonic factory require corn? I suspect that it is a ruse, and hidden beneath it are ingredients for Mr Heep's cure-alls. As they likely do not wish that barn to be connected with this factory, they make deliveries at night."

Soon enough, the clip-clop of hooves faded into the night. Rather than call out to Toast, the ladies continued to wait. Sable would emerge from the factory within minutes.

Cold air swirled at their ankles, snaking into the gaps in their clothing. Walt shivered. "If you had accurately described the working conditions this position entailed, I would've said, 'Thanks, but no thanks.'"

"Oh, really." Penelope peered over the wall. A shadow crossed the yard towards the lane: Sable had left the factory.

"Yes." Hunched low, they skirted the wall in the direction of Toast. His leaf-like wings rose over the waves of grass.

"And would you have preferred I not rescue you from certain death at the theatre that night years ago?" Cupping her hands over her mouth again, Penelope called to their companion. He bounded towards them like a mink.

Walt raised her hands overhead and stretched. "Death would've been more restful, so probably."

When Toast arrived, he discovered the ladies sharing a grin. As he had grown accustomed to their eccentricities, he did not comment on the matter.

Their trek across the fields to the barn was unremarkable. They hatched a plan, which Walt was made to repeat twice. Though the scheme would rely heavily on improvisation, it was sound (more or less).

There was nothing especially unusual about the brick barn set into the hillside. Its shingles had a respectable collection of moss coating them. Obliging vines crawled up its walls, forming an archway over its door. A door in the ground suggested that it had a cellar. It even housed a barn owl, who darted in and out of a gap left by a splintered board near the roof.

What was unusual was the number of men prowling about with rifles. Had Penelope not been certain that the barn contained more than feed and horses, the presence of at least three burly men would have convinced her. One was perched on a platform among the branches of a tree. Another sat in the gable's window, swinging his leg over its edge. And a third leaned against the wall near the door, his rifle propped against the wall.

Rather than enter with guns blazing, which would result in the removal of the Folk to another den, they weaved noiselessly through the forest to approach from the rear. Walt would enter from the north and sweep the barn itself. Penelope would sneak past the guard in the tree to investigate the subterranean portion of the barn. Toast, well, he would make enough mischief to distract a whole regiment of men.

A drake's howl (not an actual drake, but Toast impersonating one) sprang the trap. From Penelope's vantage point, she had a clear view of the man perched in the tower housed in a tree.

When the cry rose over the mist, the man might have needed a change of trousers, or he might have simply looked as though he did. His eyes shone like silver plates in the moonlight. Weapons such as guns were useless against drakes, and yet he lifted his all the same. Consumed with the potential man-eaters lurking in the shadows, he missed the actual threat, a woman with the face of a pixie, darting beneath his roost towards the barn.

At the edge of the treeline, she hid behind a fallen log. Thunderous footsteps beating past announced the movement of the second guard. A pair of muscular arms scaling the ladder to the platform above confirmed as much. Gunshots tore through the countryside.

Penelope winced. Though she had half a mind to dispatch the men herself, nothing says "Gotcha!" like a pair of dead guards shot through the heart. Instead, she sprinted to the cellar door. Locked. Layers of rust and undisturbed moss suggested it had not been opened in years. Rather than pick it, she moved on.

Though she discovered a door which bore evidence of recent use, she dodged this too. A snore from the other side suggested that a guard slept within.

A window no larger than a porthole offered her a third opportunity to spy what lay beneath the barn floor. As she approached, a burst of light shot through the window. No doubt whoever lurked within had heard the shots and drawn aside the curtain.

Another faux drake cry shook the forest. Penelope pressed her back into the icy wall. A minute passed, then two. Nothing. Not so much as a shout. Likely the guards felt disinclined to leave the stone walls in favour of rescuing the poor sods out of doors.

With care, she inched forward. She drew a slow, measured breath. The scene that spread before her when she peered through the smudged window was worse than she had feared. A well-swept hall stretched the length of the building. Like in Mr Heep's factory, not a blade of dried grass nor a scuff mark besmirched the whitewashed walls and stone floors.

At least a dozen doors, bolted and locked, lined the hall. Lamps along one wall lit the space in a bright glow that would have been cheery if not for the half a dozen pairs of hands gripping the bars at the windows. One pair in particular drew her eye—they were the hands of a child, perhaps twelve or thirteen at most.

A shadow stretching from an adjoining hall alerted her to the approach of a guard. Though she would have loved nothing more than to charge into the hall with pistols blazing, she did not. Instead, she turned and sprinted towards the treeline.

She signalled to her friends that it was time to retreat. As she plunged into the forest, she vowed to return. Not only did she intend to free the Folk imprisoned here, but to burn the Heep empire to ash in the process.

Chapter 20

THE CHAPTER WITH THE FIRST DANCE

"Tremblingly alive to a sense of delight, and
unchilled by disappointment, the young heart
welcomes every feeling, not simply painful, with a
romantic expectation that it will expand into bliss."

Ann Radcliffe, A Sicilian Romance

When Penelope crossed the threshold of Birch Hallow in 1781 the following evening for the ball, she felt as if she were coming home. The staff, in their usual fashion, had tucked away her father's chemistry experiments, scrubbed the smoke stains from the walls, and hidden the pet reptiles. While the Sedgewicks' eccentricities were legendary, escaped grass snakes tended to discourage dancing (which Penelope knew firsthand due to the infamous ball of her twenty-first year). It did cheer her to discover a handful of oddities tucked between books or poorly hidden for the purpose of entertaining the guests. After all, what else would they gossip about the following day?

Like the other guests, she waited her turn to greet the hosts and hostess: her uncle, father, and aunt. Within the hall, she spotted several future acquaintances—Mrs Dewar, her house-keeper; Mrs Stevenson, her aunt's dearest friend; and Walt.

{Narrator's Note: The astute reader may wonder how Walt procured an invitation to the ball. A valid question. Not to disappoint, but it was simple. Bribery, sleight of hand and a teaspoon of Mr Heep's "Smooth Poo for You" were enough to tempt a neighbour to remain home, thus liberating an invitation.}

When Penelope's turn came to be introduced, a flock of hummingbirds whirred through her body.

"Brothers, this is Miss Clearwater, a recent acquaintance." In addition to speaking, her aunt signed for the benefit of Uncle Archie. "Miss Clearwater, my brothers: Mr Charles Sedgewick and Mr Archibald Sedgewick."

Penelope curtseyed, willing her expression to not betray the whirlwind of grief mixed with elation that swirled in her chest. She mustered a satisfactory, "A pleasure." Her father's hazel eyes held hers for an instant, smiling, before they slid past her.

While she paid a compliment or two to her aunt, her father's gaze periodically wandered to a spot near the door. Niceties were observed. After she pressed a scrap of paper into her aunt's hand, containing a request to speak later, she curtseyed and stepped past her. When she reached the stairs, she turned, her eyes searching the crowd that still littered the hall. The source of her father's interest stood laughing beside Mrs Stevenson. Her mother.

Penelope stepped aside, tucking herself into an alcove containing a vase that she would one day demolish in a game of tag. Though she could not hear their words above the din, she did not care. To see her mother, a mirror of her own petite frame and precocious expressions, chit-chatting with her friend . . . It fulfilled twice over every whispered wish she had made upon the stars.

Minutes passed before her father and mother stood opposite one another in greeting—he clumsy, and she uncertain. Penelope knew that tonight they would share their first dance. And under these candles that burnt overhead, her father would lose his heart, never to reclaim it.

After a bow and a curtsey, her mother took Mrs Stevenson's arm and departed, a grin dancing in her eyes. Her father glanced over his shoulder as she passed. He watched her until she stepped through the doorway and into the ballroom.

As Birch Hallow had been Penelope's childhood home, she knew its nooks and crannies. Her feet led her to a wing that was reserved for the family. It was where her uncle would one day build a flying machine during a bout of foul weather and construct a woolly mammoth skeleton from plaster.

In the shadows, memories of her mother flitted past her. One in particular materialised. Her father and uncle had secured a swing to the oak just outside. Though it was for her own particular use, throughout her childhood nearly every member of her household had enjoyed a carefree moment soaring beneath the canopy of green.

On one such day, she had knelt on a bench in this hall, her elbows resting on the windowsill, to watch her father swing with her mother. The look in their eyes ruined her for everyday romances. No mere flight of fancy would induce her to marry. Until she experienced whatever sort of love she witnessed that day, she would not give her heart to another.

The lilt of music weaving through the house reminded her that she had not come to reminisce but to plot the overthrow of a tyrant. Her eyes swept the hall once more, comparing the furnishing and art to those of her time. They were unchanged, except . . .

Her mind flashed back to the scene of Bonnie's death. She had been dressed in a gown unequal to her station—a silk dress—and her hands had been bound by a sash of blue brocade. The same blue brocade that dressed the windows of this hall.

Heat washed across her skin. Of course that pattern had felt familiar. Until her seventh or eighth year, when her mother and Aunt Josephine had convinced her father to update the furnishings, these drapes had adorned the halls of Birch Hallow. Blast!

Penelope waved aside the rising tide of disquiet. Until Bonnie materialised wearing the dress she would fall to her death in, it was none of her concern. Of their own volition, her feet guided her to the ballroom once more.

Despite her abhorrence of balls, she had to admit that her aunt had created a fairyland (and Penelope ought to know, as she had once visited one). Across the black and white diamond tiles stretched two lines of dancers. The ladies, in their gossamer gowns, floated like dandelion seeds caught by a breeze. Candelabra encrusted in crystals adorned the white walls. Their light shimmered, setting loose constellations to roam the world below.

When the first chords of the music swelled into a harmony, her eyes rested on the second couple in line—her father and her mother. They stood opposite one another, he in a blue coat with tails and she in chiffon. According to the bedtime tales her mama had told, he would ask her whether she had a favourite bird. She would reply, "Osprey." As she did now, or so Penelope presumed, when her mother spoke.

Reportedly, her words would cause him to blush, which he did. Her mother had been a faithful narrator, for as in the story, her father then stammered, "Did . . . did you know that they mate for life?" They shared an embarrassed blush.

She paced alongside them as they moved across the room, watching their expressions. So this was what falling in love looked like. It was not comets and starlight. Nor was it trumpets and gongs. Instead, it was shy glances. It was whispered wishes. It was the quiet rapture of two souls knitting into one.

A single tear slid down her cheek. She wiped it away.

After the dance had finished, her father led her mother from the floor. Unwilling to be parted from the other, they both spoke of nothing substantial, which, to two people falling in love, is everything.

Penelope's eye caught Walt across the floor. They walked parallel paths to the dining room. Each laced their way around clusters of mamas brokering their children's marriages and knots of girls fluttering their lashes at hapless men. Here and there, she caught a hint of a charm: bold choices considering the era.

By the time she stood before the refreshment table to accept a crystal glass of ruby liquid from a footman, the wonderland-like scene had faded, and she was reminded that in general, she loathed balls. If the false civility and social manoeuvring were not enough, the odour alone would have been sufficient for her to wish to avoid them for the rest of her days. Musky sweat mingled with copious quantities of rose water—blech!

Cup in hand, she wandered back into the ballroom. Walt stood at a window. With expressions that suggested they were thinking of nothing more than lace and ribbons, they stepped apart from the throng to convene.

Penelope soothed the tightness in her throat with a sip of punch. "We must discover Bonnie. I suspect this is the night she is killed."

Walt knocked back her entire cup whilst her eyes surveyed the room. "Is that your mother?" Her head tilted towards her mama.

Penelope's father stood at her mother's elbow, gesturing wildly—in all likelihood regaling her with his most recent scientific discovery. Little did he know she adored the study of anatomy as much as he did, if not more.

"It is." Her throat grew tight. She stamped on the sensation until it grew quiet. "This is the night they met."

"By the looks of it . . ." Her friend's eye flicked to hers. ". . . this is also the night they fell in love."

"Utterly and completely."

Neither woman spoke; they simply watched. Her mother's hand was claimed by a new partner for the second dance. A curtsey. A bow. A glance cast over her shoulder as she was led away. A shy smile spreading across his stubbly face. The seeds of a love that would last their lifetimes.

Once her father had vanished from sight, Penelope thanked Walt for not muddying the moment with trite condolences. "You truly are a wonderful friend."

"Don't let that get out. You'll tarnish my well-earned reputation as a layabout and a hooligan." She scowled at a lady who dared catch her eye. She recoiled, retreating to another room.

Penelope chuckled. "Perish the thought."

As they were unacquainted with the other guests, Walt and Penelope were left to themselves, which suited them well. Unencumbered by the niceties of polite society, they engaged in the time-honoured tradition of slighted ladies and wallflowers alike: gawking.

One couple after another claimed their places in the line. While they waited, the ladies swished their skirts, reminding Penelope of Canterbury bells caught on a breeze. Whirls of lilac, soft pink, and lavender added to the scene. Like peacocks in the spring, the gentlemen lifted their chins.

Among the dancers stood Mrs Stevenson in a periwinkle gown, opposite the impeccably groomed Mr Heep with his salt-and-pepper hair and pleasing smile. Had not Penelope already respected her uncle's future love, the sight of her mustering a grin for the scoundrel despite her knowledge of his deeds would have qualified her for sainthood. Beside her was Mrs Dewar, curtseying to a baron.

"What's Mrs Stevenson doing with him?" Walt asked.

Penelope suppressed a grin. "Likely gathering information."

Mr Heep's gaze slithered up and down his partner's full figure before it drank in the ladies on either side of her as well. Ugh! Not only did he imprison Folk for gain, but he was a rake.

Unwilling to shoot an unarmed man (or ruin her aunt's ball), Penelope turned from him. Further down the line, she spotted Sable on the arm of a country knight. Despite having seen her twice, she was still astounded by the change time had wrought on the healer.

"Is that Bonnie over there?" Walt asked, her voice tainted with concern.

At first, Penelope could not spot the young woman among the throng. However, when she recalled that the shop girl had died dressed as a lady, she found her. Dressed in the gown she would die in stood Bonnie, her golden hair and porcelain features enhanced by the candlelight.

"It is." Penelope set her cup on the windowsill.

"Crap."

Chapter 21

THE CHAPTER WITH THAT BUSYBODY, FATE

"To yield is grievous, but the obstinate soul that fights with
Fate, is smitten grievously."

Sophocles

Destiny, it would appear, preferred a dramatic musical score
to underpin the unfolding scene. For at the precise moment
Penelope and Walt spotted Bonnie, a snappy melody filled
the ballroom. The chipper tune belied the impending doom.

Our sleuth's hazel eyes trailed Bonnie as she darted through
the room. The girl's gaze was locked on Mr Heep, who, unfortunately, was a fabulous dancer. She paid no heed to others.
Doubtless, her lover had fallen into the cure-all pedlar's clutches or worse.

The downturn of Walt's brow, as well as the lack of bravado in her voice, suggested she felt uncertain. "What's the plan?"

Perhaps it was the punch, which was a tad strong, or the
foresight she possessed as a visitor from another time. (Or,

dear reader, perhaps our heroine had learnt, at last, to trust herself.) Regardless, she blurted, "To hell with plans."

To say that Walt was thunderstruck would be putting it mildly. Stunned would also be an ill-fitting adjective. Even incredulous would fall short. No; even though her assistant kept company with a yeti and had been known to play ten-pins with gnomes, she was thoroughly and utterly flabbergasted. After the shock had worn off, a wicked smile transfigured her face. "Oh, this should be fun."

With care so as not to draw Bonnie's attention, they slid nearer her position. Rage roiled behind the girl's chestnut eyes. While Mr Heep preened and flirted with his partner and her neighbour, Mrs Dewar, Bonnie seethed. Had the two met in a less public setting, Penelope had no doubt the girl would have choked the life out of him and enjoyed it.

Walt slipped her hand through the crook of her associate's arm. "Whew! If looks could kill."

"They very well might." Penelope composed a brief list of suspects from the guests in attendance. One of them, or a member of the household staff, would murder Bonnie tonight.

"Could he do it, to protect himself against her?" suggested Walt.

"Unlikely, unless Bonnie happened upon a charm timed to transport her to the balcony of the teahouse at the precise moment she tripped with her hands tied."

Though the girl rested in a chair at the edge of the dance floor, her eyes still tossed daggers at Mr Heep and his partner as they flitted across the floor like butterflies caught in the wind.

"Could happen." From her pocket, Walt withdrew a stack of shortbreads wrapped in her handkerchief.

How her assistant maintained a never-ceasing supply of treats, Penelope could never understand. At times, she wondered whether Walt had a yet undiscovered gift of magicking food out of thin air.

After savouring a second bite, she continued, "Last night, I met a man who could play the harp with his feet."

"And how is that related?" Penelope signalled that she, too, was famished. A second handkerchief materialized and was handed to her with a smug grin. It contained another stack of shortbread.

"It's not." Walt dusted the crumbs from her lips as a proper lady might. "I just hadn't had the opportunity to work it into our previous conversations."

Though the dance was not at an end, Bonnie's patience was. Not halfway through the set, she rose to dart from the room, her skirts billowing behind her. Several of the guests were astonished at the sight of a young woman running, as evidenced by a rash of clutched pearls.

Penelope led the way to a shortcut through the parlour. With any luck, they would intercept the girl before she disappeared once more. Walt trailed beside her, her hand in her pocket, either to grasp her pistol or to protect her snacks. Let us be honest; it was probably the latter.

Clusters of ladies lined the hall. Flowers, feathers, scales, and gauze adorned powdered hairstyles that defied gravity. Though Penelope ardently longed for the day women could wear breeches in public without being labelled harlots, she had to confess that fashion had leapt forward when it had abandoned false rumps and hair cushions in favour of the silhouettes of her time.

After navigating the hall without incident, they dipped into the parlour. The scene that spread before them was a familiar one to Penelope: the cosy fireplace, the writing desk at which she had composed her first dissertation on livor mortis, and the squashy chair ideal for napping. Tempted as she was to pause and rest, circumstances would not permit such extravagance.

With care, she crossed the room, heading for the door that led to the hall lined with blue curtains. A melody of string instruments mingling with the hum of voices reverberated across its polished floors. It was empty save the huddled form of a girl. Seated on a bench was Bonnie, her head in her hands, weeping.

Penelope gave a tip of her head, signalling to her assistant that they ought to retreat. She left the door ajar. "I shall speak with my aunt while you remain near Bonnie. Though I doubt we can prevent her murder, or that we should even try, we may be able to discover her killer."

Walt adjusted her stays and checked the pins holding her dress in place. From her pocket, she withdrew a well-polished spoon: one from this very house, if Penelope's memory served her well. She held it in front of her face to inspect her hair. "Not sure I can watch a girl get murdered without stepping in."

"Do not tempt Fate." There was a sharpness to Penelope's reply. Her time in the void and the incident with the branch had taught her not to cross the forces that governed the universe. "If she warns you to retreat, do so."

Like a lass told not to touch a fresh batch of ginger snaps, her friend replied with a noncommittal "Um-hmm."

"I swear, Walt." Panic tinged the corners of her voice, betraying the sudden sense of foreboding that swelled within her. "If you nearly die attempting to defy Fate, I shall finish the job myself."

"'Course you will." Despite her snappy retort, Penelope could sense a shift in Walt's demeanour. While her friend was a chaos magnet in satin who threw caution to the wind with glee, her sense of self-preservation was keen.

"Seriously, please, do be careful." She clasped her hand and squeezed.

Walt shrugged.

After her assistant had drawn a chair near the door and reclined with her feet over the arm, Penelope approached a nearby bookshelf.

Birch Hallow, like all proper estates, had several hidden passages and secret rooms. One such passage would permit her to pass through the house undetected in search of her aunt.

The lever was hidden by a row of novels. She slid it with ease, causing the whole bookshelf to pop outwards like a door. A quick glance at Walt, who observed her yet pretended she did not, and the sleuth slipped into the dark passageway, careful to close the doorway behind her.

As expected, the narrow passage was well-swept: evidence of its recent use. Candles were not necessary due to peepholes interspersed throughout the space. After an hour of facing the dreaded horde of merrymakers, she paused. The dim light and relative silence soothed her. She promised herself a day of respite when she returned home. Perhaps she would organise the library or polish silver. Such tasks had always proved restorative.

Beginning with the drawing room, she stepped onto a stool near the wall. The pair of eye-shaped holes, disguised by a painting, looked over the room. Card tables had replaced the usual furnishings. Men of all ages gathered about them, wagering, telling poorly constructed jokes, and smoking. Since there wasn't a lady in sight, Penelope moved on.

After a glance through another peephole confirmed that the study was unoccupied, she crept further down the hall. It was in the dining room that she discovered her aunt entertaining her guests.

A rose-red satin gown added a liveliness to Aunt Josephine's face. Rather than tease her hair into oblivion, she had styled it in a refined fashion in keeping with her tastes. She conversed with the guests with an ease she typically reserved for family and dear friends. Penelope had failed to appreciate it before, but her aunt was a natural hostess.

Before rushing from the passage into the servants' hall, she paused to capture the vision of her aunt dressed in colour—vibrant and bold colour—and catalogue it among her fondest memories.

Thankfully, the corridor into which the hidden passageway spilt was free of servants. Seconds later, she entered the dining room and stood across the room from her aunt, awaiting an opportunity to gain her attention. She did not have to wait long. After thanking a pair of twins enjoying their first Season, her aunt crossed the room.

Once the usual compliments and courtesies had been observed, Penelope leaned near and dropped her voice. "I discovered where they are keeping the Folk."

Aware of the people nearby, they threw their heads back in laughter, as though she had told a hysterical joke. Taking her niece's arm, Josephine led her through a door towards the kitchens. "Brilliant. Tomorrow, we shall organise their release."

"And I fear that Bonnie's life is in danger." A footman rushed by laden with a tray of cakes.

Once he had passed, Josephine replied, "All who fight against—"

"No." To the best of her knowledge, only three people ever had dared to interrupt her aunt, and, well, let us say it went poorly. Penelope steeled herself. "I am certain there will be an attempt on her life tonight. And while I do not believe it can be prevented, it is imperative we discover the identity of the murderer."

{Narrator's Note: By poorly, I meant one man *may* have lost a foot; however, as it was injured when he fled from the force of her stare, she cannot be held responsible. Had he simply endured her wrath instead of fleeing, he would not have been left with a peg leg.}

Josephine took a step backwards to better appraise her. She lifted a brow. "How did you come by your information?"

"I cannot tell you."

"Then how can I trust your word?"

At that moment, Penelope knew that her aunt knew (or, at the least, suspected) that they were related. Despite Josephine's question, her trust had been too easily won. And though she was prevented from unfolding the entire tale by a sensation that felt rather like a horse bit wedged between her teeth, she supposed she ought to call a spade a spade.

She whispered. "I suspect for the same reason you have trusted me thus far."

Shock soon gave way to delight as a mischievous grin enlightened Josephine's eyes. "What shall we do?"

A quarter-hour later, a patrol of the halls, balconies, and grounds had been initiated. It was womaned by members of Aunt Josephine's league, as well as a few gentlemen. They were instructed to keep their eyes open for the following:

Bonnie

Mr Heep

A & B together

Any curtains without a sash

As it was nearly eleven and time for the evening meal, Josephine was relegated to the role of hostess; however, she did instruct a maid to deliver updates. Walt, having been supplied with two plates piled high with treats, remained at her post, watching the hall.

Within Penelope swelled a rising caution that mounted to a shout. It would be unwise of her to remain within the house; of that, she felt sure. Instead, she paced the gardens bordering the hall. With every passing moment, a certainty grew within her. She would not be able to prevent the young woman's death. But perhaps she could avenge her.

Half an hour passed with nothing of consequence having transpired. Bonnie had left the hall. Her path suggested that hunger had gotten the better of her or that she wished to confront Mr Heep in public. As no shouts had filtered through the partially opened windows, she might have chosen to scowl at him instead. Since Penelope had observed one of the foot-men tailing her, she remained glued to her post.

After an hour, she lost sensation in the tip of her nose due to the chill. She started for the balcony near the ballroom. She would sweep the upper floors before returning to her post outside. One by one, she glanced through the windows as she passed. Empty. It was not until her hand reached for the balcony's carved stone bannister that a movement at the window furthest from her drew her eye. One of the drapes swished closed.

In spite of her gown, which had more ruffles and padding than ought to be permissible, she jogged the length of the wing. At each window, she paused, her eyes roving the hall. Nothing. When she looked through the window opposite the door to the parlour, it was closed. Whether Walt had abandoned her post, she could not tell. Heat swept through her body in waves, driving away her inhibitions. With no heed to propriety, she plunged towards the end of the wing. A woman's cry pierced the hush of the garden, spurring her on.

As she approached the final window, a gust caught the pane the staff had left open. Desperate, Penelope stretched her arm to prevent it from closing. Like water passing through a cupped hand, Time marched on, spiralling into inevitability. The window slammed against the frame. She dared not touch it or attempt to gain access to the hall through a door—Fate had given her hints enough; she was not to interfere. Instead, she hid behind the frame and watched, hoping she had been wrong yet knowing she was not.

Opposite the window, a door stood open. Lamplight sliced through the darkness, spilling into the hall. Beyond the glass, she observed the shifting of shadows within. The rise and fall of muted voices filtered through. Down the hall, a pounding at the parlour's door indicated that Fate had blocked Walt's interference as well.

Seconds ticked by. Tempted to try once more, she reached for the window but was halted; the lace on her sleeve caught on a vine she had not noticed before. The lace tore, hanging loose at her elbow. Contrite, she folded her hands at her waist and waited.

It was the hem of a dress that confirmed her fears. With her hands pressed against the window, she caught a hint of silk fan out as though its wearer had lost her footing. Penelope's body hummed with expectation, knowing what would come next and that she was powerless to stop it.

Without warning, Bonnie stumbled backwards across the space of the open door as though she had been shoved. Then she vanished. Penelope waited. Not a hand nor so much as a shadow appeared.

Thirty years would pass before the girl would appear again, broken on the cobblestone beneath a balcony at the foot of the teahouse steps.

Chapter 22

THE CHAPTER WITH THE SLEEP SERUM

"While the presence of magic has been recorded throughout the course of human history, its prevalence has grown with each generation, beginning in the latter half of the sixteenth century.

Today, it is estimated that one in every two-hundred men and one in every fifty women possess a gift."

A History of Magic Across the British Empire,
Sir William Ravensburger

"Remind me again why she gets to play the wanton seductress, and I have to lie in the dirt with *you*?" whined a disembodied voice under a night sky.

Had a farmer overheard those words, he might have thought he had drunk too much at the tap room that evening. A glance across the fields that stretched outwards from the forest would have confirmed their vacancy—well, vacancy of anything besides tilled soil (which does not make a habit of speaking aloud). Unless he had brought a lantern, he would have missed the two women dressed in breeches lying on their stomachs in the ruts.

"It is my aunt's plan; therefore, she has the right to decide who plays what role."

If the reader has yet to guess, the first voice was that of Walt and the second that of Penelope. From the tips of their toes to the crown of their heads, they wore black. Her aunt had provided them with the clothing, and with dark handkerchiefs, which they tied about their mouths.

"She scares you a little, doesn't she?" Though Walt's face was obscured, the wry grin in her voice was unmistakable.

"Just a tad, yes."

"Me too."

They adjusted their coats, drawing them under their chests to protect against the cold. Mother Nature had shown mercy by not letting loose a torrential downpour in the two days since the ball. Despite the absence of mud, the sharp nip of an autumn night leeched through the woven fibres of their clothing.

Penelope stared across the ridges towards the barn. It loomed, unchanged. A guard still reclined on a chair at the front. His head bobbed with fatigue. In the window above sat a second man. And though its shingle roof and wooden boards obscured the third watchman, perched above the ground in a platform at the rear, she would have bet he was there. Little did he know that no fewer than three intruders were closing in on his location.

Her aunt had hand-selected a team of skilled men and women from within her trusted circle. The manor-size man who had accompanied them to the meeting was among them, as was the nursemaid from the same gathering. Apparently, she was not only excellent at rearing young children whilst indoctrinating them with values like equality and justice, but she threw daggers with deathly accuracy. A few others made up their party, and though Penelope did not know them by name, she recognised two faces from her aunt's sewing circle.

A jab in the arm drew her attention to the appearance of a cloaked figure emerging from the mist that clung to the lane. Though a hood was drawn across her face, they knew who hid beneath the folds of wool: Josephine. With only a chorus of crickets to keep them company, they watched as she approached the barn.

Her presence roused the watchman from his broken slumber. A grin curled at the corners of his mouth as her aunt stepped into the circle of light cast by the lantern. At the sight of a woman dressed in a petticoat that revealed her ankles (Scandalous! I know) and in a gown cut low, the man smoothed his hair. The second man nearly toppled out of his window.

Although the content of their conversation was swallowed by the melody of an October eve, Penelope assumed it went according to plan, for the guard hanging out of the barn window waved them up. The first man permitted himself to be led by the collar to a side door. The poor bloke was in such a dither he left his rifle leaning against the front wall.

"Are you nervous?" asked Walt as she pulled herself into a squat.

Our heroine, who loathed squatting nearly as much as she abhorred disorganisation, stood. "About my aunt?"

Walt dusted the dark soil from her chest and thighs, leaving half of it behind. "Mm-hmm."

"Not in the least." Penelope, spotless and unwrinkled, watched the barn's window for the signal.

Walt cocked an eyebrow in reply.

"Truly, I am not." She dusted the palms of her hands against one another. "Certainly she can handle two groggy men blinded to her lethality by the curve of her ankles."

"Yeah, 'cause that's what they'll be looking at." As half of Walt's face was covered with a kerchief, Penelope could only see her eyebrows. They waggled like two caterpillars chasing one another.

With herculean fortitude, she resisted the urge to elbow her assistant in the ribs for her pert remark. "Besides, she is armed with a draught that would knock out a woolly rhinoceros."

Another minute ticked by before the slender silhouette of her aunt stood at the window humming a tune—a call to signal that all was well. In reply, Penelope impersonated a barn owl's cry to alert her conspirators. The ladies jogged across the field to the barn.

As planned, Walt assumed the guard's post, taking up his seat and rifle, but not before she dimmed the lantern that hung overhead. Penelope, keeping to the shadows, edged around the corner of the building to meet Josephine at the side door.

When she rounded the corner, another gentleman of their party met her. He dipped into the building to take up the post at the window. Seconds later, her aunt emerged, a key dangling from her finger.

"Did they give you much trouble?" Penelope asked.

"Not in the least. They were like clay in my hands."

With the lantern dimmed to a flicker, passersby would be hard-pressed to spot the young lad in black and his lady acquaintance trot to the front of the building. At the door, Josephine inserted the key into the lock. A look passed between the women, carrying with it well wishes and cautions. Her aunt turned the key.

It turned with a creak that ought to have awoken the man snoring on the bench just inside. To their utter relief, he did not so much as stir. Josephine withdrew a lacy handkerchief doused with a liberal dose of sleep serum and pressed it to his nose. It would be an hour at least before its effects wore off. With any luck, they would be long gone by then.

A narrow hall framed by rough-hewn timbers stretched before them. At one end, it intersected with a second hall-way: one that she suspected led to the cells. Two doors stood on either side of the passage. Its low ceiling and stone floor reminded her of a cavern.

Equipped with a candle to light their way, Penelope nodded a farewell to Walt, but not before she whispered, "Walt, I must know . . . Why the spoons?"

With her hat tipped low over her face, she leaned back in the chair, putting her hands behind her head. "Well, miss, if you must know, I intend to fashion a suit of armour and sit for a portrait the way the gentlefolk do."

A tut from within reminded Penelope of the task at hand, permitting her mere seconds to scoff before drawing the sturdy door closed, leaving Walt outside to keep watch.

They would explore the front rooms first to minimize the risk of encountering a guard while freeing the prisoners. This was to be a bloodless escape. When shots were fired, it was often the innocent who fell in the crossfire.

Setting a candle on a nearby table, Penelope stepped to the door of the first room. If there was a guard on the other side, a lad would raise less suspicion than a lady. With one hand resting on the knob, she took a steadying breath before pushing it open. Her aunt followed close behind.

A quick glance about the room revealed it to be a chamber for the guards' particular use. In addition to various hooks and a rifle on a rack above the desk, the room was furnished with a wingback chair and table. The faint light of a lone candle burning low revealed a slumbering man tucked beneath a wool blanket on a cot near the stove. Through the grate on the door, streams of orange light lit his pox-scarred face.

With the dose of sleeping draught in her hand, Penelope crossed to the man. She pressed it to his nose. He stirred for an instant before stilling once more. A bead of saliva dribbled down his lip. For good measure, she secured his hands and feet.

An iron hook beside the door held a set of keys. Handy. Penelope relieved the hook of its burden. The keys clanked against one another as they settled into her pocket.

Josephine kept watch on the hall through the door she had left ajar. "The hall is clear. I doubt there is another guard around at this hour; however, we ought to check the room across the hall to be certain."

The column of light spilling through the door lit her aunt's eyes. In them, Penelope perceived the same spirit that dwelt in the woman who had raised her—the determination, the strength, and the passion. Her mind flitted to the vision of smoke and ash. After discovering this prison, Penelope had felt certain that the factory would fall by her own hand, and yet, the fire that burnt within her aunt made her wonder whether *she* would be the one to set it ablaze.

Her aunt slipped past Penelope into the hall. "As the upper floor of the barn contains empty crates and boxes of bottles, I suspect it is a workshop."

"Agreed." Penelope crossed to the second door. Like the first, it was not locked. She slid the door open, prepared to pounce, though she doubted it would be necessary. Met with nothing more terrifying than a darkened room and the odour of oils, she stepped inside.

She sat a candle on the table nearest the door. Its orange glow revealed a cramped workroom. Though the room was organised with pristine furnishings and neat rows of bottles lining the shelves, all of its perfections could not compensate for one detail: secured to each table leg was a pair of shackles.

Moments later, she slid the door shut.

Her aunt had not entered, but had peered down the adjoining hall instead. She looked concerned. "What was in the room?"

"Tables, stools, and ingredients." Penelope's nails dug into the palms of her hands. Her eyes flicked to her aunt. "And shackles."

Josephine drew a breath. "Then we had better release the victims of Mr Heep's twisted schemes from their cells."

Without needing to subdue any more guards, they slipped into the final hallway. Her aunt moved to the first cell and whispered through the bars, "You must be silent. We are here to free you." She continued, warning the prisoners one by one.

Keys in hand, Penelope approached the first door. Two pairs of chestnut eyes stared back at her, terrified. The lamps hung on the walls cast black stripes across the captive's face. She lifted a finger to her mouth and winked before turning her attention to the lock.

It did not take long to free the Folk, twenty-five in all. Among them were men with grey beards and a woman with child due in a matter of weeks. Like the woman they had discovered in the forest, each wore black with slippers rather than boots. Two of the captured were children.

Not a word passed between them. They huddled against one another for support. Though they were well-fed and groomed, Penelope suspected it was due to Mr Heep's obsession with order rather than out of kindness. A man who enslaves children sees them only as tools, not people.

Josephine gathered the Folk near the door to the hall. Her voice was the soothing one she would use when a young Penelope skinned her knee. "We will exit through the side door and escape into the woods. About a quarter of a mile away, I have three carriages waiting to take you to safety."

"What about the factory and this barn?" At the back of the crowd stood the ginger-haired man from the square—Bonnie's lover. By the hollow look in his eye, Penelope guessed he had been informed of his sweetheart's disappearance.

"What exactly are you considering, sir?" her aunt replied.

"If they're left standing, won't he just find others like us?"

One of the men and a middle-aged woman nodded.

All eyes shifted to Josephine, for she exuded an undeniable sense of authority. "I cannot condone such a course if it places others at risk." She paused. An exhale spread across the room. Most of them did not seek a fight, only safety. The young man and two others, though, did not waver.

Josephine took a measured breath and continued. "However, the destruction of both properties would exact upon Mr Heep a blow from which he may not recover." A spark flared in her eyes. "So who among you wishes to take a detour on your way out of Alderwood?"

Chapter 23

THE CHAPTER WITH THE KISS

Stand facing her.

Look dreamily into her eyes.

It is well to sigh a couple of times
at about this stage of the game.

Whisper softly that her rosebud lips remind
you of Cupid's bow.

Do not hurry.

Draw her towards you.

Incline your head towards her until your lips align
— BUT WAIT!

Do not kiss her until you know that she uses Mr Heep's
Peppermint Lozenges.

Do You Know How to Kiss a Girl? Then Learn!

Apparently, chemicals, oils, and dry hay, mixed with vigilante justice and loathing when ignited, create a stunning blaze. Penelope certainly thought so when she stood in the field near the factory, watching as a glow like the sunset burned in the distance.

Of course, the guards had been bound and removed (unfortunately), left to wait for aid in a field. To ensure that the blaze did not spread to the forest, Toast stood guard at its edge. And everybody, except three of the Folk, had been whisked to safety. All in all, a tidy affair without violence.

{Narrator's Note: It is rumoured that the guards were discovered dead the next morning. This tale is utter nonsense. Yes, a pile of ropes was discovered, torn to pieces and left lying in the field. And yes, the men were never seen in Alderwood again. However, that does not mean they died. They could have fled. In fact, two of the men may have made it as far as the Americas before they met a sticky end. *IF* a field dragon was spotted licking a bone that resembled a human femur that week, it does *not* necessarily mean the men were eaten alive. It only suggests that *one or two* of the men may have been devoured.}

As they approached the factory, the moon hung low on the horizon, shining a brilliant blood orange. Though the building was made of nothing more nefarious than brick and wood, a sense of evil leaked out from its walls, soaking into Penelope's bones. She shivered, sensing that a moment was coming, one she had both hoped for and dreaded.

At the wall, their party gathered: Aunt Josephine, Walt, and Penelope, as well as three of the liberated Folk. These were Bonnie's ginger-haired lover, a middle-aged woman wearing an apron, and a greying grandfather who stood a head above most gentlemen. Toast had promised to meet them once he felt sure the forest would not be harmed (or once its protectress, a she-dragon called Hallstrom, arrived to manage the situation).

As the most adept lock-picker, Walt hopped the wall and scurried across the yard whilst Penelope and her aunt kept watch. In their time together, she had not learnt the names of the rest of their party, nor had she shared her own. The less they knew of one another, the better. However, she had learnt that the matronly woman and wizened man were healers, while the young man was a seer.

Less than a minute later, Walt waved them through an open door into the factory. A cavernous space stretched before her, supported by hewn beams. Shafts of moonlight cast spotlights upon the floor. The slits in the cast-iron stoves interspersed throughout the factory glowed, their tooth-like grates grinning menacingly. Without the pots of boiling liquids or the steam of fifty tinctures, Penelope could almost taste the magic entombed within the walls.

Due to the tidiness of the factory, it took mere minutes to glance under the tables and peer behind the shelves. Not a soul inhabited the building save themselves. After a plan had been laid, Penelope, Josephine and Walt stepped outside. They felt that the captives deserved a moment to themselves before they burnt the work of their captor's hands.

Penelope trailed behind her aunt and Walt as they filed through the rear door. She had not yet closed it when the click of a gun's hammer brought her to a halt. From the shadows stepped Mr Heep, a pistol aimed at her aunt.

"Thought you could burn this building as well, did you, Miss Sedgewick?" Unlike other villains, malice did not contort his handsome features. Instead, it enhanced them. Could the man *be* any more perfect?

"Not at all, Mr Heep." A nervous giggle erupted from Josephine's lips. After clapping her hand over her mouth to stifle the "outburst," she raised her arms above her head, as did Walt, who stood nearest her. Penelope, unfortunately, was still stuck by the door. Had his pistol not been trained upon her aunt, either Penelope or Walt could have immobilised him in seconds, even without a weapon.

"My friend and I made a bet . . ." She tilted her head towards Walt, who waved at the gentleman. ". . . that none of us were brave enough to enter the factory at night."

Lord, her aunt was a genius. Once, when playing lawn darts with a distant family relation, Josephine had instructed her niece, "Always permit the weak to underestimate you. It makes them much easier to exploit." The bet an eight-year-old Penelope placed later that day earned her two shillings, a marble, and a slingshot.

Mr Heep's disdain wavered. Since he was a businessman, it was unlikely he had socialised with her aunt. With her uncle and father, perhaps—but the ladies of the family would have been nodding acquaintances. Perhaps he had heard of her brilliance. But had he, like most, undervalued it?

The look of predator closing in upon his prey flashed across his face. "A likely story, and one I would have believed had not I questioned the men you left tied in the field."

CRAP! It was at that moment Penelope considered revising her stance on leaving prisoners alive.

A rustling sound near the corner of the building gave her hope that the Folk within knew of their predicament and had come to offer aid. That, or Toast lay in wait nearby.

"According to them, a woman dressed as a lady of ill repute mystified them with her womanly wiles and a dose of sleep serum." His gaze raked up and down her aunt's body, causing Penelope to wonder what would be the most excruciating way to remove a man's eyeballs.

Her aunt shrugged. "It was worth a try." She spoke with a nonchalance even Penelope admired. "So what will you do with me now? Shoot me?"

"I could." A wicked grin made him even more devilishly handsome. "In fact, I think I shall."

The charge exploding in the barrel rent the night in two. Her aunt stumbled into Walt. While Penelope's mind insisted that a round fired at that distance could have missed its mark, her heart protested adamantly. Only when her aunt's knees buckled, forcing Walt to cradle her in her arms, did she accept the fact that Josephine had been wounded.

Wisps of smoke trailed from Mr Heep's pistol, which was still trained on its target. He chuckled. "That was more fun than I expected."

Heat clawed up Penelope's neck, roaring in her ears. She dropped to her knees beside her aunt. Blood bubbled from a wound in her shoulder, drenching her linen dress. Walt's hand pressing against it did little to staunch the flow. Penelope tore her coat off, folded it, and clapped it to the wound.

The determination on her friend's face as she support-ed Josephine against her body lent Penelope strength to still her trembling hands. For a frantic moment, she considered seizing the locket pressed to her chest under her clothing and returning to the moment before they had exited the door so that she could immobilize Mr Heep. However, Fate stayed her hand. A voice called over the blood whooshing in her ears. The locket remained where it lay.

Since they were focused on her aunt's wound, they had neglected to take stock of their surroundings. Which was why the appearance of Mrs Sable Heep stepping from the darkness to stand beside her husband was so jarring. Especially since she held a rifle designed to fell Irish elk, and had it aimed directly at his temple.

"Good evening, darling." Sarcasm dripped from her voice like honey. "Do be a lamb and hand that pistol over before my trigger finger experiences a nervous tic, or before I become so bored I shoot you simply to pass the time."

"Of course, my dove." Mr Heep snarled. As he extended the grip of the pistol towards his wife, Penelope could feel her aunt begin to shiver. Hot blood seeped through her jacket. Walt shed her own, rolling it tight before layering it over the first coat.

They exchanged a knowing look. Walt's caramel eyes reflected Penelope's rising panic. Without aid, her aunt would not last the night, perhaps even the hour. A hundred memo-ries of her aunt kissing her bumps and bruises nudged her. She bent near Josephine to whisper, "Hold steady. You make it, I swear."

Hope, as well as a hint of amusement, flitted across her aunt's face. She nodded.

Sable stuffed the gun down her stays with a look in her eye that shouted, *Go ahead and try.* Quite unexpectedly, and to the confusion of all, no sooner had the gun been stowed than she grabbed her husband by the collar, pulled him to her, and pressed her lips against his.

Chapter 24

THE CHAPTER WITH THE AHA

Horacio Heep's Tooth Powder, a pure,
fragrant, non-gritty tooth powder for all who
value the appearance of their teeth. Now with
dragon tooth. Sold everywhere.

A box of Onoto, c. 1780

Sable released her husband, who swayed on the spot. "You were always a terrible kisser," she scoffed.

With impeccable comedic timing, he swung his head towards his wife as though he were drunk.

"Thankfully, that will be the last I'll ever have to suffer the taste of your breath." She spat on his polished shoes.

With eyes unfocused, he staggered first in one direction then the next, before falling like a felled tree to land on his perfect face. When his nose crunched on the stone path, not a single person shuddered.

"Is he dead?" asked Walt, hopeful.

"Unfortunately, no." Sable's lip curled into a sneer. She wiped her mouth with the cuff of her sleeve. "Just unconscious. I used one of his own tinctures against him. Perhaps he should have written in the instructions that one shouldn't use it as a lip stain."

The door smacked against the building, revealing the matronly healer. Her eyes flicked from Sable, who still held the gun at her side, to the prone Mr Heep and then to the knot of women on the ground. Rather than demand an explanation, she dropped to her knees, whisked her greying hair behind her ears, and shooed Walt aside. Her strong arms lifted Aunt Josephine's body onto her lap. Penelope relinquished the compress to her able hands.

With her palms pressed against the wound, the woman's eyes fluttered closed. Walt's hand reached out, fumbling for Penelope's bloodstained one. Though they did not look at one another, they stood together, friends, or perhaps, if they survived the night, nearer sisters.

"We will need to combine our strengths as healers," the woman shouted to the elderly gentleman who stood in the door. Though her voice remained calm, there was an urgency to her words. "Neither of you would happen to be Folk, would you? I'm not certain that two will be enough."

In the chaos, our heroine had not noticed Sable slip away. Her shoulders unmoving, she strode to the end of the building, determined.

A gust stirred the curls at the nape of Penelope's neck, carrying with it the fragrance of herbs, wisteria, and soil on autumn morn. In a blink, the factory vanished, replaced by a garden. The bright melody of crickets mingled with the calls of songbirds.

She pressed her hand to her chest, sensing the warmth of the locket pressed to her skin. Sunlight heated her face.

As though it called to her from a great distance, she heard Mr Scott's voice say, "Sable, how were your gifts discovered?"

The healer's voice, frayed with age, rang across the decades. "Had not I and two other healers combined our gifts, she would have succumbed to her injuries."

At the clap of the factory's door as Bonnie's lover exited, the vision disappeared. Mrs Heep had not yet turned the corner when Penelope called out, "Sable!"

Her call did not break the healer's stride. Pfft! She always had been an insufferable witch.

Of course, Penelope appreciated the risk. To abandon one's husband was not unheard of. To threaten him with death was common enough. But to give oneself away as a healer after doing either of those things—suicide.

Though Penelope would have fallen on her knees, begged, pleaded, and promised her half her estate, Fate prodded her to utter a single word, "Please."

If magical words had existed, an observer would have thought she had used one. The crunch of gravel under Sable's boots ceased. Without turning, she exhaled a breath. It swirled around her neck and shoulders.

"I suppose," she began, her voice resigned, "as I have parted with my husband . . ." At last, she spun on her heel. ". . . I might as well do it thoroughly."

Gravel flicked behind Sable's boots as she hurried to Aunt Josephine's side. After casting a final glance at Penelope, she fell to her knees. Without removing her leather gloves, she pressed her hand atop the wound. Her lightning-blue eyes fluttered shut.

Time did not stop. It ticked on. Like sand funnelling through an hourglass, it passed. And Penelope waited, wishing on the unknown galaxies spinning above her.

A thump behind her alerted her to Toast's arrival. Though she did not turn, she noted Walt jog past her in his direction. A toasty snout (pun intended) wiggled its way beneath her arm. His presence lent her strength, enough to keep her misgivings at bay.

Curiously, it was not the bead of sweat that trailed down the elderly healer's cheek and disappeared into his grey beard, nor the pinched look on the woman's face that buoyed her hope. Instead, it was the compulsion to sneeze that flooded her body with relief.

In all of her years, she had never sensed magic untethered—untied to an object or a magical being. Yet tonight, under a swirling river of stars, the power fanning outward from the trio seeped into her skin. The fragrance of it was so full-bodied she could taste it rolling across her tongue. It reminded her of fresh air driving away the stench of a long-neglected room.

Moment by moment, Aunt Josephine's strength returned. The tension drained visibly from her body—her breaths became surer, and her eyes less lined. When the healers' eyes snapped open, only the sticky blood drenching her stays and dress revealed that she had ever been injured.

With care, the healers helped Josephine to her feet. Walt and Penelope each took an arm to support her as they moved away from the building to lean against the wall. Though her wound might have healed, time and rest alone could restore her to complete health. They settled her onto the grass with care.

"Do all future Sedgewicks keep forest dragons as friends?" Aunt Josephine spoke through cracked lips. She peered at her niece from the corner of her eye. "Or only the ones who are sniffers?"

"Ha!" Walt's outburst was accompanied by a knee slap. She wandered away with Toast, the pair of them sniggering. Traitors.

Of course, she had suspected her aunt had cobbled together a near-accurate theory. Why else would she have trusted her? Penelope grinned. "What betrayed me?"

"Your appearance, for one. You resemble my aunt, or your great-aunt; the likeness is uncanny."

The young seer, Bonnie's lover, jogged across the yard to hand Josephine and Penelope coats he had found within the building. They accepted his gesture with a smile.

Once he had trotted back to his fellow captives, who were eagerly tying Mr Heep's wrists and feet (and not being gentle about it, might I add), Penelope helped her aunt with the sleeves. "I have never seen a portrait of her within Birch Hallow."

"It hangs near my bedroom. However, I suspect that before you are born, I shall have to tuck it away." She gestured for Penelope to sit beside her. "And may I ask when I should expect to become an aunt?"

With her head resting against the stone wall, Penelope tapped her finger to her mouth.

"Or which of my brothers will be your dear papa?" She raised a questioning brow.

A shake of the head sufficed as an answer.

"Blast. Had you divulged the date and time of either occasion, I suspected I could have won several hundred pounds."

Aunt Josephine's lips turned upwards. "Alas, I shall have to content myself with betting on who will dance with whom at my annual ball."

"You? Bet? On that?" Penelope blinked several times. "Is that why you force us to endure such life-sapping crucibles?"

Her aunt, with a face so wicked even pixies would be impressed, elbowed her niece's arm. "This Season, I won one thousand pounds."

Had they had mugs of ale in hand, they would have clinked them together. Instead, they shared a hearty chuckle, though it cost her aunt a wince.

A comfortable silence fell between them, one they would share nearly every day of Penelope's life. Whether they read novels at one another's side, practised mathematics, or played chess, they would share hundreds upon hundreds of silences. Until that moment, our heroine had never appreciated them for what they were—islands of refuge in a sea of societal expectations.

After several minutes, Penelope, still staring at the Milky Way overhead, asked, "And what is the other reason you trusted me?"

Rather than answer with words, her aunt tugged on an object in her pocket. Before it had freed itself from its fabric prison, Penelope knew what it was—her locket's twin, unbroken and polished. "The likeness is of my aunt, Mary Prudence Sedgewick, whom you take after. You would have liked her."

"I suspect I would have."

Without her permission, her throat tightened. Part of her wished to remain in this time for a few more days. She might drink tea with her mama when she came to call for the very first time. She might laugh with a younger Uncle Archie, console him when Mrs Stevenson married her husband, and promise him that his day would come. And perhaps, even, she might have the opportunity to hug her maternal grandmother one more time. She could not, of course. Fate stood over her shoulder like a mama hurrying her children to church.

When she turned to her aunt, she met glacial eyes studying her. She tried to grin but did a poor job of it. "It is time for us to return."

Aunt Josephine sighed. "I suspected as much."

"And I shall need your locket to do so. It permits us to navigate through space and time."

"Navigate through space and time? Curious." Without hesitation, her aunt handed it to her.

Penelope rose and then helped her to her feet. They joined the tight circle their companions had formed—away from Mr Heep, naturally. Walt eyed her. A half grin reassured her assistant. They gave their attention to the Folk, who were weighing their options.

"With all of those chemicals, alcohols, and oils, I'm not certain it's safe, dear," pled the matronly healer. Though the elder gentleman nodded his head, Bonnie's red-haired love was resolute.

"I don't care." Jaw clenched, hurt seeping from every pore, he would not budge. "It needs to be destroyed."

Gently, as his own mother might have, the woman stepped nearer him, face to face, and rested a hand on his arm. "But she would care." In reverence of the girl who had paid the ultimate price for their freedom, they hung their heads in silence.

After a minute had passed, Penelope caught an exchange between Walt and Toast. A glance from her and a nod from him meant they had concocted a plan. She stepped forward. "We do have a dragon."

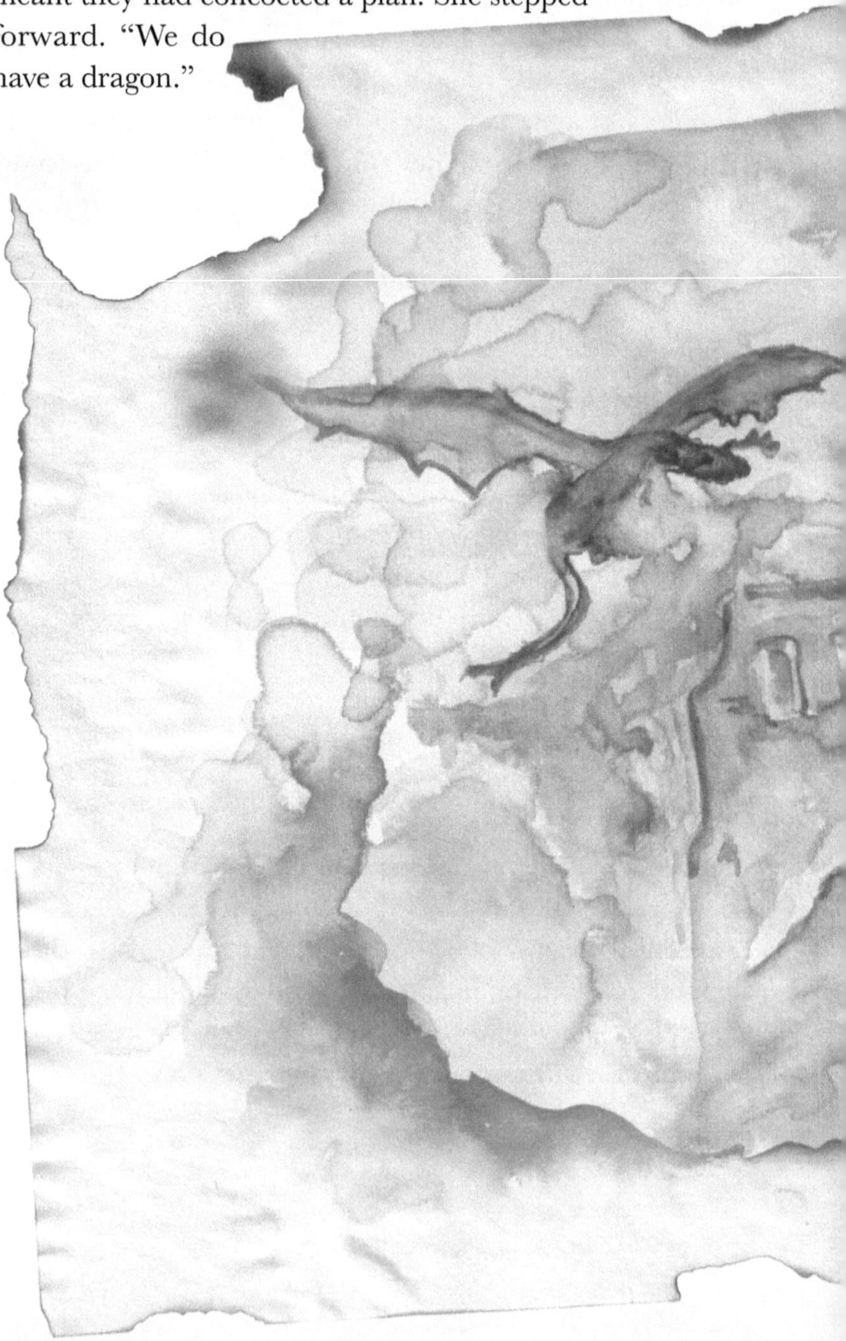

Chapter 25

THE CHAPTER WITH THE GOODBYES

"Charms are created when the practitioner fastens a piece of their gift to an object. The strength of a charm is correlated to the durability of the charm itself, making metals, stones, and crystals preferable to cloth or leather."

James Hutton – The Father of Modern Geology

Once Josephine had sent the Folk on their way to a nearby safehouse, Walt, Penelope, Josephine, and Sable stood in the field whilst Toast soared overhead.

While they waited, Penelope stepped towards Sable, who stood apart. "Thank you."

"'Twas nothing." Sable shrugged. "By the by, why did you call me Sable?"

As the healer had sacrificed much to save her aunt, Penelope felt she owed her an explanation of sorts. "It is what everyone will call you one day."

Sable's eyes danced with amusement. So she had suspected that Penelope had gifts that day in the shop. "My name given name is Crucible."

- 229 -

Of its own volition, Penelope's lip curled.

"Ghastly, I know." Her pursed mouth restrained a smile. "However, my governess, knowing how I loathed it, called me Sable. Has a nice ring to it, don't you think?"

"I always have."

Though Penelope had questions yet to ask, the sight of Toast barrelling down on the factory, fire glowing in his chest, proved a distraction too marvellous to resist. Orange flame poured from his mouth, setting ablaze an inferno intent on devouring the building. Flames licked the brick walls greedily. Heat billowed across the yard.

A final turn about the field, and he landed, his head held high. A scratch under the chin from Penelope and a punch on the shoulder from Walt was praise enough. Even Aunt Josephine curtseyed and gave her thanks.

In the excitement, Sable had disappeared. It was just as well. She had an adventure of her own to begin. Perhaps, in thirty years' time, Penelope would barge into her home for a cup of tea and a tale or two.

At the horizon, the sky had begun to lighten. She sensed it was time to leave. Besides, it would not do well to be caught at the site of an inferno with a bloodied gentlewoman, a dragon, and a tied and gagged Mr Heep.

Penelope, carrying a weight she would gladly have left in that field, turned to her aunt, who stared at the blaze, enraptured. Her posture was precise, her dress was perfect (if not for the blood), and the barely bridled fire in her eyes was terrifying. Though she was thirty years younger and lacked a few lines and silver hairs, she was the same in the essentials—her tenacity, her intellect, and her love.

With a tug, Penelope freed her locket, the broken one, from her pocket. She held the newer, whole one in her hand. A breath helped settle the nerves stampeding up and down her limbs. So, Walt had been correct—only a woman could be diabolical enough to create such a charm. Her eyes slipped shut, winking out the present.

Though she often had to wrestle a memory from an object, on that early morning, the past welcomed her with open arms. With ease, she sped through the lockets' earliest moments. Flickers of familiar faces, her uncle, father, and aunt, brushed past her.

The night they had arrived in 1781 presented itself to her, but from the vantage point of the bedchamber, where, she discovered, Aunt Josephine had hidden. Through the cracked door, Penelope caught a glimpse of herself and Walt. She chuckled at the sight of Walt pinching a spoon as they exited the room.

As she had learnt during her study of the creation of charms, she drew a piece of her magic from her heart as one might tug on a loose string. She knotted it to the moment, holding the other end in her hand.

When a familiar country lane came into view, the time traveller paused. Arm in arm, her aunt and Mrs Dewar strolled down the lane between two gardens. Once again, she fastened a knot, knowing mere seconds would pass before she and her assistant would materialise.

Further memories sped past. At last, she arrived at the factory. It had been her aunt's skirt that had whipped around the corner that night. Had Sable's appearance or the presence of the wagon spurred her homeward, or had she ventured out that night for another reason entirely?

It mattered not. With care, Penelope secured a final bow, tying the locket to that moment as well. With the strands clutched in her fist, she connected the lockets' memories, creating bridges across which she and Walt would inadvertently stumble. As sunrise approached, she relinquished her hold on the past, falling headlong into the current moment.

Like a swimmer breaking the surface of the water after a dive, Penelope gasped for the present. She drank in the brightening sky in the east and the rustling of grass on the wind as a drowning man might suck in air. Never had she submersed herself that long. With her hands on her knees, she breathed deeply, sensing the earth's strength beneath her.

Josephine placed a hand upon her back and rubbed it as she would when Penelope was ill. A pair of boots, her assistant's, appeared beside her, caked with mud. Neither woman spoke. They let her recover without suffering their trite comments.

When Penelope rose, she cast a reassuring smile for their benefit. It smoothed the worry from their brows. She turned to her aunt and extended the locket. "Keep this hidden and safe for a while." The chain slithered through her fingers into her aunt's open hand.

"And when shall I give it to you?" Josephine fastened it about her neck.

"I hesitate to give you a definitive time and date . . ." Her aunt pinched her lips in a manner that suggested she objected. "However, as I cannot leave you without any direction, let me give you a clue: a morning will come when you and a woman you will know as Mrs Stevenson will take a walk in the woods. We will cross one another's path. I will tell you that Uncle—"

She caught herself. Drat! Aunt Josephine leaned forward keenly, aware of her misstep. Penelope played with a curl tucked behind her ear. "I will tell you that my uncle, one of your brothers, is studying temporal displacement. Much to the entertainment of your friend, I shall also discuss him practising escapism."

"Ha! So we are as odd a bunch as ever."

"Worse." A smile spread across Penelope's face.

She had not forgotten the matter of Toast, of course. Nor had her friends. Apparently, they had been bickering about how to best extract one of his teeth to make into a charm. Walt had been in favour of tying a string to it and then fastening the other end to a horse, which she would spook by discharging her pistol. And though he had conceded it would have been hysterical to watch, a much simpler approach would be for him to shed a tooth (which, apparently, forest dragons can do. Who knew?)

Like the locket, Penelope dove into the fang's history to tie a knot about the moment he would appear in the forest to rescue them from the drakes. As dragons have a magic of their own, he could navigate the charm home, or so the ladies understood from an intricately drawn series of pictures.

He bowed to Josephine.

"Thank you for your help." She curtseyed low. "I look forward to making your acquaintance one day."

Ever the gentleman, he bowed. After an eyebrow waggle and a wink, the flirt vanished.

"It was a pleasure *not* to make your acquaintance." Walt held out her hand.

Josephine took it, amused, apparently accepting that she would not learn its owner's name for years to come. "A pleasure."

With her hands stuffed in her pockets, Walt stepped aside to kick at clods of dirt near the still-unconscious Mr Heep. (Alright, <u>on</u> the still-unconscious Mr Heep.)

The aunt and niece turned to one another. Though Penelope would see her again that evening, she would miss this Aunt Josephine, who was more colourful, less stern. Rather than offer a handshake, she opened her arms. Her aunt willingly stepped into her embrace.

It would be three years before these arms would first hold her. Seven before these hands would help her to lace a pair of boots. Another four before they would teach her to dance. And then there was the number fourteen, the year they would take on the mantle of motherhood.

As Penelope stood there, held in those arms, she wondered how Josephine bore it all. She blinked back tears, proud to have this woman as her second mother.

In her aunt's ear, she whispered, "Love us well."

They stepped apart. Not an eye among them did not shine with emotion. The sun peeped over the farms, transforming the smoke belching from the factory into a coppery funnel of ash and soot. A steady stream of townsfolk poured into the lanes to inspect the blaze, but not to fight it.

Penelope collected her half of the locket and extended her hand. Her friend took it. With a parting grin, she said, "When you gave me the locket, you asked me to remind you to hug my parents often." And then she closed her eyes.

Josephine Sedgewick stood alone, a question on her lips and concern in her heart. She turned and hurried home.

Chapter 26

THE CHAPTER WITH THE GRAVESTONE

M.T. 1775-1781 — Ever Parted

A Gravestone discovered in the Forest of Dean near Alderwood

When they arrived home, everything was as they had left it, only a tad colder and darker. Penelope had meant to arrive a minute or two after they had departed; however, an error in judgment landed them in their chambers an hour later instead.

Walt quickly stripped from her bloodied clothes and slipped into her bottle-green banyan to lounge in her chair with her pipe in hand. "The tea's gone cold."

"The horror." After having spent several hours traipsing through fields at night, Penelope had looked forward to a warm fire. Ever pragmatic, she only paused to shed her waistcoat before kneeling at the hearth to coax the dying embers to life.

Walt stuck her tongue out at her employer, who was too engrossed in fanning the infant flames to notice. Her mind was occupied with one final mystery: who had killed Bonnie, the gentleman in the forest, and perhaps others?

Though the ability to read minds was not a real gift, Walt possessed an uncanny aptitude for discerning the thoughts and motives of others. Which is why Penelope ought not to have started when she asked, "You're wondering who committed the murders, aren't you?"

"Yes." The flicker of the coals mesmerised her. They rippled with heat, shifting in intensity. Warmth fanned across her face, though she did not sense it. Her mind had folded in on itself. When she spoke, her voice was but an echo of its usual self. "Who had the means and the motive?"

Walt riffled through the bag she had intended to bring on their escapade, seeking the tin of biscuits. After stuffing one in her mouth, she observed, "Mr Horacio Heep is an obvious suspect."

"Which renders him innocent." She stoked the flames before adding another log to the fire. After brushing her hands on her breeches, she turned to her friend. "Of those crimes, at least."

As the cold tea had not proven too repulsive to wash down the dry biscuits, Walt downed an entire cup. Her cheeks puffed with the bitter liquid. She waved her hand to indicate she wished Penelope to continue.

"Had it been him, my aunt would not have needed my aid to bring him to justice." She crossed the room to the washbasin in the bedchamber beyond. She stilled her hands before she poured icy water into the bowl rimmed with painted flowers, careful not to slosh it over the edge. "I suspect he kept an associate. Several, perhaps. One of whom is adept at moving through time."

"One who handled the dirty work for him, eh?"

"Or was the mastermind himself."

"Or herself," Walt corrected.

"It would explain the missing seers and listeners." Blood-tinged water soon filled the basin. Penelope wetted a cloth to wipe her neck and face. "Bonnie's murder required a knowledge of this afternoon's events. Perhaps, like us, her death was a part of the perpetrator's past—a loop."

After exchanging her filthy clothing for garments more suitable for an heiress in 1811, Penelope tossed her shirt and breeches into the hearth. She watched as the fire blazed orange. Tongues of flame licked the fabric greedily.

When she reached for the kettle to boil water in the kitchen below, her hand paused, hovering at the handle. Her voice, distant and hollow, murmured, "How did Bonnie arrive on the balcony?"

"Didn't you say she wore a charm?" Walt skimmed the morning edition while puffing on her pipe.

"Yes . . ." Penelope leapt to her feet to pace back and forth, startling her assistant, who toppled the tin of treats. "But in order to create a bridge between the past and the present, it would have been necessary for its twin to have been on the balcony when she fell this afternoon."

Her assistant exhaled a ring of smoke. "Like the locket. We could only travel to those times and places because your aunt had done so while wearing it."

"Precisely!" Penelope ripped the locket from her neck, snapping the chain. "When I created this charm, I could create anchors within its own history. However, I could not cause us to appear in France in 1781, because the locket was in England for the entirety of that year."

"But I thought you said the balcony was empty and the doors closed."

"Meaning—"

"A future or past version of the pendant is, or was, on the balcony." Walt leapt to her feet and began to pace the length of the opposite side of the room, parallel to her friend.

Though Penelope usually scowled at interruptions, her mind had already somersaulted to several conclusions. It raced onwards. She rubbed her hands together. "And the gentleman in the forest, the duchess's lover. He must have had a charm; however, by the time we had reached him, it had been removed."

"By the same person?" Walt snatched what had been Penelope's teacup and knocked it back as though it were a serving of cheap spirits.

Our sleuth ignored her question (Rude!) and raced to her desk, where lay a tidy stack of letters. On the top perched the letter from the duchess. Penelope's irises darted back and forth, devouring each word.

Rather than enlighten Walt, she let the letter fall to the desk, and crossed to the bookshelf. Her trembling fingers danced across the bindings until they alighted on their target— an olive-green cover with gold embellishments. She yanked it from the shelf.

Without bothering to sit, she cracked open the tome and flipped through the pages. The troop of hummingbirds had returned, swirling through her chest and into her arms, causing the cover to shake. Walt moved beside her to steady the book.

At about the middlemost page, Penelope stopped. She muttered a list of names and dates to herself before she handed the book to Walt and raced to the shelf once more. A second volume was tugged from the shelves. Once again, she remained glued to the spot. Page after page was turned before she paused at a handful of entries. Colour drained from her face as she let the book slip to the floor.

Without explanation, she flew to the desk. She scribbled a hasty note, which she folded and addressed. She snatched her pistol from the table and bolted to the door. One arm then the other shrugged on her holster and spencer. "Get dressed and be ready should I send for you. But first, deliver the letter."

"Should I be armed?" Her friend returned the volumes to their shelves.

Penelope yanked out the blade Walt had accidentally embedded in the door earlier that day and sheathed it in a holster on her thigh. "To the teeth."

"Do you know who did it?"

The ladies' eyes met—Penelope's brimming with concern. "Intimately."

Walt's lips curled into a grin. "Give 'em hell."

With that, Penelope wrenched open the door and ran down the stairs.

A lady stood under the canopy of a grandfather oak, golden tresses shining in the moonlight. Her hands were clasped at her waist, her eyes fixed on a simple carved headstone framed by a border of leaves and moss. A barouche and thoroughbred stallion stood tethered nearby.

A petite figure emerged from the mist like one of the fae at solstice. Veiled, the pixie clad in muslin approached. "Thank you for coming."

"I appreciate your prompt response." The lady did not turn.

Little did she suspect that it had taken our heroine swathed in black gossamer threads several days and three decades to respond. With a tread so hushed that one might have suspected she had bewitched the forest and bent it to her will, Penelope approached the grave to stand beside her client. The humble stone read, "M.T. 1775-1781 — Ever Parted." River stones encircled it.

"I take it those are his birth year and initials." A leaf, shaken free by a breeze, swirled to the earth below. Penelope let it fall.

"Montgomery Thomason." The Duchess knelt to brush the dust from the stone. She caressed the carved letters lovingly. "We were lovers. Childhood sweethearts, actually."

Though the lady could not see the rise of Penelope's brow, she answered it. "My husband knows. It was one of the terms of our marriage." She pressed her hand to the stone. "We were partners and keepers of one another's secrets. He satisfied his tastes in London while I had Montgomery."

Penelope nodded. "And when did Montgomery disappear?"

"Last week." The Duchess rose, drawing her regal figure to its fullest height. It was no wonder the Duke had selected her. Poise glowed from her skin. She would fill every room she entered, driving forth all speculation and doubt.

From her pocket, Penelope withdrew a gold pocket watch. She held it aloft. It spun, reflecting the silver moonlight.

Her client's delicate hands flew to her mouth, covering it. The chain slipped through Penelope's fingers as it dropped into her hands. She clasped it to her chest; a tear trailed down her cheek. "It was a gift."

Of course, our sleuth had guessed as much. In the hours since her departure from her offices, she had paid a visit to town and nipped to the night of his death to reclaim the watch, mere minutes after her past self had examined the gentleman's body.

She need not have, of course. And yet, she could not bear leaving it to be pocketed by the constable's hands. It alone could provide the closure his lover sought, as well as prime her to answer Penelope's lone question.

Before she asked it, she stepped aside, permitting the duchess a moment to compose herself. As though drawn by an unseen tether, she wandered to the headstone once more. Crystalline cracks in the stones encircling the grave shimmered in the moonlight. They drew her in, beckoning her. For a reason she could not name, Penelope slipped one into her pocket.

Minutes passed before she turned to her client once more. "A seer or a listener?"

"I beg your pardon?" The lady shook her head.

"Which was he, a seer or a listener?"

"A listener." Her ladyship answered. "When his uncle discovered his gift, he was disinherited. It was the reason we could not wed."

Hidden beneath a curtain of midnight, a wry grin crept onto Penelope's face. Her fingers fluttered with excitement. She hid her emotions as she said in a sombre voice, "Please accept my condolences."

With a curtsey, she turned to depart, suspecting that the Duchess wished to grieve alone. However, she had not taken ten steps when the lady called after her. "Do you know who murdered him?"

"I do."

The lady turned. "And do you intend to reveal their identity to the authorities?"

"Worse." She walked on. "I intend to obliterate them."

Chapter 27

THE CHAPTER WITH TEA

"I always cry over spilt tea. Do you know how long it takes to make a pot or how hard it is to wash out the stains? You'd cry too if it were left up to you to brew it."

Florence Bobbington, Housekeeper, 1809

A rhythmic *tap-tap-tap-tap* of Penelope's boots rang through the hall of Birch Hallow. According to the footman, her aunt was in the library, taking tea. Not an unusual practice for a family that kept an odd schedule, chasing their flights of fancy into the wee hours of the morning.

Though Penelope had removed her coat, her holster remained secured to her side, furnished with a pistol. It clung to her, offering little reassurance.

Without pausing, she fixed a pleasant expression on her face, grasped the door handle, and slid it open. The heads of four two-legged friends and two four-legged companions turned to greet her. Blast! Bystanders.

On the canapé sat Aunt Josephine and their housekeeper, Mrs Dewar—reviewing menus, by the looks of it. Plans for the annual ball appeared to be well underway. Uncle Archie and Mrs Stevenson had each claimed a chair near the fire. Their feet brushed against one another's. As for the scaly companions, they curled together on a pillow near the hearth.

"Good evening, my dear," her uncle signed, his characteristic smile enlivening his features. His hair was especially ruffled this evening, indicating he had spent much of his day thinking. Despite the tension that had wound her shoulders into more knots than a fishing net, his presence soothed her as always. "And where have you been today? I have not seen you since breakfast."

"Well. It has been a busy . . ." *several days tramping through the mud and muck* ". . . day." She noted the position of each lady in the room, as well as their proximity to the throwing knives (hidden nearest Mrs Stevenson under the table on which her teacup rested), the pair of pistols (tucked under the sofa near her aunt), and the rifle (hung in a panel hidden in the bookshelf). The presence of bystanders complicated her plan; however, perhaps witnesses were preferable. Even if weapons were drawn, four of them could likely prevail without casualties.

After Cerberus and Ambrose paid her a polite nod, they turned back to the fire, snuggling together under a quilt. The ladies signed a "Good evening" to her in turn. Her aunt's eyes lingered on her for a moment before flicking back to the paper she held in her hand. "I suppose we must serve tongue, though I loathe it."

"Indeed, ma'am." Mrs Dewar jotted a note in her journal. A pair of wire-rimmed glasses rested on the tip of the housekeeper's nose, enlarging her round eyes. Though her station had changed, her bearing had not. She still moved like a lady, with a grace even Penelope admired.

Penelope wandered to the sideboard where cakes and tea had been laid. With care, she poured herself a cup and swirled in a spoonful of honey, then downed it in one go. The bitter liquid burnt her tongue.

While she nibbled on a berry, she stole a glance out of the window overlooking the garden. She spied the golden glint of a dragon crouching in the shadow of a hedge. As promised, Toast lay in wait, prepared to aid her if it all went to Hades in a handbasket.

The hum of unrushed conversation between her aunt and housekeeper, accompanied by the rustling of pages and the crackle of the fire, conspired to create an illusion of safety. Her eyes swept the library. The peculiarity of the room—the bell jars containing poison frogs, the skulls-turned-bookends, and the miniature of Pompei—reassured her. This was her home; she would defend it.

She meandered about, perusing the shelves, before pausing at the edge of Uncle Archie's line of sight. A quick wave caught his attention. His curious hazel eyes met hers. Rapidly, she signed, "Careful. We are not safe. An enemy—"

"Penelope, dear." A voice as rich as chocolate forced her hands to fall to her side. Mrs Stevenson glanced up from her novel. "Did you ever happen upon anything more thrilling than webs? A bandit or even an everyday rake, perchance?" Mischief danced in her eyes.

Clearly, Fate felt she had dawdled long enough. Very well, then. For the benefit of all present, she spoke and signed simultaneously, enlivened by excitement (and a touch of fear, perhaps). "Something infinitely more delectable." Since dramatics demanded it, she paused. "A murder. Two, in fact."

Uncle Archie, whose rumpled appearance travelled down the length of his wrinkled sleeves to infect the newspaper he held in his hand, patted the pistol hidden beneath his waistcoat. He winked before responding, "A murder? Anyone we know?"

Her aunt and Mrs Dewar, still engrossed in figures and shopping lists, paid her little mind, or so they wished her to believe. Mrs Stevenson, on the other hand, turned to her. Through a veil of dark lashes, she scrutinised the trembling of Penelope's hand, the sharp rise and fall of her voice.

"Yes, Uncle. I suspect everyone in this room is acquainted with the first victim. Though none have seen her in three decades. " She cleared her throat. "Her name was Bonnie."

An unnatural strain settled over the room, similar to a fiddle whose strings have been wound too tight. Lips flattened into lines. Jaws were clenched as though bracing for a blow. Knuckles blanched. Scarcely a breath was drawn.

"Thirty years ago," she began, "a young shop girl named Bonnie disappeared at a ball. The annual Birch Hallow ball, to be precise."

Subtly, it would appear, so as not to draw attention, Mrs Stevenson moved to the edge of her seat. "Yes, she vanished. We feared she had been discovered by her employer, Mr Heep."

"She may have been. However . . ." Her finger traced the barrel of her gun. ". . . her death had nothing to do with that blackguard."

"Has she been in hiding this entire time?" Though Uncle Archie's tone was relaxed, as evidenced by the nonchalance with which he formed the words, a glimmer in his eye reassured her that he, too, perceived the danger.

"No. She died due to a fall from the teahouse balcony in Alderwood today." Penelope's eyes flashed to her aunt. A wall of ice met her gaze. "Temporal displacement was the cause of her death." She turned to her uncle, a grin playing on her lips. "Or, as a brilliant scientist has christened it, time travel."

Though Uncle Archie slapped his knee good-naturedly, tension had settled over the library like a soupy fog. Whilst Ambrose, ever the faithful friend, coiled his sand-coloured tail about his companion's feet, Cerberus hovered between her friend and Mrs Stevenson, eyeing her. And as for Mrs Dewar, she sipped her tea. A slight tremor of her hand was evident in the rattle of her cup as it met the saucer.

Penelope pressed onwards. "As you hypothesised, Uncle, listeners can navigate time through the bridges created by objects. Unfortunately, dear Bonnie upset the wrong person and was sent careening through time to her death via a charm."

Her left hand slipped into her pocket. Inch by inch, she unfurled a brocade curtain tie. "With her hands bound by a tie like this one, she was shoved. A silver pendant fastened about her neck created a gateway between that moment and another this afternoon. Therefore, when she stumbled in 1781, she did not simply land on a rug, but tumbled through time to collide with the bannister of the teahouse balcony in 1811. Since it had been tampered with, it gave way under her weight."

"And how have you come by this information?" Mrs Stevenson, her coral lips pursed, all but named her suspicions. Her gaze flicked to her lover. A knowing dawned behind his eyes as well.

As a contrarian, Penelope would not be so easily induced to spill *her* secret. Instead, she began to pace. "And then there was the other murder: a gentleman whose body was discovered mere days before the ball. He had been shot. His death was conveniently placed at the feet of a seer who had taken refuge in a burrow near the scene."

Her words entranced them, beckoning them to connect the dots themselves, to finally see the patterns they had overlooked. "A humble gravestone lies hidden under the oak where he died. Curious, considering he was a stranger to Alderwood in 1781, and yet his birth year and initials were correct." The smooth stone in her pocket pressed upon her thigh, beckoning her.

Uncle Archie, inquisitive even in the presence of a murderer, tapped his foot to gain her attention. "Did he, too, wear a charm?"

"Yes. However . . ." She pivoted to her aunt. Through the wisps of grey at her temples and the black gown she wore, a younger, less refined spirit shone. ". . . it was removed, I suspect, by his murderer after he was shot."

Penelope continued, her words spilling out like grain from a split sack. "A brilliant plan, is it not? Transport a person to decades before or after the moment they were last seen—long after or well before all efforts to discover their whereabouts would cease. So brilliant, in fact, that the murderer would be tempted to replicate the pattern dozens of times, across continents and decades, until . . ."

Not a soul breathed. Even the breeze outside had ceased to rattle the window panes.

"Until what?" asked Mrs Dewar.

Emboldened, Penelope stared at her. "Until her hubris would lead her to foolishly bury one of her victims under the tree where he and his lover met in secret."

"A coincidence?" offered Mrs Stevenson. Her hand slipped into the pocket of her gown.

"More like spite, I would hazard. But can anyone tell me who would have been responsible for the remains of unclaimed bodies in October of 1781?" She folded her hands like a teacher awaiting her pupils' replies. One by one, her uncle and then her aunt, and finally, Mrs Stevenson turned to face the housekeeper.

Though no weapons had been drawn, the steel in her aunt's voice could have slaughtered a battalion. "The late magistrate, Sir Henry Dewar. Is that not correct, Agnes, dear?"

Mrs Dewar did not whimper nor weep. She was the picture of a stalwart English housekeeper and criminal mastermind. Instead, she sat with head held high, a rod of propriety jammed down her spine.

Penelope stepped towards the housekeeper. "He was, Aunt. That is, until he went missing the next month. It would not surprise me if the body of a gentleman matching his age and description has been or will be discovered one day."

As the wyrm had been let out of the bag, pretence showed itself out. Fluidly, as though it were a choreographed dance, weapons were drawn. Uncle Archie stood facing Mrs Dewar, the barrel of his flintlock trained on her head. Cerberus crouched at his feet with teeth bared, her willowy facade dropped at last. Fury rolled across her peacock-blue scales. Had she the opportunity, Penelope felt certain she would gladly relieve the housekeeper of her head.

Though the back of the couch blocked her view of Mrs Dewar's hands, the fact that Ambrose coiled his pearlescent scales like a shield against her aunt's chest told her everything she needed to know—a weapon was trained on Aunt Josephine.

"Agnes, dear, do be a dove and lower your weapon before my brother willingly mistakes one of my gestures for a signal to shoot you." Unable to resist her impish streak, even in the face of death, her aunt teased, "And consider the rug. Bloodstains on a Persian rug are not to be taken lightly. Besides, my niece has not had the pleasure of presenting the rest of her evidence, have you, love?"

"No, Aunt. You are quite correct."

When Mrs Dewar did not lower her weapon, a boisterous thought wiggled its way to the forefront of Penelope's mind. Drawing a gun on a room of Sedgewicks was a bold move, unless of course one possessed the means to escape. Penelope inched nearer the couch. "On the night the gentleman's body was discovered in the forest, Bonnie had ventured there to meet her lover. Her trek homeward was intercepted by a lady cloaked in a hood and riding a steed."

"Was not her lover arrested shortly before the ball? On charges of murder, if I recall." Mrs Stevenson slid nearer the door, a muff pistol held at her side. Blasted woman. She even held a gun seductively.

"Yes, for the murder of the nameless stranger. Convenient, is it not? Bonnie crosses paths with a cloaked figure fleeing the scene of a murder. Her . . ." Penelope paused. Her aunt's eyes narrowed, then flicked to the murderess' neck, where hung a gold cross, before they snapped back to her niece. The necklace was a charm—a temporal one, of course. "Her lover was arrested the following day."

With a sneer on her lips, Aunt Josephine's gaze slid up and down Mrs Dewar's body. "Doubtless, Bonnie put two and two together—that you instead of her lover had shot the unknown man in the woods. Was that the reason you killed her, Agnes? To bury, quite literally, the evidence?"

At last, the traitorous viper in lace spoke. "All of you are mad, and the entire town knows it." Oh, delightful! A grab at sympathy. Such fun. Though Penelope could only observe her in profile, the indignation rippling across her features was impressive.

Penelope laughed. "Well, of course we are mad. Why would we wish to be otherwise?" As her hands were free, she signed as she spoke for the benefit of her uncle. He chuckled. "Regardless, the evidence against you is insurmountable."

"Impossible," Mrs Dewar spat. Her free hand rested on her chest, mere inches from the charm. "Justice will prevail."

"It already has." Penelope's own hand trailed to her pocket. The stone beckoned her. "An hour ago, the magistrate, as well as the Earl of Alderwood, received twin notes apprising them of certain facts."

For the first time during their little tête-à-tête, fear blanched Mrs Dewar's features. Penelope danced on a knife's edge, gleefully and with the utmost rapture. "Namely, that embedded in the balcony of the teahouse was a charm identical to the one worn by the dead girl. The note included instructions to have the charm appraised by a skilled listener."

With care, Penelope signed for her uncle and Mrs Stevenson to hold fire. "As well as directions to investigate the purchase history of the teahouse, which—spoilers—is owned by a Johnston." She rose to the balls of her feet. "Is that not your maiden name, dear?"

Counting on her youth and sheer determination to propel her, she leapt for Mrs Dewar. Her right hand reached for the housekeeper's shoulder as her left squeezed the stone from the grave. She pressed her eyes shut.

As the crack of a pistol discharging rent the hush of the night air in two, a tangled mass of muslin slammed onto dark soil. Penelope somersaulted over her disoriented adversary. With an impressive degree of dexterity, she landed on her feet. Mrs Dewar lay on her back, gasping for breath on the forest floor.

Overhead, a waning moon conspired with the clouds to cloak the world below in darkness. The stars fled. Even the grandfather oak who loomed overhead denied admittance to what light remained. They were utterly alone, without a soul to intervene.

Our heroine stormed to her adversary's side and ripped the charm from her neck. With her foot, she sent the discharged pistol skittering across the dried leaves. The chorus of a thousand martyred Folk coursed through her veins as she grabbed Mrs Dewar by the collar and dragged her to her feet.

At the base of Mr Montgomery Thomas's headstone, she stopped. The humbly hewn marker circled by river stones stood as judge and jury. "Why him?" Penelope spat. "Tell me why he had to die."

"No." Mrs Dewar savoured the word, permitting it to roll across her tongue like wine. Loathing curled her lip. "That riles you and your inflated sense of morality, doesn't it . . ." She folded into a mock half curtsey. ". . . Miss Sedgewick."

Disdain's frosty grip snaked into Penelope's chest. It infused her veins, tempting her to heed the siren's call of the cold steel of her pistol pressing against her ribs. Reason, though, stayed her hand. It shushed her baser instincts, reminding her that she was a Sedgewick, and they did not kill in cold blood (especially without answers).

With a tad more force than necessary, Penelope released her collar. The lady stumbled. Her gaze did not dart this way or that, seeking an escape. Instead, she smoothed her dress and folded her hands at her waist. Penelope half expected her to ask whether she ought to serve the scones.

"Clearly, it was personal. Why else would you place his gravestone under *this* tree? Did you convince your husband to select the burial site, or was it as simple as writing a letter bearing his signature?"

Her opponent's eyes remained placid, unwilling to betray her.

"Your husband was not a confidante, was he? Merely a pawn. Mr Heep . . ." Penelope appraised her expressions for flickers of emotion. None. "I would hazard that he was a middle-man?"

Her gaze drifted down the length of Mrs Dewar's body. "And you were not the one calling the shots." With intention, Penelope's eyes snapped to hers. A wry grin tugged at the corner of her mouth. "Obviously."

For an instant, the housekeeper's thin lips pressed together. Penelope pressed onward. "A lover? Unlikely, who would want . . ." She let the silence linger. It rang across the grove, taunting her opponent. ". . . you?"

A flicker of hatred flashed across Mrs Dewar's pleasant features. Just as Penelope had hoped.

"A parent then. Did they die?" She feigned an exaggerated frown, tilting her head to one side. "Or simply not care enough to raise you above your position?"

Through puckered lips, Mrs Dewar spat at her. No sooner had the saliva hit its mark, did steel press itself into her forehead. Penelope stared down the barrel of the pistol at her, unflinching.

Malice unfurled itself across Penelope's skin, blanketing her in a shadow not perceived by the eyes but by the soul. Her heart thrummed, crying for vengeance. The rhythm mingled with the voice of Montgomery, whose body rotted beneath her feet. It harmonised with the rage of the young seer who would never hold his beloved again. Even Bonnie's laughter as she pressed kisses to her lover's lips shouted for justice.

Mrs Dewar's contempt faltered.

Death very well might have come to call that evening had it not been for this fleeting display of frailty. In the terror that shone through the hag's eyes, Penelope caught a glimpse of the monster she would become if she committed such an act. She lowered her weapon to her side.

To Penelope's surprise, hysterics possessed Mrs Dewar. She threw her head back in laughter. No longer was she a woman, but a demon set free from the pits of hell. "I knew you didn't have it in you. You Sedgewicks, with all of your bravado, are—"

The crunch of Penelope's fist colliding with her jaw silenced her. When her body struck the ground, the blanket of leaves did little to cushion her fall. Pity. Though she still drew breath, she slipped into a twilight, hovering between consciousness and nightmare.

Our heroine stood over her form, a suppressed grin on her lips. "Take that, you witch."

> {Narrator's Note: Except she did NOT say witch, though she did use a synonym ending in the same three letters.}

The Epilogue

WITH THE MISSPELT INVITATION

At nine the next morning, the butler entered the library with a fresh pot of tea. A proper Englishman to the core, he did not roll his eyes at the spectacle unfolding before him.

The room had been rearranged. Unsurprising. The Sedgewicks moved furniture about so often that the seasoned butler retained three strapping footmen to aid with such endeavours. Steven, a skeleton covered in fluffed cotton and fabric, had been hung by a hook from the ceiling. (Whose skeleton he was remains a mystery.) Even this was not unusual. In fact, if Sir Steve the Stiff (as he had been named by the staff) was not dragged forth at least once a week, the butler would have felt pressed to alert the family's personal physician.

No. What the butler, with his creased coat and perfectly parted hair, disapproved of that morning was his master's lady companion dressed in trousers, cursing.

"Next time, remember to squeeze your fist when you throw a punch so as not to damage your hand," Aunt Josephine called from the breakfast table drawn near the window. "And keep your elbow bent at a ninety-degree angle."

With her lips pursed, Mrs Stevenson flapped her injured hand. "Perhaps I would remember had I a more convincing target." She settled onto her chair, crossed her legs at the knee (Scandalous, I know), and pivoted to her friend. "You wouldn't fancy volunteering, would you, Jo?"

"Perhaps next month after the ball." Aunt Josephine topped up four cups of tea. "At present, my schedule is too strained to accommodate another attack by an enemy posing as a friend."

Penelope, whose knuckles were perfectly intact despite the glorious right hook she had planted on Mrs Dewar's chin the evening prior, executed a brilliant spin. Her bare foot connected with Sir Steven's painted mouth, snapping his neck. When her family, led by Uncle Archie, burst into polite applause, she blushed and hurried to her seat, but not before pressing a kiss to the crown of her uncle's head.

"Well done, my dear." A grin stretched across her uncle's face. "You do us all proud."

Despite her age, Penelope felt at times as though she was a girl teetering on the edge of womanhood. She wondered whether she would ever feel grown. The twinkle in her uncle's eye when he peppered Mrs Stevenson's injured knuckles with kisses convinced her that she likely would not. All the better, she supposed.

After a protracted sip of tea intended to shoo away the colour in her cheeks, she patted her lips with her handkerchief. "Have we had word from the magistrate this morn?"

"Not as yet." Aunt Josephine glanced over the morning paper at her. "Which reminds me . . . you failed to elaborate on how you connected the body discovered in 1781 to Montgomery Thomason."

Indeed she had. Once she had returned with the former housekeeper, the family had settled around the table to share a pot of tea while they awaited the magistrate. Over copious amounts of honey and cake, she had unfolded an abridged version of her misadventures through time.

Of course, she omitted Walt from the retelling, though Aunt Josephine's expression confirmed she had not forgotten the nameless conspirator with raven hair. Though her employer had extended a standing invitation to tea, Walt preferred to remain in the shadows (at least, for now). Begrudgingly, Penelope respected her wishes.

That their niece was a sleuth who investigated matters for ladies was also conveniently passed over. It had not felt pertinent, or perhaps that was simply what she had told herself.

She did, however, confess her gifts to her uncle and his beloved. Despite decades of trepidation, she was not met with disappointment or judgement, but with understanding.

"Are you not displeased?" she had asked, her head bowed low.

A calloused hand reached across the table to enfold hers in its grasp. When she lifted her face, the love her uncle felt spilt down his cheeks. "My soul loves all of the pieces of you, even those you hide or deny," he signed. "When I held you the first time, I gave to you every bit of myself I could spare. I have never regretted, nor shall I."

So when the matter of Montgomery Thomas was brought forth once more, Penelope answered it with a precocious grin. Her clients trusted her to keep their secrets, and she would not divulge them even to her loved ones. "Perhaps I shall tell that tale another time."

After their bellies were satisfied, each turned to their own pursuits. Uncle Archie and Mrs Stevenson wandered to the comfortable chairs near the fire to grin at one another like lovesick children. Invitations commanded her aunt's attention. And Penelope, well, she combed the bookshelves for records, as she had done late into the night.

Lingering questions still orbited around her former house-keeper: questions Penelope intended to solve. With a cup of tea in hand (her fourth that morning), she tucked into a book of heraldries.

She had not read three pages when her aunt observed, "Mrs Dewar troubles you, does she not?"

Penelope's finger danced down a page depicting an ancient coat of arms. "She does. Did you know that it was a Mr Johnson who sold that barn, the one we burned, to Mr Heep?"

"I did not." Her aunt crossed tongue from the menu. Thank the heavens. "However, her maiden name was Johnston, not Johnson."

"True." Penelope pressed her lips together. "However, I have discovered that the names Johnson, Johnston, and Johnsten keep popping up in records, especially those connect-ed with murder and illicit activities. Curious, is it not?"

"Curious, indeed."

"Furthermore, before I went to bed, I nipped into Mrs Dewar's chambers." She waited. On cue, her aunt set aside the menu. From between two pages in her journal, Penelope withdrew a scorched scrap of paper she had discovered on the hearth. Though she could discern little of interest, the words "keep an eye on Miss Sedgewick" shone through the smudges left by the smoke.

The scrap of paper was laid on the table between them. Her aunt studied it. "Have you discovered with whom she corresponded?"

"Not yet. However, it confirms a suspicion I have held."

Her aunt returned the blackened paper to her niece. "You do not believe she worked alone?"

"No. I suspect her poverty was a ruse." Penelope tucked the paper between two pages of her journal.

"To permit her unfettered access to this house?"

"And your work, perhaps?" She flipped through several pages of the heraldry book. "On that topic, whatever happened to Mr Heep?"

"He disappeared." Aunt Josephine crossed a line from her guest list. "Shortly after the fire, several papers published articles exposing Mr Heep and his illicit business practices. Reportedly, an anonymous lady provided proof of his misdeeds."

Though neither spoke her name, the ladies exchanged a knowing look. So Mrs Crucible Heep's midnight outings to the factory had been for more than fresh air.

"Though he was arrested," her aunt continued, "he later escaped. A man fitting his appearance has been connected to several crimes over the last thirty years, yet he has never been caught."

"You suspect, as I do, that he and Mrs Dewar were connected?"

Aunt Josephine nodded. To discover that a member of their household, a confidante, a friend was, in fact, an adversary, well . . . such knowledge requires time and tea to come to terms with.

Penelope laid her hand on the table. Her aunt accepted it, giving it a gentle squeeze. "We shall discover it together."

After they had both stared at their respective papers for several minutes without attending to what they read, Penelope felt as though she would burst if she did not tie up one mystery that remained. Without glancing up, she asked, "Aunt, I do have two further questions."

"Yes, dear." Aunt Josephine perused the guest list for the eleventh time.

"Why do you wear black?" For the first time in her life, she felt she had earned the right to ask. Perhaps it was because she had interacted with her aunt as an equal. Or perhaps it was because she finally appreciated her aunt's brilliance. Whatever the cause, Penelope waited patiently, offering acceptance, not judgment.

A boisterous "Ha!" erupting from her aunt startled Mrs Stevenson, as well as dear Ambrose, who had stolen in after a morning romp to visit Toast. A pat on the head and a handful of sugared berries served as an apology to her scaly friend. The lady simply returned to her flirting with Uncle Archie.

"Do you know that no one has ever asked me that question before?" She swirled in a spoonful of honey into her tea, just as Penelope was wont to do, and as her mother had before her. Taking honey in tea, our heroine supposed, must be a trait shared by Sedgewick women.

"Your proclivity for maiming men and women may discourage such inquiries." A grin peeped out from behind her teacup as she took a sip.

"Come now. That reputation is wholly undeserved." Not a hint of irony crept into her voice. "To the best of my recollection, I have not disfigured anyone these last three months."

"Would you like me to applaud your restraint or order you a medal to wear on your spencer?" her niece replied boldly. The tart.

At the sight of her aunt flashing her an offensive sign, Penelope burst into laughter. Her aunt did not acknowledge the outburst.

Once her niece became a sensible lady once more, a breath of grief crept into the corners of Josephine's eyes. Penelope quieted; she mirrored her aunt, inviting her honesty by proving herself trustworthy of it.

"The year before you were born, the country was swept by a purge the likes of which I had never seen the like." Her eyes stared unfocused past Penelope's shoulder. "Despite our best efforts, we lost many. At the height of it, the *Gloucester Journal* printed a headline boasting the number of Folk and their associates who had died or been imprisoned. I swore to dedicate one day apiece to mourn each of the nameless victims."

"And how many days have you left to mourn?"

"Once I added those reported on the Continent and in the Americas, I have 32 . . ." Her eyes flicked to her nieces, the ghosts of legions swirled behind them. ". . . years until I have mourned them all. It is the reason I continue my work. It is why I did not force you to divulge your secret."

Penelope blinked back tears. "I have never admired you more than I do at this moment."

Shock registered on her aunt's face. Embarrassment, though, soon overtook it, tinting her neck in red. Her hands fumbled with her papers. At last, a brief smile curled at her lips. "Thank you." She righted her glasses on her nose before she continued, "And you had a second question?"

After emptying her cup and settling it into its saucer, Penelope said, "Yes. I was wondering whether you would consider permitting me to join your work. I can boast an excellent list of references and a splendid right hook."

Rather than answer her, or even acknowledge her, Aunt Josephine scribbled a hasty note on a scrap of paper, folded it, and rose.

After requesting Mrs Stevenson stop flirting with her brother and direct his attention towards her instead, her aunt signed, "Could you please review the invitation to the ball and check it for errors?"

The folded note plopped into Penelope's lap as her aunt brushed by. She watched as Josephine crossed to her brother. He accepted the invitation with a grin.

Penelope unfolded the paper under the cover of the table. It read, "Thursday. The back room of the parsonage. Say the phrase 'The dragons are rioting again' to gain entry."

An ember of pride glowed in Penelope's heart. It shone through her hazel eyes. She wandered to the fireplace and tossed the paper onto the coals.

"Sister, dear?" her uncle signed. A hint of mischief tugged his lips upward. Penelope noted the same expression mirrored on Mrs Stevenson's face. "You have miswritten the names of the host and hostess. They should read 'Miss Josephine Sedgewick and Mr Archibald Sedgewick, and . . ." He paused, beaming. ". . . his wife, Mrs Abigail Sedgewick."

Dear Aunt Josephine, who had inopportunely swallowed a mouthful of tea, spat it across the Persian rug. A pity, considering it had narrowly avoided bloodstains the evening prior.

At the sight of her uncle taking his beloved's hand, Penelope covered her mouth and may have actually squealed with delight. She flung herself into her uncle's arms. Her free hand reached for Mrs Stevenson's—scratch that, Mrs Sedgewick's hand. The lady's eyes swam with delight. Even her aunt joined the huddle of misty-eyed Sedgewicks rejoicing in a love thirty years in the making.

When Penelope pulled away to pat her eyes, she signed, "When?"

"A month ago," replied her uncle's wife—her second aunt, she supposed. "But do not worry, Jo. I have no intention of living here. Nor does Archie plan to leave you either." She squeezed her friend's hand reassuringly. "We rather like having our own spaces—his for experiments and mine decidedly free of canned appendages."

And with that, our story comes to a close. That is, until, the author makes time to record how Mr Scott became a yeti or who had held Toast captive. Or perhaps, until she has the opportunity to divulge the greatest mystery of them all—why the spoons?

Farewell, and until then, keep calm and carry a snack, for you never know when you may be stuck in a tree.

The Author

K. Starling creates stories set in a reimagined Regency Era, overflowing with dragons, intrigue, and magic.

When she is not writing witty female heroines or delicious villains, she will hit the trail with her family or the open road in her tent. And though she does not have a pet, her kids have a menagerie of dinosaurs, stuffies, monsters, and dragons.

An avid reader, she has long nurtured a dream of penning a novel in her name. After twenty years of writing articles, novels, and blogs for organizations and clients, K. Starling is thrilled to publish her second novel Memories, Magic, and Mayhem.

FIND HER ON. . .

Threads: @authorkstarling
Instagram: @authorkstarling
Website: authorkstarling.com

OTHER WORKS. . .
Talismans, Teacups, and Trysts